I0690289

THE SOLSTICE REALM

GLAVEN

FIRAE

NETHER

AQUARTA

THE FOG

THE CITY MOUNTAIN RANGE

OLYMPUS

DWARVENSHIRE

BANISHED BY DARKNESS

Daphne Paige

EMILIA OF THE
SOLSTICE REALM

BANISHED BY DARKNESS

Copyright © 2024 by Daphne Paige

First Edition September 2024

Find the author on Instagram @daphne.paige.books

Cover design by GetCovers

Chapter designs by Daphne Paige

Editing by Jackie Marie and Brenda Woody

All rights reserved. No part of this book may be reproduced or used in any manner without written permission from the copyright owner except for brief quotations in a book review.

This is a work of fiction. Names, characters, places, and incidents are either the product of the author's imagination, or are used fictitiously. Any resemblance to actual events or persons, living or dead, is entirely coincidental.

Published by Popcorn Publishing in the United States of America

Popcorn Publishing

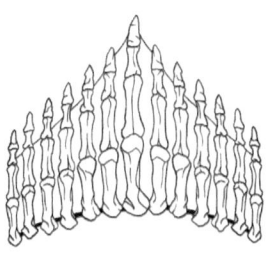

To Jacob, for all those times you've looked at the stars with me, and for all those times we will in the future

BANISHED
BY
DARKNESS

Magical Definitions from the *History of Magic*

The Veiling: A curse that turns someone inhumane and Dark

Unnatural: A species that's not human

Aridam: The cursed Sword of Death

Eve: The Sword of Life

The Solstice Realm: A realm of allied kingdoms

The Banished Realm: A realm for the banished Unnaturals

Runespeaker: A mage who creates runes with magical properties

Soul Sight: An ability that allows someone to decipher the truth

Depiction of the mutated chimeras in Nether, illustrated by Daphne Paige

Chapter One

The sunlight reflects off the butterflies' shimmering wings as they flutter about the conservatory.

I watch them with my mouth slightly parted, in awe of their beauty, of how far they have come since I first suggested the idea to Adriene. In just under two months, he's taken all of our captured butterflies—destined for meals and nothing more—and turned them into our Dark spies. We have eyes everywhere now, watching and waiting for whispers about Nether.

Someone tugs on the black lace train of my dress, and I glare over my shoulder at them. My stare only lightens by a fraction when I realize it's Adriene. "You've outdone yourself," I admit.

Adriene watches the butterflies flap freely around the newly constructed conservatory. He knows how much I love seeing the outside and being close to nature. Over the past two months, I've grown close to my right-hand man. The

1

executioner, the alchemist, and the gentleman. A rare and odd combination.

Sunlight dapples his snow-white hair, glinting across the dome of his black eyes. "It's nothing, Emilia."

He hardly ever uses my formal title—*queen*. If it were someone else, I would make them kneel before me in apology. But it's not. It's Adriene. So, I don't say anything.

"Emilia," he adds, hesitantly. By the tone of his voice, I'm not sure I want to hear what he has to say. But I turn to face him, nonetheless. He glances at me, then quickly away. "It's been almost two months since their funerals. Are you sure you don't want to visit their burial sites?"

I shoot him my most *how-dare-you-bring-them-up* glare, even though a part deep inside me pangs at the very thought. I know I cared about them before I killed Aaron. I just can't remember why or how much. I also can't decide if forgetting is a gift or a curse. "Not yet, Adriene."

He dips his chin. "Alright, Emilia."

We stand in silence, watching the butterflies. There are trees planted in the sections of the conservatory that aren't covered by stone walkways; pale branches stretch toward the sky, unaware that they'll never reach it. Cherry blossom trees are one of the prettiest aspects of the Earthen Realm, so

Adriene brought a bit of my prior life here…for me.

A bench rests underneath the tallest cherry blossom tree near the entrance to the conservatory. I take a seat and pat the other side of the bench for Adriene to join me. We sit, enjoying not feeling alone. It's something we started doing even before Adriene finished mutating the butterflies. Each of us finding comfort in each other's presence.

I sense Adriene watching me, studying me. I don't know what he expects to find—maybe a fragment of my old self. Though I know—better than anyone—that she's gone. I am now Queen Emilia Strazenfield of Nether. Queen of the Shrouds. A woman of Darkness and unwavering cruelty.

I shift, meeting his stare. "You're not going to find her, Adriene. Why do you bother looking?"

His lips thin, and a sliver of white rings the black of his eyes. "Because you find the good in me even when I'm like this, and I'm determined to find the good in you too." He reaches over and takes my hand. His pale skin is unusually warm. "I'm not going to give up on you. I know that you don't like the effects of the Veiling, and that you wish you didn't kill Aaron."

"Don't say that," I hiss, tearing my hand from his grip. I rest it in my lap, feeling the absence of his touch more than I would like to. "Aaron deserved to die. I'll never regret being the one brave enough to kill him."

"Even when you feel like this? Like violence is the only way to fill the cavern where your heart used to be?"

I hate that Adriene can voice my thoughts—my fears. I won't give him the satisfaction of knowing he's right, so I stand up, dust off my gown, and command him to release the first batch of butterflies into the Solstice Realm. We need to know if there are any whispers of war. The entire realm was gearing up to take on Nether—and Aaron—but would they stop since *I've* inherited *all* his evil…? I wonder.

Adriene stands up too. "The butterflies should return within two days. I'll notify you when they do," Adriene promises, linking his hands behind his back. He heads toward the doors of the conservatory, but stops to glance back at me. "I know you're in there, Emilia. And I won't give up until you're freed."

I want to scream at him that freeing me is a waste of time, that it's impossible, and that I'll forever be stuck in this ghoulish prison. But hope vanquishes my voice. So, I watch him leave, turning my attention to the butterflies flitting around me.

I know that the rest of the realm will want to get a look at the new Nether queen—and the war that was rallying on the horizon *may* still happen. Nether

—and the curse that comes with it—will always be a danger to those surrounding us.

I should want them to vanquish this forsaken kingdom, to unleash their blood lust upon the Shrouds that inhabit this palace and the small village nestled alongside, but the Veiling flowing through my veins and the crown of bones perched atop my head makes me want to protect these awful people. By law. *My people.*

Eons ago, it seems, I was surrounded by *my people.* At least people I claimed to have felt most at home with.

I don't know what that feels like now. Now, I'm a shell full of violence. Will I ever feel at home again? Or will I have to live the rest of my life as this hollow being? The soulless queen of black-hearted people.

I sigh, tilt my chin high, and follow Adriene. I'm queen… I suppose it's about time I get to know my flock.

I manage to catch up to Adriene in the main hallway, right outside the grand sitting room, where the high-class Shrouds are cackling amongst themselves, clinking silver cups that slosh with a foul-scented liquid. He's leaning against the door frame, watching them with an eerily human expression on his pale face. Longing, almost. Since when does a Shroud long for anything?

"Adriene," I say, my voice sounding sharp and commanding. I try to soften my tone, but it feels unnatural on my tongue. Adriene slowly pivots to where he's facing me, expressionless.

"What?" his voice is bitter. He must be angry that I brushed him off so easily. I roll my eyes to the black-stone ceiling. I don't have time for this, nor should I care. I should have him flogged for annoying me, or exiled for a week in the bog surrounding this kingdom. But Adriene… Flashes of him in a dark hallway, of his finger brushing mine to comfort me, to tell me that he's there… Adriene is the one person in this entire palace that doesn't irritate me to no end. If Adriene wasn't here…I'd go even more insane from sheer boredom. He's competent, calculating, and measurably cruel.

At least, that's what I tell myself. A queen cannot have a soft spot for her executioner.

"I want to see the village," I say quietly, tediously, wondering how he'll respond. It seems only right that I see the village, see my people.

Adriene tilts his chin up, though that's as much of a reaction as he's going to give me. "We can leave in an hour after I'm done releasing the butterflies. Does that sound acceptable to you?"

I give him a curt nod, and he pushes off the door frame, not sparing another glance toward the Shrouds drinking in the sitting room. I watch them.

They all look so different—dark and light, blonde and brunette, thin and fat—but they all have tar-black eyes and cruel grins stretching their lips. They lift their silver glasses again and clink them together, cheering for another era of Nether. Cheering for me, I realize.

I narrow my eyes, disgruntled and unaware of how to react. Should I feel...*glad* that they're worshiping me so easily? I shake my head, deciding that I should change my outfit, and start back toward my room. I run my fingertips across the black beads of my corset, ignoring the squeaks of surprise from palace servants as I stalk by, a Veil of evil seeping from my aura.

As soon as I make it to the monarch's suite, I slam the door and lean against it, taking a deep breath of the musty air.

Blanketed with lichen, the slick stones of the upper floor are alive with creepy crawlies. A wardrobe carved from the trunk of an ancient black tree stands alone on the wall to my right, with arched windows on either side. And across from the wardrobe is the bed; blood-red drapes hang from the matching black-wood bed frame. My nightmare-plagued sleep left my sheets rumpled.

I haven't been able to rest ever since I slayed Aaron and inherited his power and position. Whenever I close my eyes, I see them.

Sophia and Jaxon. Soph…my sister. And Jax… my friend. Though, in my dreams, the person sliding the blade across Sophia's throat and thrusting it into Jaxon's heart…is *me*. I pinch my eyes shut, wincing as I bite my cheek and blood coats my tongue.

Adriene constantly reminds me how much they meant to me, of who they *were* to me. But my feelings for them have slowly ebbed as the Veiling settles. I'm aware of things—of how I *should* feel about their deaths. But…this curse hasn't only drained the white from my eyes, it has also stolen the emotions from my heart.

I know they're dead. I know I should be grieving. But *knowing* does nothing with this Dark curse flowing through me.

I bite my lip and shake my head. I need to go down to the village and face my people with clarity.

I push off the door and head toward the wardrobe, throwing it open to reveal the packed row of gowns, all in varying shades of red, black, or the darkest of greens.

I select a forest green gown made of silk with a ruffled high collar, along with a pair of black riding boots. I peel off my black outfit and toss the dress in a mound on my bed; the train falls down the side and across the stone floor like the limp body of a serpent.

My fingers run nimbly up the corset, fastening pearl buttons as I stand in front of the floor-length mirror. I stare at myself; at my pale, thin face and my sunken, black eyes. My lips are barely a shade darker than my skin, and the hollows of my cheeks are ghastly with how prominent they are. I resemble nothing more than a corpse.

I blink, fixing the crown of bones upon my head. My dark brown hair hangs down my shoulders like the hide of a dead animal. And, like a dead animal, it's lost all its luster.

I tilt my chin up, refusing to cower from my appearance. I turn my head toward the writing desk pushed against the center window, watching the cloudy sky outside as it broils with the beginning of a storm. My journal is open on the desk, turned to a blank page. I haven't had the dedication, nor the urge to write anything down since… Well, since that day, months ago. That blank page has been haunting me. I slam it shut, glaring at the pale blue cover.

There's a knock at the door, and my spine stiffens. I run my hands down the skirt of my dress, smoothing the non-existent wrinkles.

The glass of the window reflects my appearance, my dead eyes, and my ashen tone, broken up into segments by the iron details. The window is dissected with black iron bars, giving the palace a

11

gothic appeal.

Rain parts the clouds, falling in fat droplets on the small Nether village below. It spatters across the roof of the palace, slipping into crevices where the roof is weak and splatting on the floor. I lift an eyebrow at the intruding puddle that's now forming, then shift my glare to the failing roof.

I thought that King Aaron took care of his conquered kingdom.

"Emilia," Adriene calls through the door. He sounds exhausted. "It's time to go."

I huff and cross under the dripping section of the roof, earning an icy trickle of rain slicking my scalp. I pull open the door and blink in surprise at Adriene's get-up.

"What's with…" I flourish my hand, indicating his entire outfit.

Adriene takes a step back and looks down at himself, brandishing a coy smirk. "It's the uniform of the Nether executioner. I can't make a formal appearance beside the queen without wearing it."

He's wearing a suit of form-fitted black leather, iron bands cinch the leather around his shoulders, hips, and ankles. Spikes protrude from the top of his shoes, and I gulp, wondering what he needs them for. Crossing his back is a sheathed scythe.

With his pale skin and moon-white hair standing stark against his uniform, he's the definition of intimidating.

"Well…" I swallow, at a sudden loss for words. My eyes flick up to meet his, and I frown at the mischievous twinkle I find there. "We better get going."

I push past him, earning a dark chuckle.

The stairway to the monarch's suite—which is basically a glorified attic—is narrow and dimly lit. I squint to make out the steps in front of me. It would be too embarrassing if I tripped and fell; Adriene would never let me live it down.

Just as the thought crosses my mind, my heel catches on the lip of the step, and I fall forward. Without a word, Adriene grabs my arm and tugs me back, catching me before I can get hurt. I look back at him over my shoulder, his hand still wrapped around my upper arm. His eyes somehow appear darker, his pale skin blossoming with the lightest pink.

"Can't have the queen getting hurt now, can we?" he asks, and I study the way his mouth moves.

The feel of his hands on me takes me back to the inn… It's been weeks since I've thought about that. About how we always end up comforting each other, being there for each other.

"You're right… We can't have that." I'm strangely aware of how close he is, and how alone we are in this stairway. I think he is too, because a teasing smirk pulls at his lips, and he leans closer. His breath warms my lips, and I part them in invitation, wondering what he's going to do.

But then a crease knits between his brows, and his eyes narrow, staring squarely at me as if he's figuring something out. I clamp my mouth shut and glare at him, tearing my arm from his grasp. I turn away before he can say anything, continuing down the flight of stairs with my gown clenched in tight fists.

What was that? That heated moment between us… And why did he stare at me like *that*? Like I had something on my face.

"Emilia…" Adriene says quietly behind me. My name on his tongue always sounds like a plea.

I don't respond, too perturbed by what just happened, of how much it felt like a rejection. I've never been *rejected* before. Blue eyes flash across my mind, and a gasp leaves my lips, getting carried away on a draft as I step into the hallway. The large window at the end is open. As the rain hits the ground, it releases the sweet smell of a storm. I take a calming breath.

Sky.

That's his name. Sky. I form his name silently with my lips, needing to ingrain it so I don't forget. I can't forget him.

Sky.

Sky.

Sky.

But what is so important about him? Why did I have such...*feelings* for him?

I furrow my brow. The only thing I can come up with is a picture of tulips and blue icing. Of my heart racing as he leans closer, a stream burbling nearby. Then his determined gaze as a crimson tie sweeps back his raven-feather hair.

Adriene's hand on the small of my back vanquishes all thoughts of Sky, whisking him away on the breeze.

"It's beautiful outside, isn't it?" Adriene asks, staring in awe as the sky cracks open, and a bolt of lightning shoots into the bog bordering our kingdom. A monstrous howl lifts through the weeping trees, joined by more and more as it carries toward the village.

"What is *that*?" I gasp, squinting at the tree line, attempting to spot a monster lurking within. But I can't see anything.

"Patrol," Adriene says lightly, holding back a malevolent laugh. "They stop anyone from getting through the bog."

"But *what* are they?"

A humored smile spreads across his face. "Creations, Emilia. They're made from blood." He leans toward my ear, whispering, "They have the body of a wolf, the wings of a dragon, and the tail of a rattlesnake. Mutated chimeras of my making."

"Your making?" I raise an eyebrow, trying to picture the winged beasts. The image my mind conjures is horrifying. I know I'm queen of this land, but I certainly hope I never have to encounter those monsters.

"The king before Aaron wanted these lands constantly guarded, so he entrusted me to make that happen." He chuckles, a chunk of hair falling across his eyes. "They will eat anyone who tries to cross."

"Will they serve us when the time for war comes?"

"*If* it comes," Adriene corrects. He straightens his posture and tilts his head, staring past the village and into the trees bordering the bog. "They're not loyal like that… They're sacrificial creatures. They're instructed to kill on sight, no matter who it is."

"So, they can't be controlled," I conclude. Doesn't that make them more of a liability than a safety precaution?

"No, they can't." His eyes glint. "Best stay out of their way then."

I nod, pulling my attention away from the bog as we continue our descent through the palace.

Chapter Two

The Nether village doesn't look as scary as I thought it would. Thatched homes are made from wood that varies from gray and black to the darkest brown. The doors all have an iron-framed window centered at the top that looks out at the trodden path leading through the village and toward the palace, and in front of each home is a small fenced garden.

We pass a few pink and black spotted pigs eating lazily from a trough, and a stable that houses a pair of stunning brown quarter horses.

Kids are playing in a puddle, throwing their heads back and bellowing with joyous laughter as their parents watch from rocking chairs under the protection of their covered porches.

I'm completely taken off guard. This isn't what I thought it would be like. I was expecting... tremendous violence, for this is a kingdom forsaken by the Veiling, is it not? The Veiling is a curse that seeps the kindness from a soul, leaving them wicked.

A shell of their former self. But this is…not *that*. This is *just* a kingdom. When I look at the people, the *families*, watching after each other, living…all my preconceptions of Nether vanish.

"It's not so bad, now is it?" Adriene asks, nodding toward the smiling children. "Nether just gets a terrible reputation because of how different we are from every other kingdom. Of how we follow our own rules and house those who aren't welcome anywhere else in this realm."

"Then why—"

"Why did I leave?" He gives me a look like I'm missing something. "I've told you before. I left for you, Emilia, to get you here, where you are now." He watches the children for a moment longer before draping my arm through his and urging us to the right and down an alley between houses. "Aaron wasn't a good king. He was feared by many. He introduced violence to the kingdom and insisted upon severing the strained relations we had with all the Solstice Realm monarchs. His obsession with… well, *you*, led Nether into a shadowed place. And his vampire soldiers—those snobbish men all comfortable in the palace—were sent to him because of a deal he made with Cyprion."

Cyprion… I've heard that name before. But where?

"Who is Cyprion?" I ask, stepping to the side to

avoid a puddle. My boots *click* on the stones that interrupt sections of the dirt path.

"Cyprion isn't a person. It's the name of the vampire kingdom in the Banished Realm. King Cassius and Aaron partnered together to bring the exiled Unnaturals back to the Solstice Realm. Cassius's son, Garamond, is residing within the palace as we speak. Though I haven't seen him for weeks…" He frowns, narrowing his eyes at the path.

Garamond… Anger sloshes in my stomach at the mere thought of his name, and it takes me a moment to remember *why* I'm so enraged. "That *tick*," I hiss between my teeth. Flashes of my sister's face flutter across the forefront of my mind; her bright blue eyes framed by long blonde hair. Her joyful smile and her constant companion, Garamond.

Adriene raises an eyebrow, then he nods knowingly. "Ah yes. He was courting your sister, wasn't he?"

"I remember trusting him…with *her*… And then he just…betrayed her. He let Aaron *kill* her," I say, piecing together the puzzle of my fading memory as I speak. I sound like such a fool—trusting a *vampire*.

"By all means, punish him. Nowhere in the contract between Aaron and Cassius did it say that Garamond is to return in one piece," he suggests. A pleased smirk tilts the corner of his mouth.

I flash him a demonic smile as well, blood lust congealing in my black heart. "I'll have to take you up on that offer."

"But first," Adriene declares, directing me toward the door of a quaint thatched building, an inviting smell drifts through the open door, and the patrons sitting at tables around the room turn to stare, recognition flickering to life across their faces as soon as we enter.

I give Adriene a questioning look. He taps the small counter at the back of the room with two knuckles. As he whispers something to the round man behind the counter, I turn to study the room, bristling at the patrons' insistent gaze.

It takes me a moment to realize that only half of them have tar-black eyes, while the others look vastly different; some are obvious humans—possibly mages—while fur sprouts from the feline ears of a couple toward the back, and scales shine on the cheeks of a pair of boys closest to me. A man sitting at a table to my right opens his mouth to take a bite of food, fangs flashing as he does.

Adriene's right. Nether welcomes all. This kingdom must risk a lot more than I thought, directly going against the rest of the realm's laws, and knowingly offering banished Unnaturals a home.

"Are you our new queen?" one of the small, scaled boys asks, looking up at me with a sandwich clutched in his webbed hands. "Are you going to make us eat those nasty bugs like you do in the palace?"

I want to laugh; I can feel one growing in my chest, but I force it down and flash him as kind a smile as I can muster. "You can eat whatever you like. Even *I* don't eat those nasty bugs."

I can sense Adriene watching my interaction with the child. I glance back at him—noting the softness of his expression—and smile at him. He returns a smile, pressing his hand against the small of my back. He directs us back through the front door and to a table on the porch, where we have a perfect view of the lightning as it streaks through the sky. It's still raining.

"Why does the palace serve insects and cha kla eyes for every meal? Surely, that's not a normal practice here." I cross my hands in my lap, enjoying the sound of the wind rustling through the trees and the thunder rumbling above us.

"It's not normal," Adriene agrees. "I personally don't have a problem with it. Though the same meal day after day does get monotonous."

"But why would someone even think of serving *that*?" My lip curls in disgust. I can still hear the terrified screeches of the creatures down in the dungeon. Music to my ears. Though I wouldn't like it if my eyes were scooped out, so I'm sure they feel the same way.

"Aaron thought it would be a better alternative for the vampires residing in the palace. It's not as if we can serve humans or goblets of blood." Adriene's gaze drifts to the tree line only a hundred yards from the village. "You're the queen—you can always decide to serve something else. Vampires are picky creatures, but even they and their dietary needs can't argue against the crown."

I mull over his words. It's true. I am queen. And it would be nice to wander through the palace and not smell urine, or see those disgusting brutes slurping up eyes at every meal I decide to attend. "I'd like it to be stopped. Immediately. And I want to help the cha klas that were mutilated."

Adriene leans over the table, and that same look he had in the stairway returns to his face.

"What is it?" I insist, glowering at him.

He sits back, opening and closing his mouth, yet not making a sound.

"That's not possible…" he mumbles, studying me with an intensity that makes my cheeks blush. "It *shouldn't* be possible. Especially because of the Nether monarch's curse…"

"*What is it?*" I command, slamming my palm on the table and scaring a couple dining at the table in front of us.

"Your eyes…" He shakes his head in bewilderment. "Emilia… Your eyes… They were blue. They were *your* eyes *before* the Veiling. In the stairway, I saw white rimming the black. But just now…your iris flashed blue."

I furrow my brow, a crease appearing between them. "That can't be."

"I know. Maybe you're stronger than either of us thought." He reaches across the table, his fingertips pushing a strand of my hair away from my face. "Emilia, I think you're fighting it."

I stare at him, speechless. Could I be fighting the Veiling? Could I be returning to my former self? Do I even *want* that?

It would be preferable to look in the mirror and not see a walking skeleton, to see my cheeks fatten and my stomach extend, to hide my now protruding bones. And it would be nice to be rid of this fog clouding my judgment and my memories.

The pudgy man from behind the counter sets two steaming bowls in front of us, as well as a little ceramic tray of hot bread. He moves to the table in front of ours, and they converse politely before he disappears back inside.

"What is this?" I ask, nodding toward the bowl in front of me.

Adriene grins, taking a piece of the wonderful-smelling bread and drowning it in the soup. "Buttered rosemary and thyme bread with chicken

Parmesan broth." He pops the entire piece of squishy bread in his mouth and swallows. "Much better than cha kla eyes and insects."

I take a slice of bread and dip the end in the broth, bringing it to my lips and savoring the mouth-watering scent. With my first bite, the flavor explodes across my taste buds, and my eyes shut in delight. "This may be the best thing I've ever tasted."

Adriene glows at the praise. "We used to have this every weekend at the palace—long before Aaron was crowned."

I smile at the nostalgia written across his face. "We will have to again. Every Saturday for dinner," I suggest.

His lips form a sheepish smirk, and he peers at me through the canopy of his eyelashes. "You're something special, Emilia. I'm so very glad you took the path you did."

"I—"

A scream tears through the village, and we bolt from our seats, eyes wide and frantic, scanning for the source of the scream.

A howl follows soon after, alongside a bolt of lightning crashing into the forest. Adriene narrows his eyes as if his suspicion is confirmed. "A chimera."

"I thought you said they patrolled within the bog?" I shoot a glance toward the windows of the restaurant, noting how everyone's either ducked under tables or cowering far away from the door. Fear is evident in the hunch of a vampire's shoulders and the tears streaming down a scaled boy's cheeks. If even a vampire is scared of a chimera… I don't ever want to come face-to-face with one. Though I may not have that luxury.

"What do you think happened?" I ask Adriene, following him toward the center of the village. He presses me against the house to our right, one hand on my waist, and peers around the corner. He must spot whatever he's looking for because his mouth hardens in a line, and his eyebrows knit together.

"One of the chimeras must have gotten hungry and wandered into the village for food." Adriene's eyes shift as a plan starts to formulate.

"Food? Did it take someone?" I try to peer around him, but he pushes me flat against the house again, his leather-clad arm holding me in place.

"One of the children who was playing outside… A little boy, I believe." He studies the scene that's unfolding in the street. I can hear a woman crying.

I gasp. "We can't just let the chimera eat him."

Adriene's head snaps toward me, and his eyes rim with white. "These chimeras are incredibly dangerous. There's no guarantee that the boy is still alive."

"But he might be," I insist. "He's a *kid*…"

25

"I know," Adriene says quietly. He removes the scythe from his back, brandishing it before him. He takes my hand and pulls me into the center of the village, where a crowd is now forming, watching the tree line and the bog within with ghostly expressions. A woman with blonde hair and deep brown eyes is sobbing, pointing a finger toward the trees.

She spots Adriene and steps toward him, hands clasped in front of her as she falls to her knees and muddies the hem of her gray dress. "Please, Adriene. Protector of our people. Please. My son—"

Adriene nods toward the woman. "We'll bring him back safely." His gaze travels over the gathering crowd, and he calls over the din, "Go back inside your homes and lock your doors. If I find that anyone follows us past the trees, then I'll make an example of them. Their blood will stain the village. Am I understood?"

The crowd starts to disperse, and equal looks of fear and awe are shot toward Adriene, the mighty executioner, as he tightens his grip on his scythe.

"Protector of our people?" I ask, quoting the woman.

"Patrol used to be my task," he answers, seeming to not want to explain it further. I let the subject drop as his fingers tighten around my own. "Let me protect you, Emilia. Once we part those trees—we are in the chimeras' territory. I don't want you to intervene. Stay back and watch."

"And if I don't? Are you going to make an example of *me*?" I question tauntingly. Honestly, I don't need *him,* of all people, to protect me from hybrid monsters. I have faced enough monsters, and so far, they haven't broken me. Not completely. The memory of Aaron falling to his knees with Aridam protruding from his heart rushes to the forefront of my mind, and I start to turn away.

Adriene's hand slips from my own, and then he uses it to lift my chin, forcing me to face him. He lowers his mouth toward mine, leaving me dizzy as his warm breath parts my lips. "I would never hurt you, Emilia," he promises. His touch is gentle, a stark contradiction to the blade of the scythe glinting in the flash of lightning and the tight leathers constricting the body of the executioner. "But I might not be so nice if you force my hand. Do remember, I am here to protect you. *That* is my job."

I swallow. "Duly noted."

He pulls away, and I kick myself for being disappointed. I'm *queen.* I don't have time for feelings... *Longing...* Anything of that sort. I shouldn't even have those feelings, not after everything that happened. My sister was *buried* a couple of months ago. I need to be on my guard. I know that the

Veiling is toying with my memories as well as my emotions.

Adriene sweeps a hand through his hair as he watches the trees, scanning between them and into the deep recesses of the bog. "Shall we go get ourselves a chimera?" He flashes me a maniacal grin. I'm tempted to match him. Instead, I give him a rigid nod and force myself to turn toward the forest.

"I think we shall."

Chapter Three

The trees sway above us as the storm magnifies, rain falling through the slits in the canopy and splashing across already sodden ground.

Right now, the ground is firm beneath my feet—but I can tell when it turns into the bog. When the ground is little more than an algae-infested pool. About a hundred feet in front of us, the grass shifts from well-watered green to a murky yellow. I curl my lip in disgust, not wanting to go anywhere near the limp grass and sponge-like ground.

"Where is it?" I ask, spinning in a circle as my eyes scan the forest. Adriene is stiff beside me, staring to the left.

Cutting through the silence is a distinctive rattle that sends goosebumps racing up my spine. Adriene said the mutated chimeras have the body of a wolf, the wings of a dragon, and a rattlesnake's tail... I narrow my eyes, searching for the mutated monster behind the eerie trees that sprout from the ground.

"Follow me," Adriene instructs, raising his scythe. He stalks forward, eyebrows lowered over his eyes. His mouth is set in a concentrated frown, and with every twig that snaps, he shifts—following something I can't see.

I grimace as we step into the yellow grass, our feet sinking into the restrictive clutches of the bog. I can hear the ghastly sucking noise the bog creates when it swallows my leg up to my mid-calf. With every footstep, I grit my teeth at the sound. The bog smells *disgusting*; it's comparable to manure, mold, or expired milk; maybe all three mixed together. My stomach somersaults.

Trees jut from the wetland, their bark varying from brown to black. The village must have cut down some of these trees to build their houses, since they appear to be made of the same wood.

Adriene stops, and I run into him; I imagine running into a brick wall would feel the same.

His posture is rigid, and his jaw is set. He's staring intently at something, tracking it with his eyes as it moves through the trees. Without warning, he pushes me behind the nearest tree, earning a startled squeak from me, then the dirtiest glare I can muster.

I grip the black bark of the tree and lean forward, trying to stay hidden yet still in a position to watch the conflict that's bound to happen.

Adriene steps forward, and the rattling sound

grows louder. The wind picks up, blowing leaves and needles from the trees. They flutter down and sink into the bog. I take a steadying breath and crane around the tree enough to see.

My eyes widen.

The chimera rears back on its haunches, gray fur shimmering from the lightning darting across the sky. Filling the expanse of the small clearing it's standing in is a pair of shadow-black wings, veined with crimson. Its tail flicks out from behind it, lifting its rattle that must be the size of my head in the air and swishing it about. That daunting sound fills the forest, and I bite my lip, wondering how Adriene is going to win.

Adriene tightens his grip on his scythe, sending me an urgent look that screams *stay put*. But as the chimera shifts and reveals a little boy hunched on the murky ground behind it, I know I'm going to have to disappoint him.

Adriene steps forward as the chimera lunges, opening its maw to reveal a set of sharp white teeth. Its yellow eyes flash with violence, with the need to tear into flesh and quell the hunger burning in its stomach. Adriene arcs the blade of his scythe through the air, slicing the skin of the chimera's front paw open. An agonized howl tears through the forest as the chimera's wings beat the air, creating the powerful wind that sways the trees. My hair flies backward, and my crown of bones tumbles from my head, landing behind me in the bog. But I don't have time to recover my crown—it's at the bottom of my list of current priorities.

The boy *may* still be alive—and I'm going to find out.

Adriene slashes his scythe through the flesh of the beast again, earning another pained howl that makes my ears throb. I move from the tree as quickly as I can, darting behind another one closer to the boy. I keep my back against the trunk as I slowly move around it, avoiding the gaze of the chimera.

My fingernails dig into the bark, tearing the smooth skin of my fingertips. The pain brings a sense of satisfaction coursing through me as I move to the next tree, getting closer and closer to my target. The Veiling does more than just toy with my emotions and memories, it also makes me feel satisfaction from pain.

A groan emits through the forest and my head whips toward the source, eyes wide as the chimera draws back from Adriene, who's kneeling in the center of the clearing, his knees sinking slowly into the bog. He's clutching his arm as blood seeps from between his fingers and drips onto the yellow grass. His scythe is cast aside, crimson painting the blade.

Adriene… He's hurt.

My heart stalls in my chest, split in half from conflict. Either I rush to my friend's side or I save the boy. I won't have time to save both, not when the chimera is near and fueled by blood lust.

I bite my lip, my eyes trailing to the helpless boy, then back to the chimera as it circles Adriene, hunger shining in its eyes.

My eyebrows lower, an idea finalizing in my mind. Greed courses through my body; I'm *queen*… why should I ever choose just one?

I crouch low, scanning the ground. I reach forward and pull a stick from the leeching bog. One end is broken and sharp. I have half a mind to cut my arm and draw the chimera to me with the scent of my leaking blood—but I'm not stupid.

I grab the stick like a boomerang and close one eye, reeling my arm back while focusing on a tree forty feet away. I have one shot—if it doesn't work— my blood will spill alongside Adriene's and the boy's. Our blood would spread through the bog like an infection, turning the yellow grass a morbid red.

I peek over my shoulder, watching as Adriene reaches for his scythe. The chimera switches from simply stalking around his prey to gearing up to eat him. The chimera's mouth snaps open, the skin of his snoot curling back and forming an impressive number of wrinkles. Saliva drips from the chimera's teeth, and before he can rip open Adriene's throat, I hurl the stick at the tree. It clacks off the trunk pitifully, sinking dread into my stomach.

But it must have been loud enough because the chimera draws away from Adriene. Its beady yellow eyes latch onto the tree forty feet away, and its fur rolls with its movement as its target changes. A hunt is more appealing than eating the meat that's kneeling right in front of it.

The chimera springs forward, pushing off the ground as its wings spread wide, pumping through the air and carrying it effortlessly through the forest.

My lip curls in terror at the image of a wolf flying right above me. *That just isn't right.*

Gosh darn Adriene and his stupid scary mutants.

As soon as the chimera is a decent distance away, completely ignoring everything behind it, I dart toward the boy. Adriene frees himself from the bog and secures his scythe, meeting me by the boy's side.

The boy's skin is pasty, and his brown hair is matted to his forehead with sweat... But he doesn't seem to be bleeding. The chimera must not have had time to sink his teeth into the boy after snatching him from the village. Which means we were closer on the chimera's trail than I thought.

Adriene studies the boy, concluding, "He'll be okay. I think he just passed out from shock."

"He's not hurt?" I ask, pressing my fingers to the boy's neck, feeling for a pulse. His heartbeat is steady beneath my fingertips, and I exhale in relief. "Let's get him back to his mother."

Adriene doesn't move, watching me again. His eyebrows lowered over his—

"Your eyes," we both say in unison.

He reels back, one hand reaching toward his face. "What about them?" he asks urgently.

"They're..." I take a step closer to him, peering up at this Shroud; this supposedly soulless immortal. I'm so used to his pitch-black eyes and the occasional white that rims them when his humanity starts to peek through—but this...this golden color circling his pupils is different... "They're golden." My voice is quiet, barely more than a gasp. The bog seems to go silent around us, the wind dying.

He lowers his scythe to use the blade as a mirror. After smearing the blood off a section with the cuff of his uniform, his mouth pops open. He sheathes his scythe just as quickly. His eyes flood back to black. "That's impossible." He shakes his head as if he can just deny what we both so clearly saw. "They haven't been golden in decades." Adriene lifts the boy into his arms, lolling his head against his chest. After scanning the boy, a small, relieved smile flits across his lips.

"If it's possible for me, Adriene, then it's possible for you too." I reach out and lay my hand gently on his arm. I don't know how I feel about this hope flaring in my chest. It's making me dizzy and disoriented. I don't think I want to return to who I was before the Veiling... I was weak and timid. Now, I'm a queen, my morals dashed to the wind. I can take whatever I want... And the power that comes from seeing the fear marking people's expressions lights a fire of satisfaction in me. Past Emilia didn't have that... I shake my head. First, we need to focus on getting out of this infernal bog and returning this boy to his devastated mother.

We both turn forward to continue our trek out of the forest, but we stop short, our eyes going wide as three chimeras stare back at us.

Chapter Four

The chimeras' muscles ripple under gray and brown fur, mouths curling back to reveal their dripping canines. The one in the middle is the biggest, with black-streaked auburn fur and scaled yellow wings protruding from its back, and curling to its sides when not in use.

The gray chimera from earlier glares at me as if it knows *I'm* the one who deceived it. It's only slightly bigger than the one on the right, which must be considerably younger since its brown wings are half the size of the other two.

It's no less intimidating as its green eyes fix us with a ferocious stare. I can almost picture what it would do to us... How it would peel our flesh right off our bones and take joy in our screams. I appreciate its aptitude for causing fear.

"How should we do this?" I ask Adriene, nodding toward the boy he has pressed against his chest, one arm protectively wrapped around him.

Adriene scowls at the territorial beasts before us.

"Take the boy back to the village—give him to his mother and tell her that he'll be okay. He just needs to rest and recuperate from such a fright. I'll stay here and take care of the chimeras." He levels his stare at me when my mouth falls open in protest. "It's only fair, Emilia, since *I* created them."

"No," I insist, shaking my head. My long brown hair falls around my shoulders, and the hem of my dress is completely ruined by the infernal sludge. My head feels so much lighter without the crown, and I find, even though I know I shouldn't, that I'm a bit relieved it's gone. "I'm not going to just leave you here. You couldn't even handle *one* chimera. There's no way you will live when there's *three*."

He shoots me a withering glare, but I only spoke the truth. "You're not a mage. You don't have magic. There's nothing you can do that will be of use, Emilia."

I cross my arms, prepared to give him a thorough tongue-lashing when a series of howls shake the forest, a crash of thunder echoing alongside.

"Don't argue with me, Emilia," Adriene demands, thrusting the little boy into my arms. He's kind of heavy, but the adrenaline from the life-or-death situation spurs me into action. I cast one last worried look in Adriene's direction as he pulls the scythe from his back and slashes it through the air. His face is twisted with determination. His scythe glints from the blast of lightning overhead, and the chimeras lunge.

I run, doing what Adriene told me to. I know that it's the only way this boy is going to get out of this forest alive—and I'm not about to make a mother mourn because I simply wanted to fight alongside Adriene. Not when I can save her son.

Though tears slip from my eyes and roll down my cheeks as Adriene's groans follow me, as the chimeras howl—not in pain, but in something terrifyingly close to victory. I clasp the boy tighter, my feet sticking in the bog, but I yank them free and stumble onward. I practically fall onto the solid ground, breaking through the trees. I sigh in relief, but the sound of fighting continues behind me, pushing me back into an unsteady run. I'm so close to the village, to saving this little boy. My lungs burn from the exertion, and my skin is damp with sweat and bog water.

I reach the village—where a crowd is waiting, completely ignoring Adriene's command that they all huddle inside.

The boy's mother darts from the crowd, wild eyes taking in her son's condition. She turns to me, lips quivering as her arms open wide.

Instead of scooping the boy from me like I anticipated, she pulls me into a hug, sandwiching the boy between us.

"Thank you, Your Majesty. Thank you for saving my boy," she cries, her thin lips pulling into an eternally grateful smile. She takes him in her arms, lovingly tucking his sweaty hair behind his ears and planting a kiss on his forehead. Her gray eyes shine.

"He's in shock," I say between gasps of air, hating how out of shape I am. "He'll need lots of rest. But he'll be fine."

She nods, running the back of her hand under her nose. Tears drip from her eyes, but her smile never leaves her face. "I'll take him home. Thank you again, Your Majesty. I'm so glad you came to our kingdom. Maybe now…things will be different."

I warm to her words, and the woman shifts, her eyebrows shooting into her hairline. Murmurs crest along the crowd as they all surge forward to get a better look at me. My hand reaches up to touch my face, wondering what they're so fascinated by.

"We've never had a ruler with colored eyes," the woman says, raising a finger to point at me. "You *are* different, Your Majesty. You will lead Nether into an era of prosperity and acceptance. I can sense it."

I frown. It happened again. Was Adriene right…? Am I fighting the Veiling? "Maybe. But right now… My friend is in that forest still, being attacked by the chimeras. I need to help him. Do you have something that will…make me more powerful?" I point toward the bog just as a chimera screams and lightning parts the sky. The woman before me steps back, hugging her son to her chest even tighter. She scowls at the bog, her eyes flashing with maternal anger.

The crowd moves to the side, all turning to stare at an older man with sun-kissed skin and russet-colored hair poking out from beneath a wide-brimmed hat. I don't know what the importance of this man is—or who he is, for that matter—but he steps forward and offers me a glass vial with a swirling green liquid inside. Slight black stubble lines his cheeks and chin. He appears to be middle-aged, though I'm not sure how accurate my assumption is. I think Adriene looks to be in his twenties, but he's actually hundreds of years old.

His eyes are pitch black, just like mine and Adriene's. He hands me the vial and nods toward the bog. His voice is humble and cracks between words. "Take this and drink it. Be *quick*… The chimeras are strong, Your Majesty. Adriene may not last for long."

I hold the vial up, watching the liquid sparkle as the overcast light hits it. It's beautiful, shimmering with iridescent blues and greens. The rain beats down harder on us and the strange man peers up at the sky, adjusting the brim of his hat. "Who are you?" I ask, tightening my fingers around the vial. Urgency flares in my chest; I need to return to Adriene's side. I need to help him—to see if he's still *alive*. But I need to know *who* this man is, and why I should trust his gift. For all I know, he could be poisoning me.

"My name is Bartholomew. Bart. I was the palace's alchemist years ago. I used to work with Adriene. I don't want him to die. So go." He nods toward the tree line, his black eyes daring me to stay here for a moment longer.

I uncork the vial, holding his eyes as I down the green contents. The liquid burns my throat as it slides into my stomach. I'll trust Bart because we both have something in common: we don't want Adriene to die.

As the elixir hits my stomach, I charge back toward the bog. My lungs burn from the exertion, and the metallic taste of the elixir makes me want to heave. I swallow, forcing it to stay down. The elixir won't do any good if I throw it back up.

I'm only ten feet away from the tree line when I start to change, pain searing through my body. It starts in my chest, a persistent, paralyzing heartburn that makes me stop in my tracks. I drop to my knees, tearing my gown, my arms falling to my sides as an agonized scream is pulled from me. It feels as if all my bones are breaking and stitching themselves back together.

Black nails pierce through the skin of my knuckles and my body shifts. Dark brown fur sprouts from my skin, and I groan as my face shifts into that of a wolf. I tilt my face toward the stormy sky, a howl dragging from my throat as my back splits open and a pair of golden wings spread wide. When I glance toward the forest, I'm overtaken by the smell of blood; my canine senses draw me toward it. My wings start to beat through the air, propelling me forward. I know I should be terrified as my paws leave the ground—as I *fly*—but when is a *chimera* afraid to fly?

My dragon wings snap off any branches that get in the way and leave gauges in the tree trunks as I zone in on the clearing where blood is oozing across the wetland. That's a *lot* of blood—whatever—*whoever*—it came from can't still be alive.

From up here, I can't spot Adriene—but there's little doubt that he's still alive, still fighting, when I take note of the original gray chimera splayed on the ground, blood spreading from the long gash in its stomach. I touch down in the clearing, digging my claws into the ground and nosing the beast's carcass to catch the scent of Adriene. I latch onto his piney scent right away, snapping my head forward. The dead chimera's dull, yellow gaze is like an arrow pointing to where the battle now takes place.

43

I hover my nose above the ground, following his scent like a dog—well, I guess more like a *wolf*. Lightning darts across the sky, following a loud rumble of thunder. The rain mattes my fur and slicks my wings, but that slight annoyance won't take my attention away from finding Adriene and the remaining two chimeras.

A howl pierces the air and the hair along my spine stands on end. I snap open my maw and charge across the bog, pulling my paws free from the suctioning ground with ease. A rattle resounds about the bog—and for a brief moment, I'm struck with fear before I realize that it's *my* rattle. My tail swishes behind me, raised like that of a scorpion, but instead of a stinger, I have a thick scaled rattle.

My wings flare around me, cutting through the branches and shrubbery that dare get in my path. I spread them wide as naturally as extending a limb, my back stretching with the extra weight. Prowling in front of me, half hidden by a felled tree, is the largest chimera, blood dripping from a cut on its leg. It rears back, claws striking forward and wings flaring wide, preparing to strike down what must be Adriene. Before the chimera has a chance to hurt my friend again, I leap, my wings gliding me over the fallen tree.

I tear my claws through the soft tissue of the chimera's back, lashing out and gauging the thin material of its wings. It screams, wings flapping in a desperate attempt to escape. But it won't get away that easily.

I sink my canines into its neck, snapping and tearing at important ligaments. I rip out its trachea and the chimera drops in front of me, its throat hanging from my bloody maw, dripping crimson onto its auburn corpse.

I finally look up, my breath coming in short gasps, and meet Adriene's eyes. His scythe is painted red as he stands with one foot on the dead body of the smallest chimera. He's watching me in shock, his mouth open and his eyebrows knitted together. "Emilia?" he asks, unsure.

I spit the trachea onto the grass and curl my lip in disgust; I can't believe I had that thing in my *mouth*.

I stalk toward him, my muscles searing with the exertion now that the adrenaline has worn off. My wings tuck back to my sides, and I lower my head in a small nod. Relief washes over his features, though there's something else flickering within his shark-like eyes... Something close to admiration or pride.

He gestures to the dead chimera behind me, nodding in approval. "That was quite impressive."

I stretch my neck, my claws sinking back into my skin. My wings shrink, and the fur blanketing my body starts to disappear. With one last shake, my rattle is gone, and I'm lying on the forest floor in a torn green gown, sucking in large gasps of air.

I blink up at Adriene, who's leaning over me, his forearm propped on his knee. He sheathes his scythe and scoops me up, holding me with reverence—a kind that doesn't have anything to do with being the queen. "I guess I was wrong earlier."

I chuckle, though the effort it requires zaps the remainder of my energy. I rest my head against his chest, listening to his strangely human heartbeat. "Say that again."

He shakes his head, a wide grin brightening his face. "You continue to surprise me, Emilia."

"Is that good?" I ask, watching his face as he carries me out of the bog.

The brightness from the lightning makes his skin appear silvery and ethereal, highlighting the sharp angles of his jaw and the way his bowed lips twist into a devilish smirk. Though he's an immortal executioner, known as an evil and immoral man throughout the realm, I've never felt safer than I do encompassed in his arms.

"Of course, Emilia. Queen of Nether and Chimera Slayer."

Chapter Five

*B*ubbles float on the surface of the rose-tinted water, the flowery smell fills the bathroom. I sigh. The hot water and soothing oils coax my muscles to relax. It's been a rather taxing day. I want nothing more than to unwind in a tub of nearly scalding hot water.

I lean my head against the edge of the stone tub, closing my eyes as my energy slowly restores itself. I breathe in the scent of the rose oils and reach over the edge of the tub, where a paperback novel and a towel are waiting. I dry my hands off and pick up the book, noting that the spine is cracked in dozens of places, and the corners of the pages are curled from wear. How many times has Adriene read this book? It's a thick story, probably 600 pages or so. I've never shied away from a long book.

As soon as we returned to the palace, Adriene carried me up here and drew me a bath, handing me a book he retrieved from his room with strict instructions to relax. Since I could hardly stand on my own without my legs threatening to give out, I was in no position to oppose him…so I didn't.

The cover of the book is faded, but I can still make out the painted depiction of a cloaked figure standing in front of a gothic palace, surrounded by tall coarse trees, a jagged sword in the figure's hand. I never would have taken Adriene as a fan of fantasy. Especially since he lives in one. By the massive amount of books lining his shelves in his small room, I suppose I shouldn't be *that* surprised.

I open the book, pinning the front cover to the back so I can hold it with one hand. Another content sigh leaves my lips as I scoot a bit farther down in the tub, determined not to get out until my skin is pruned and I've at least come to understand what this story is about. I love taking book recommendations from friends; it allows me to take a peek inside their minds… Adriene is still such a mystery to me, so maybe this story will help me unveil more about the immortal executioner.

I'm recovered enough to join the rest of the Shrouds for dinner in the glass dining hall; the hall where dinner is served every night for those in the monarch's inner circle. There's another dining hall to the west of the palace that serves everyone else. I wouldn't care if we all dined together, finding the difference between the two groups more annoying than anything. I want to see *all* my people—not the divide between them.

Adriene meets my eyes as the silver domes in front of us are removed with a grand flourish by maids and butlers, revealing a bowl of chicken Parmesan broth on a plate rimmed with thin slices of buttered rosemary bread. Something shifts in his gaze as the rest of the Shrouds curl their lips in disgust—the fangs of the vampires in attendance flash in the waning sunlight that drifts through the glass ceiling of the dining hall.

"Is something wrong?" I ask, directing my stare toward a particularly irritating vampire two seats down from Adriene.

He cowers away from me—and my bone crown that Adriene fetched from the bog while I bathed. I wouldn't have cared if the thing disappeared, swallowed whole by the murky bog. But it *is* probably better that I wear it, keeping those below me in line, lest they get any ideas in their empty skulls, however unlikely *that* is.

I return my attention to Adriene, who's blowing gently on a spoonful of the hot broth, before happily lifting it to his lips and grinning when he senses my eyes on him. He watches me as he drowns a slice of bread in the broth and brings up the saturated carcass to plop into his mouth. "Emilia," he says quietly, disbelief and gratitude dripping from every syllable. "This is wonderful. I was growing quite annoyed at eating things with wiggling legs."

I lift an eyebrow, trying not to laugh at how odd that is to hear. "To be fair, this was mostly a selfish act. I never did finish my meal in the village."

The corner of his mouth lifts in a subtle smirk. "Well then, I'm very glad you acted so selfishly and messed with the kitchen's repertoire."

I match his smirk, lifting my spoon and taking a sip of the broth. The savory smell tingles my nose, teasing me with how delicious the smell is alone. But as the broth slides across my taste buds, I almost jump from my seat and squeak with delight. Adriene meets my eyes and gives me an *I-know-how-you-feel* kind of look.

The rest of dinner goes without a hitch—as in, none of the Shrouds revolted against me because of the sudden switch in meals—so Adriene and I make our way to the conservatory, where the moonlight reflects off the thin wings of the butterflies flitting about the enclosure.

I remember being afraid of these things, of how they look up close, and how they aren't afraid of landing on people—unlike a lot of other insects. But now…they're peaceful in a way I don't think I could have appreciated before the Veiling slid through my veins.

They're just *being*. Living and thriving in the only way they know how.

"Did you enjoy the book?" Adriene asks, crossing his hands behind his back as I settle onto the bench beneath the cherry blossom tree. The fading sunset casts a golden glow throughout the conservatory, highlighting the soft pink blossoms on the tree above me. Adriene tilts his head, his white hair falling to the side and grazing his jawline.

I pat the spot next to me and Adriene tracks the movement, an intensity buzzing between us like it hasn't before. He slides into his spot beside me and rests his forearms on his thighs, ready to listen. I appreciate that about Adriene—how he listens and pays attention. How he cares enough to put weight on every word that leaves my lips.

"It was…interesting," I say, furrowing my brow as the first fifty pages I read flit through my mind. It wasn't what I expected when I cracked open the book, and it doesn't strike me as something Adriene would read over and over again, bending and creasing the spine *that* many times. "I don't understand the main character. She seems…"

"Lost?" he suggests, raising his eyebrows.

I nod. "And…sad. Going about everyday tasks with a lack of…clarity, of care. It's as if her world is missing color." I don't know how else to say it, to put words to the dullness of the main character's life. But if the cover truly does reflect the story written within, how does she go from being so mundane to a warrior in a fantastical land? "How many times have you read it?" I ask, turning to him with a small smile ghosting my lips. "The spine is basically *destroyed*."

He shakes his head, chuckling. When he changes the topic, I don't question it. "Earlier, you were—"

"Crazy?" I supply, remembering the metallic taste of the chimera's blood running across my tongue. I cringe, feeling the need to spit in an attempt to clear my mouth. I can't believe I dug my claws into the monster's back, and then tore its trachea from its neck using my *teeth*... I can't believe I transformed into a mutated chimera, let alone *flew*.

"How did you do it? You're not a mage—*are* you?" He shifts, bringing one foot up on the bench and wrapping his arm around his leg. He tilts his head, studying me with an intensity in his black eyes that brings heat to my face. It's as if he's seeing into my bones... Seeing through me to everything that lies within. My fears. My faults. My insecurities.

"No, I'm not," I say. "I went to the village and delivered the boy to his mother. And I asked them for help so I could go back for you." Pink blooms across his cheeks, but his eyes don't drop from mine. An immortal executioner like Adriene doesn't seem capable of blushing, yet here he is. "A man named Bart—well, *Bartholomew*—said you worked together. He gave me a vial that changed me into...*that*."

A crease forms between his brows, and he chews on his cheek in thought. "Bartholomew... I haven't seen him in years."

"Were you both friends?"

He nods, smiling sadly. "He was our best alchemist. He taught me everything I know, which pales in comparison to his vast knowledge. He helped me create the chimeras lurking in the bog, so it's no wonder he knew how to make that elixir. I thought he moved to the Banished Realm, but apparently, he's back."

"The palace would love to have him back—if you would like to focus on your other tasks besides alchemy," I say, shrugging one shoulder. My draping, thick black sleeves pull on my still sore muscles. I regret my outfit choice—but I wanted to choose something that commands respect. Something worthy of the title Queen of Nether. Suddenly, however, I want to be in nothing but a pair of linen pajama pants and a t-shirt.

He nods, pulling his lips to the side. "I would appreciate that, Emilia. I would rather spend my time bending to the will of the new queen and perfecting my scythe-work." He flashes me a teasing grin that has me swatting at his chest. He catches my hand and the heat of his palm against mine sends a blush creeping up my neck. Tension flares in the space between us, and my eyes flicker momentarily to his lips, which seem too close to my own to be safe. And safe would mean ignoring anything between me and my executioner. *Safe* would mean slapping him in the face for *that* look he's giving me. Safe would mean not pulling him toward me and smothering his lips with my own.

But *safe* doesn't describe me anymore.

So, I slip my fingers around the stiff collar of his leather executioner's uniform and pull him toward me, closing the distance as I press my lips to his. I can feel him smile against me as his hand gently cups my cheek. His kiss is kind and tender, barely more than a caress, but it's enough to make the walls I've been carefully constructing around my damaged heart crumble. A tear slips down my cheek, and he pulls back, worry flickering to life in his golden eyes. He wipes the tear away with the pad of his thumb and tries to get up and leave. But I don't let him go far. I reach up and gently touch his face, drinking in every detail of his golden eyes; small, dark brown flecks circle his pupils, and ringing the breathtaking golden-color is a green the shade of grass under a spring sun.

"Your eyes," I whisper again for the second time today. "They're so beautiful."

His fingertips linger above my cheek, right below my left eye. "And so are yours, Emilia."

Chapter Six

"You said they would be back in two days…" I say inquisitively, cocking my head and inspecting the little blue butterfly Adriene has captured in a glass jar. It's flitting about, the light from the lamp on his desk catches on the vibrant teal in its wings, making them appear paper-thin and ethereal. Blue magic, the color of the sea, pulsates around the creature. I watch tendrils of magic push against the glass like they're searching for a way to escape.

"Whoever attached that magic to it must have increased its speed too," Adriene explains, tapping the tip of a quill on the piece of parchment before him. He leaves behind little splotches of black ink. He gently presses his front teeth to his bottom lip, while white pieces of hair catch on the thin sheen of sweat on his forehead. The gears in his head are whirring, trying to figure out what the magic is and who it could have come from. "It's a message binding. Mages and other magic-folk used it on pigeons and crows long ago." He runs a hand through his already disheveled hair. When he glances at me, a monocle framing his left eye with a thin silver chain dangling from it, I want to break into laughter. But his expression is serious, stone cold with concern that has my stomach flipping.

I force my nerves and fear away, needing to know the answer to two very important questions: "*Who* left the message, and *how* do we reveal it?" I nod toward the butterfly again, the light bouncing across the desk with its every frightened move.

With a quiet hum, Adriene gets up from his desk chair and paces across the length of his room. He stops in front of his bookshelf and removes a thick leather tome. He spreads it open on his desk and flips to a dog-eared page, pointing to a section that is sprawled in ancient, black ink. "A message-breaking spell," he reads aloud. "It requires a pinch of salt and a dash of sugar." His head snaps up at me. "I'll run to the kitchen and grab the supplies we'll need. Can you read through this and write down anything else that's important to know?"

I nod, and he quickly scurries from the room, not even bothering to put on a pair of decent shoes; what will the palace staff—let alone the Shrouds—think of their executioner running about the palace in a loose shirt, trousers, and slippers?

I sit in the chair he left, studying the butterfly

closer. Adriene had summoned me to his room as soon as he noticed the butterfly returned. None of the butterflies were supposed to return with any word about Nether or the happenings of the realm until tomorrow. I wonder what the message is, that the mage—or whoever it was—needed us to hear it as soon as possible; especially at such an unholy hour. Everyone in the kingdom should be asleep, including me.

I focus on the book, running my finger under the sentences as I read them. With the quill, I write down any information that seems important.

The Message-Breaking Spell:

-Requires a pinch of salt, a dash of sugar, and a steady tongue repeating the incantation.

> *Locked words be unraveled*
> *intentions be known*
> *thee note that's traveled*
> *shall find thee way home*

Once the spell has been done properly, the message will only be said once.

There doesn't seem to be much to it, so I let out a relieved breath, eager to find out who captured one of our butterflies and sent it back to us with a message.

How did they even realize that the butterfly's cursed and was sent from Nether? Will the message be a threat? It certainly could be... Every kingdom was ready to wage war on Nether when Aaron was sitting on the throne. I don't believe they would stop now, when I've inherited all his evil.

I furrow my brow as I stare at the butterfly. It could be *anyone.* I jump when Adriene's hand sneaks around me and places a little ceramic bowl of sugar and a matching one of salt on the desk. He gives me a perplexed look before shrugging it off and reading my notes.

He sighs. "Well, that's easy." He scoots the bowl of salt toward me with a cheeky grin. "Care to go first?"

I raise my eyebrows. "But I'm not a mage…"

"It doesn't matter for the first part—just the incantation," he explains.

I purse my lips, taking a pinch of salt between my fingertips and doing as he directs—quite literally sprinkling it over the lid of the jar. It rests in a tiny mound on the top, and I find it a little silly that this is what magic looks like. "But how much is a dash?" I ask, grimacing at the bowl of sugar.

Adriene frowns, eyebrows pulling over his black eyes. "I'm not sure actually…" He blows out a quick breath before clawing his hands through his hair again. It flops across his forehead in disheveled chunks. "When something is…*dashing*…it's supposed to be moving fast, right? And I think a dash is a *bit* more than a pinch."

"So…you want me to throw *slightly more than a pinch* of sugar really quickly at the top of this jar?" My voice drips with skepticism. But then he smiles sheepishly and my stomach does a back flip; are we *ever* going to hear the message? I comply with his odd instructions, grabbing a bit of sugar between my fingers. I stare at the jar and pray that this works, and then I flick my wrist, sending the sugar spraying across the jar.

Adriene whispers the incantation, which parts through the air like a crack of lightning. The hair on my arm stands on end, and I balk as the blue magic pulsating around the butterfly starts to untangle itself like a ball of string. It unfurls into the air and floats above us like a cloud, casting our faces in a vibrant blue light.

I gawk up at the magic as it swirls above us, so close yet completely out of reach. I have a feeling that if I tried to touch it, I would make the magic whisk away like smoke.

When the message begins to play, I immediately recognize the voice that's heavy with authority. King Hanson of Aquartia.

"All the monarchs of the Solstice Realm are meeting in Olympus tomorrow. Queen Emilia, your attendance is required." Then the blue magic dissipates and his chilling voice is left ringing in my ears.

He does *not* sound thrilled about this meeting.

I narrow my eyes in disdain at the ceiling, hating the way his tone—and his command—make me feel like a chastised child.

"I know what you're thinking, Emilia, and it's not a good idea," Adriene says calmly, standing over me. His shadow is thrown across the floor, and I watch as it moves.

"You can't possibly know what I'm thinking," I say, leveling him with an unwavering stare.

He leans against the lip of the desk and looks down his nose at me. "You're thinking of not going simply because he instructed that you do."

I glare at him, which is answer enough that he's right. He smirks, though there's a tightness in the action.

"What's wrong?" I stand up, brushing my hands absentmindedly over the skirt of my dark purple nightgown. The velvet fabric is heavy, making me feel like I weigh a hundred pounds more as I walk, but it's fitting for a queen with a crown of bones— and surprisingly comfortable to sleep in. I used to borrow my Mom's weighted blanket back in the Earthen Realm, and the thick, draping velvet gives the same effect. I remember that much…though the memory is fuzzy like a dream I'm reaching toward, but can't quite grasp. I hate how the Veiling is playing with my memories. I only had two years' worth before this infuriating curse, and now it's all slipping away…

"All the monarchs haven't held a formal meeting since your sister was appointed," Adriene says, sighing when I frown at the mention of Soph.

"So, you're saying that the meeting is because of *me*?"

He nods. "Precisely. And I have a feeling that nothing good will come of it."

I roll my eyes to the ceiling, earning a laugh from him. A groan tears from my throat, and I shake my head. "We better leave now then. How long will it take to get to Olympus?" A light bulb flickers on in my mind when I recall copying Jax's map down in my journal; though the momentary relief I feel is outweighed by the dread of opening it again, peeking into a life that was stolen out from under me. It feels as if it's been years since I was traveling around the realm with my friends, happy and determined to repair Glaven. But it's only been two months.

Two agonizing months where I felt like I was losing myself.

"A week by carriage. It *is* on the other side of the realm, after all." Adriene leans his elbow on his desk, watching the butterfly try to escape the jar. He narrows his eyes, chewing thoughtfully on his bottom lip.

I close my eyes in disbelief. What a complete

scumbag move of King Hanson to tell us about a meeting we *have to attend* whilst leaving us no time to even get there. There's no way we can get to Olympus by tomorrow when it's on the other side of the realm!

Adriene must see the question written across my face because he adds, "Samantha the Runespeaker is stronger than any other mage with the same power. Most Runespeakers can only carry a couple of people at a time—and need a significant recharge between leaps—but I'm sure she can get us and our guards to Olympus first thing in the morning." He shrugs one shoulder, quirking the corner of his mouth up in an *I-hope-so* gesture.

My face scrunches in protest. "No. *Absolutely not.*" My chest clenches in anger. I will never run to Samantha for *anything.* Not after she betrayed me. Not after she pretended to be my friend for years, only to spill everything about our relationship to Aaron. I can never forgive that kind of deceit. That kind of *violation.*

"You're going to have to talk to her eventually, Emilia. She's the only Runespeaker we have in Nether." He pushes off his desk and heads toward the door, looking back over his shoulder at me. "If you won't talk to her—then as your second, I'll be forced to."

I glare at him, furious that he's forcing my hand.

How would it look to her if I sent Adriene to talk to her, instead of going myself? Like I'm a *coward*? I am *not* a coward. A queen *can't* be a coward. A queen has to hold her head high and do the things she doesn't want to if it benefits her people... Right?

But what do *I* know of being a queen?

I grit my teeth and curl my hands into fists at my sides, storming after Adriene. The door to his room swings shut behind us.

Chapter Seven

I don't know how long I've been standing in front of Samantha's door, but Adriene sighs beside me and raises his fist to knock. I catch his wrist and shoot him a withering glare. He grins, and his black eyes sparkle with mischief. He likes it when I challenge him, and he likes to challenge me in turn.

I take a steadying breath of the musty air that permeates the dank hallway, wondering why the kingdom's only Runespeaker is tucked away in the shadows of the dungeon, only two right turns from Adriene's room. I suppose, if she's as important as Adriene, she's a good resource to have down here with the prisoners—especially if they need to be taught a lesson.

But as far as I can tell—we don't have *any* prisoners. The cells are only occupied by an occasional violent drunk—locked down here by Shrouds who know what kind of trouble the drunk would get into if they were allowed to roam. Using the dungeon as a cage to sober irresponsible Shrouds is a disgrace. There should be enemy spies, captured war criminals, or village thieves... Something *exciting*, at the very least.

I grit my teeth and knock on the door, steeling my nerves and forcing my anger aside. The door creaks open after a few seconds, and Samantha peers out at us. Her hazel eyes widen. Her blonde hair is tied in a ponytail, and she ditched the Dark mage attire for a gray crop top and black leggings. The torchlight from the hallway floods into her room and makes the green flecks in her wide eyes stand out. Her attention lands on my crown, and her face pales. "Your Majesty, how may I be of assistance?" Her voice is clipped, and she tries to wipe her sweaty palms inconspicuously down her pants.

Does she think I've come down here to punish her for betraying me? I *should*. I loathe being deceived. But if she's our only Runespeaker, then I can't just *kill* her. I'll need her, much to my dismay.

"Can you take us to Olympus in the morning?" I ask, raising an eyebrow challengingly. Adriene crosses his arms beside me—ever the intimidating executioner—even if he's only wearing his night clothes and not pitch-black leather.

Samantha furrows her brow and glances back into her room as if the answer lies there. I follow her gaze and note that her room is set up much like

66

Adriene's, though her shelves are mostly empty, and a little dish of candy sits on her desk. She whips her head back toward us and smiles sheepishly. "I believe so…"

"Then meet us in front of the palace as soon as the sun rises," I demand, turning on my heel and leaving her gawking at my back. I hope I appear regal and dangerous, like a queen who will behead anyone who challenges her. Maybe that will prevent me from being betrayed again.

"We will need a few guards to accompany us," Adriene says, crossing his hands behind his back as he trails after me. My stride is determined as I walk up the stairs, though I don't have a clue where I'm going. I just need to look like I have a destination in mind. I need to look as if I'm too busy being queen to dwell on my broken friendship with Samantha. However, my foggy memory makes it hard to remember why we were friends to begin with. Everything is becoming muddled… I'm losing pieces of myself. *Am I going mad?*

The night in the inn months ago—right after I met Adriene—pops into my mind. His disheveled face floods my thoughts. His lips quiver as he asks, *"When would 'eventually' ever come for someone mad?"*

My blood runs cold. Am I going to turn out like Adriene? Am I truly going mad?

"It *will* get better," Adriene says as if he can read

my thoughts, though he must have caught on by my scrunched face. He's standing in front of me. I don't recall stopping and leaning against the wall near the stairway to go to the main level, but I am. "It's only like that in the beginning. It'll take a couple of months before the Veiling settles in your system. Then you will be able to remember your past—well, the last two years, I suppose." He grimaces. "It was like that for me too. Though there *should* be signs of your memory block clearing by now." He rests against the wall beside me, and we watch the torch across from us flicker, creating moving shadows.

His declaration comforts me. My heartbeat calms as my anxiety releases its clawed grip.

Genially, I turn to face him. He's already looking at me, studying me in the dim light. "Thank you, Adriene. That means a lot more than you think."

"I know. I was there, Emilia," he says quietly, reaching out and tucking a stray strand of my dark brown hair behind my ear. His fingers linger on my cheek. Visions of last night, of the conservatory bench and our first kiss, race to the forefront of my mind. Heat blooms up my neck and across my cheeks, and soon his lips are on mine. Tucked in the alcove of the stairwell, I don't want anything else but to feel human again.

His kisses are gentle and sweet like a spring

breeze caressing my lips. The moment doesn't last forever—no more than a minute—but it's enough to ground me and stop my mind from spiraling. At least, for now.

When he gasps and takes a step back, I'm already reaching toward my face. I can feel the shift in the color of my eyes now. It's subtle and comparable to a tear welling on my waterline.

Adriene and I lock our gazes, mouths slightly parted in awe as we watch the change happen to both of us. His eyes are golden like the hide of a deer under a summer sun. The moment freezes as we stare at each other, confounded, still heated by our interaction seconds ago. I watch as his golden eyes slowly turn black again.

"How is this possible?" I ask, shaking my head in disbelief, interrupting the swelling silence. "Are we both—"

"Fighting the Veiling?" Adriene finishes, closing the gap between us. He peers down at me, his cheeks still flushed from our kiss. "I think we *are*... Somehow, when we're together, it pushes away the Darkness."

"Do you think...we can free ourselves from the Veiling?" I'm not going to explore the possibility of Adriene and I being meant for each other yet... But it can't be ignored. What if Adriene and I are destined to be together, to help each other out whether it be an anxiety attack or a Dark curse? The word "soulmates" comes to mind, but I shake that thought away. It sounds too silly and too fantastical for the dreary situation we're both stuck in.

"If we stick together... Then I would say we have a pretty good chance."

"No. No. *No*," I growl, glaring at Adriene. "We are *not* taking *him*."

"He will be great protection when we face the rest of the monarchs, Emilia," Adriene tries to reason, gesturing to the wooden door in front of us. It's dark, much like the rest of this palace, and foreboding. I thought knocking on Samantha's door was the worst it could get.

"He betrayed me. He betrayed my sister. He's the reason she's dead," I spit out, turning to storm down the main hallway of the fourth floor. There is *no way* we're taking Garamond to Olympus with us. I spin back around and throw my hands to the side. "*Besides*, once the monarchs find out he's a vampire, we're dead anyway. You know vampires can't be there."

"But they already know we have vampires. It's up to them to decide if they want to punish us or not. Now, it's just about our protection. You have to admit, if push comes to shove when we're there, having a vampire as an ally will only benefit us." He raises an eyebrow, and I get the feeling that a lecture is already forming on his tongue.

Before he can chastise me further, I insist, "Pick another vampire then. There are hundreds in this palace. Pick someone *else.*"

Adriene relents. "Fine. I'm going to go change into my uniform…" He scans my sleek, black dress with a slit on both sides, revealing a sliver of my legs. "I suggest you change as well. Maybe something more…*ruthless.* I'll meet you in front of the palace with our guards in fifteen minutes."

I glance down at my dress and shoot him a glare. Who is *he* to tell *me* what to wear? I don't give him the satisfaction of responding. Instead, I watch him as he walks back down the hallway. I wander to the other end and take the stairs up to my room, still boiling with anger over Adriene even *suggesting* that we bring Garamond. The thought of that traitorous vampire makes me want to stake *myself* in the heart.

Once I'm in my room, I slam the door and toss my crown of bones onto my bed, combing my hands through my hair and leaving it cascading down my back in a tangled web. I never wanted to be queen—and now I remember why. I may be in charge, but I'll never be in control.

I throw my head back and groan at the leaky ceiling above me. What would I be doing right now if I never killed Aaron? Would I be rotting away in the dungeon, or crowned as queen alongside him? I frown, knowing my life is way better than it would be if Aaron were still alive. If I didn't take the opportunity that presented itself and shoved Aridam through his heart.

I throw open my wardrobe and select a pair of black leggings and a dark green top that flows into a mesh train behind me. The corset is beaded with little blue flowers and the sleeves are billowy, gathering around my wrists. For the past couple of months, I've been choosing gowns for their appearance. It will be nice to finally choose something for flexibility.

I study myself in the wall-length mirror. My cheekbones are defined, cutting harsh lines across my face and casting shadows that make my face elongate. My eyes are big and bulbous compared to my skeletal appearance. I'm withering away, turning into a husk of my former self… *Terrifying* is the first word that pops into my head.

But perhaps it's also *ruthless*.

"Are we ready?" I call to Adriene as I hurry down the front steps of the palace and to the group waiting at the bottom. The sky is overcast from the storm yesterday, but I can see people in the village below in the streets, in their yards, and talking to their neighbors—enjoying the day.

Adriene glances up at me, a smile curving his lips. He's clad in his black leather executioner's uniform. Two vampire soldiers are standing next to him; a tall man with curly black hair and petrifying red eyes, and a shorter girl with shoulder-length auburn hair. Her eyes are equally as red and petrifying.

Standing to the right of Adriene is Samantha, who's doing everything she can to not look at me.

"Emilia," Adriene says in greeting, nodding toward the two vampire soldiers whom he's taken on as guards for the time being. "This is Orville and Ella. They'll be our protection during the meeting."

Orville's dressed in a silk suit with a matching midnight-black cloak clasped around his neck. The clasp seems to be an insignia of sorts. It looks like a little silver skull with a mole rat perched on top.

That's…oddly specific.

Orville smiles, revealing a pair of fangs, as he catches me looking at the strange insignia. "It's my family's crest," he explains, gently caressing the sides of the clasp with a gloved hand. "The Sentarias are a

73

powerful household in the Banished Realm."

I purse my lips before moving on to the girl. I'm not exactly sure what there is to be said about a powerful vampire family with a mole rat as a mascot. The girl watches me with wide, red eyes. She has a heart-shaped face and ashen skin. The tips of her ears are slightly pointed, and her thin lips are pulled to the side in a shy smile. She's wearing a pair of crimson leggings and a knee-length shirt with skin-tight sleeves. Strapped to both of their waists are sheaths for daggers, the delicate handles of which glint menacingly.

"This is the best you can do?" I ask Adriene, skeptically.

Adriene smirks. "They may not look like much, Emilia. But they're the most powerful vampires Aaron recruited—besides, *well*, Garamond."

I glare at him, and he chuckles, enjoying my annoyance.

I cross my arms and scan the two vampires again. I know vampires are exceedingly more powerful than most other Unnaturals, so we're probably in good hands when it comes to protection, but vampires give me the heebie-jeebies. And it doesn't have anything to do with their Veil… Not this time. Now, it's the fact that I can't read them like other people. That must be the only explanation for why I didn't sense Garamond's betrayal. *That must be it.*

"Are we ready to go then?" I ask, frowning at our little conglomeration.

Adriene reaches out and gently squeezes my shoulder. "Yes, we are."

Samantha removes a white stone from the pocket of her trousers and whispers a string of lilting words, sliding the rune stone in front of the group.

Warm white light flickers out from the portal, caressing our skin invitingly. I close my eyes and allow myself to be overcome by the blanket of light. Adriene's hand finds mine, comforting me with his warm touch. We're in this together. And I know, for a fact, that he's on my side, no matter what.

Chapter Eight

Olympus, the beating heart of the Solstice Realm, is vibrant with every color of the rainbow. I blink, clearing disorienting white spots from my vision—the result of traveling via rune stone. A tremendous marble path sprawls before us, cutting right through the center of a lavish village and snaking up a snow-capped mountain to a great white palace.

Encircling the mountain like a fairy tale dragon is a patch of roiling white clouds. I peek over the edge of the path—a better term would be *bridge*—and gulp; a cloud flows under the path and around it, blocking any view of the land far beneath.

"What is this place?" I ask Adriene, his hand still firmly clasped in my own. I know he said Olympus is located on the opposite side of the realm from Nether, but why didn't I know that there's a massive mountain range encompassing the west side of the realm?

Adriene smiles, smoothing his thumb across my

hand and sending a bolt of electricity up my arm. I hate to admit it, but I'm growing increasingly fond of my executioner. "Olympus is located among the Gods' Mountain Range. It's on the opposite side of the Solstice Realm from Nether. Olympus is also quite a difficult kingdom to get into unless you can open a portal or know the right path to take." Adriene nods toward a gaping black cavern punched in the mountain that's rising up behind us. "It could take a person weeks to find the right path and climb up here. Just as the chimeras are to us, this is Olympus's safety precaution."

Orville and Ella station themselves in front of us. They keep their chins high, backs straight, and hands calmly resting at their sides. I'm impressed by Ella; she's so small and bone-thin, but I have a feeling that she could challenge any beast and come out on top. Maybe that's just because she's a vampire —but I get the impression that she's more ferocious than she appears… I suppose that's why Adriene chose her as one of our guards for the meeting.

Orville and Ella start the long walk up the marble path and through the village, clearing our way with their intimidating Veils. The village is a conglomeration of smooth stone buildings con-structed on the side of the mountain; some of the buildings have missing walls, allowing anyone to walk through and browse their goods, while others are high up on rocky outcroppings with windows shuttered and doors firmly locked. The houses far out of reach of the main path must be residential, allowing the villagers to maintain their privacy.

The sunlight is bright, reflecting off the clouds that envelop this kingdom like a hibernating dragon. The people who live here must be used to the extraordinary light. I don't think I ever could be.

I study the people as we near the village. They shoot curious glances at us, stepping closer to their homes and ducking quickly behind doors, wary of the humanoid creatures with the powerful Veils. I remember the first time I was thrust under a vampire's Veil. It was terrifying. I wanted nothing more than to flee.

Most of the people who live here have long, silky hair trailing from underneath a headscarf and down to their waists. Their skin tones vary from cloud-white to dark caramel, and there's something about their eyes that shines with impenetrable intelligence.

"Isolated from the majority of society, they mainly spend their time studying. They're known as the scholars of the Solstice Realm. Most grow up to become professors at the Solstice Academy, if they do decide to leave the mountain range," Adriene explains, gesturing to a group of school children who are huddled on the floor in one of the open rooms, smiling intently at a woman in the front. They're all wearing matching dark blue uniforms with white ties situated squarely on their collars.

I find it so interesting how every kingdom in the Solstice Realm is so vastly different. Glaven—if my memory serves me—is more homely than Olympus and Nether. Nether is known as the kingdom of the rebels and outcasts. Olympus, according to Adriene, is the kingdom of the scholars.

A little girl glances up from the group, following the eyes of the surrounding adults. Her gaze settles on me. The silvery blue of her eyes and her long brown hair remind me of myself. Of what I imagine I looked like when I was a child. Suddenly, out of seemingly nowhere, I'm angry that Aaron stole all those memories from me. Stole my entire childhood from me. Erased everything that made me who I was.

I want my mind to be mine alone. I am done with people tampering with it.

Adriene's hand slides to my lower back. He starts to rub a slow circle, studying me with his intense shark eyes. He leans closer, his breath warming the cuff of my ear. "What's wrong?"

I swallow down my rage, needing to find the energy to speak and not shout. "Nothing. It's... nothing."

He doesn't seem convinced, but he doesn't push

it either.

Orville and Ella part through the sea of pedestrians before us, plowing their way up the mountain and toward the palace, where the monarchs are waiting. I'm not eager to see them… To see the fear, judgment, and repulsion in their expressions. Mere months ago, I was the blue-eyed, naïve Emilia —the lost princess who was miraculously found. And now, I'm Queen Emilia. Cruel, soulless Emilia. Queen of a kingdom everyone hates.

"It'll be…" Adriene whispers under his breath. I know his words are meant for me, and me alone. "Fine. It'll be fine, Emilia. I won't let them hurt you."

"I'm not scared about them hurting me."

He gives me a long, searching look. "Then what are you afraid of? Hurting them?"

His voice cracks in the last sentence. It pushes away the fog blanketing a memory I've tried dearly to hold on to: Adriene is standing in his room at the Kase Inn, admitting to me about how he's scared of himself…of his desire to hurt those around him. Adriene's been nothing but honest to me. Maybe it's time I return the favor.

"I…don't want them to judge us… They don't even know us, Nether, and what it's like to have this infernal Veiling coursing through our veins." I cross my arms, hating how vulnerable I feel. The cold wind at this altitude plays with my hair, sending it blowing over my shoulders.

Adriene does the last thing I expect him to do: he smiles. "Emilia. You're right. They don't know what it's like to be cursed, to be Dark. So, why don't you tell them?"

I arch an eyebrow. "Do you even think that'll do anything?" We mount a flight of enormous stairs, constructed from gold-veined marble, that leads to the palace gates.

The Olympus palace is breathtaking in its splendor. Tall, white spires jut into the sky as ominous as lightning bolts. The outside of the palace sparkles from the sunlight and golden rays trickle into the numerous open windows, offering a glimpse inside. From here I can make out hedges bordering the palace's private gardens, contained behind the pristine gold gates.

Adriene shrugs, turning to face the palace that towers before us. The gate stands twice as tall as the behemoth of guards posted before it. "It doesn't hurt to try."

I scrunch my nose in protest. The guards step forward, burly faces hidden behind large gold helmets. I can just make out their squinted eyes through the slits.

The first guard—a man who stands before us, almost as imposing as the palace itself—lets out a primal growl. "Vampires aren't allowed here. Let alone anywhere in this realm." He starts to step forward, tightening his gauntlet-covered hand around the hilt of his broadsword. "We're obligated to arrest you and take you down to the dungeons. Any form of protest gives us the right to use deadly force."

"We're here for the meeting with the monarchs," I hiss, stepping toward Orville and Ella. They don't even seem scared by the guard's threats.

"Only those *invited* are allowed in—and their *kind* are definitely not invited," he says, jerking his chin toward the vampires.

"I am Queen Emilia of Nether, and these are my guards. Are you really going to deny access to the newly crowned queen?" I challenge, flashing him my most sinister smile. I feel my eyes shift as they darken even more—into pools of cursed obsidian.

The guard tightens his hands on the hilt of his sword again. I wait for my words to finally form in his pea-sized brain, and when they do, he swallows and steps aside. The other guard, who remained still and silent throughout the entire confrontation, pushes open the gates for us. I nod toward him in gratitude, which leaves him as straight as an arrow with fear. A genuine smile finds its way to my face.

Orville and Ella walk ahead of us, unphased by the entire ordeal—which is certainly impressive given the fact that they don't cut the most intimidating figures.

We pass between two tall hedges that line the pebbled path to the front doors of the palace. From this close, I notice the little white flowers that bloom along the sides of the hedges. An archway cut from the hedge to my left leads to a marble fountain, where a carved cherub spits an arc of water into the basin at its feet.

Another guard is standing beside the palace doors. His hand rests deftly on the hilt of his sheathed broadsword, ready to remove it at any given time. I don't think he sees much action up here. Not only would the uninvited guests have to find their way up the mountain and through the village, but they would also have to pass the guards at the gates. Without uttering a word, he turns sharply and pushes open the doors for us. They fall inward, revealing the luxury of the Olympus palace.

A maid with a crimson headscarf squeaks and darts into a room to her left. Light music drifts down from upstairs, but at the sound of the startled maid, it quickly cuts off. Suddenly, the entire floor seems to go silent as if everyone and everything is holding their breath.

Footsteps echo throughout the pristine hallway, bouncing off the crystal chandeliers and cloud-patterned walls, dragging our attention to the stairway at the very end.

"It's about time you arrived," King Hanson says, leveling his enchanting green eyes at me. "We're all gathered on the second floor, in the Monarchs' Meeting Room." He scans the vampires in front of us, but doesn't say a thing.

Adriene and I exchange a look, both our mouths pinned in a grave line.

We trail after King Hanson, taking the marble steps one at a time, though he has the distinctly un-fair advantage of just floating up them. His scales sparkle in the sunlight from the windows that line the stairway, casting exotic green light onto the walls.

King Hanson's posture is stiff, his hands firmly locked behind his back, and his merman tail barely swishes with the action of propelling air. I don't know how he's surviving up here—on top of a mountain and not in the depths of his lake—but the Aquartian merfolk are smart. I'm sure they engi-neered some way for them to survive in arid condi-tions.

He stops at the second door to our left; the only one on this floor with a golden glow seeping from underneath it. The entire hallway seems to be dimmed, sucked of life. They must've whisked ev-eryone away from the palace for this meeting. How private does a meeting with the monarchs have to be?

I gulp down my rising anxiety, knowing I shouldn't be *too* nervous. What's the worst that can happen?

King Hanson opens the door, giving me the first glance at the assembled party. My mouth pops open and my eyebrows knit together. Memories push through the fog, flooding the forefront of my mind like water through a broken dam. Before I can stop myself, I whisper, "Sky?"

Chapter Nine

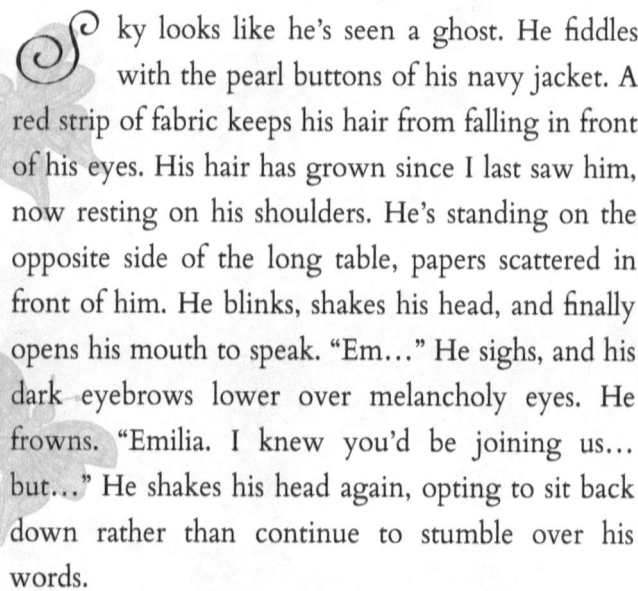

ky looks like he's seen a ghost. He fiddles with the pearl buttons of his navy jacket. A red strip of fabric keeps his hair from falling in front of his eyes. His hair has grown since I last saw him, now resting on his shoulders. He's standing on the opposite side of the long table, papers scattered in front of him. He blinks, shakes his head, and finally opens his mouth to speak. "Em…" He sighs, and his dark eyebrows lower over melancholy eyes. He frowns. "Emilia. I knew you'd be joining us… but…" He shakes his head again, opting to sit back down rather than continue to stumble over his words.

I take an empty chair beside King Jayden. His mage, Rebecca, is standing against the wall behind him, fiddling nervously with the hem of her cloak. When she catches sight of my eyes, she pales before offering a hesitant wave. A kind smile flits across her face, but I can still tell she's scared—of *me*.

"Emilia," Jayden purrs, giving me a conspiratorial smirk. "You look different. Is there any sun up there in Nether?" His brown eyes twinkle with mirth.

I pair his smirk with my own, leaning back in the chair to give the appearance that I'm calm. "Have you succeeded in getting any girls with your little drink trick?"

He flushes, but I swear a proud smile curves his lips. Rebecca behind him frowns, her blue eyes dimming. I wonder why she never confessed her feelings for the king—I'm sure he feels the same way. Maybe she did, and I just don't know. It's been months since I've seen any of them.

"Now that we're all assembled," Hanson interjects, shooting Jayden a disapproving glare, "we should start the meeting." He clears his throat. A woman with tan skin and a yellow headscarf sidles up beside him, handing him a glass of water. He drinks it greedily, passing the empty glass back to her. She proceeds to squirt him in the face with a spray bottle. Little droplets of water slide down his dark skin.

I blink in confusion. Hanson takes a steadying breath, and, if it's at all possible, his scales and hair seem to grow even more luminous. It clicks: whatever magic is in that liquid must allow him to survive for extended periods of time outside of his habitat.

He flicks his gaze over to me, his lip curling in unbridled disgust.

Once upon a time, I believed that we could be friends—but I suppose that changed when I became something he doesn't approve of.

Adriene's comment buzzes through my mind, but before I can do anything, Hanson is talking again.

"As customary, a meeting is held in this very room, following the crowning of a new monarch within our realm." Hanson lays his hands palm up on the table. "This meeting is especially important, considering the introduction of not one—but two—monarchs."

I tilt my head. *Two? Who's the second?*

Then it dawns on me.

Why else would *he* be here?

My head snaps toward Sky. "What is *he* the king of?" I hiss. Sky glances up at me and quickly away. He bites his lip, looking like he wants to be anywhere but here.

"After the unfortunate assassination of Queen Sophia Strazenfield," Hanson winces as my face scrunches, "and the next in line for the throne reigning in a different kingdom… Someone had to rule Glaven. We left it up to the kingdom to decide." He nods toward Sky. "He was the unanimous decision."

"Since when is the Solstice Realm a democracy?"

I snort, leaning back in my chair and crossing my arms. I don't know why the thought of Sky ruling Glaven eats at me so much. Maybe it's because he's sitting on *her* throne, ruling *her* people, taking *her* place. None of this should have happened. *Sophia* should still be alive. *Jax* should still be alive. If they didn't rescue me, then *everything* would've been fine.

"What's done is done," Hanson decrees, glaring at me again. "I have something very important to discuss that demands our attention."

"So, spit it out, Hanson," Jayden insists, resting an elbow on the table and his chin in his hand.

"What is so important, King Hanson?" a woman with long blonde ringlets and soft pink lips says, leaning forward in her chair. She's wearing a sleeveless baby blue dress and a matching headscarf. That color on her makes her matching eyes astonishing. She shakes her head and sighs when Hanson doesn't immediately start talking again. She turns to face me and offers me a demure smile. "It is lovely to finally meet the fabled Emilia Strazenfield. I'm Hera, Queen of Olympus." She extends a hand across Jayden, who just playfully rolls his eyes. Her grip is gentle, but I can still sense the extraordinary power she must possess.

"I've heard many things about you, Queen Hera," I say.

She chuckles, raising her thin, blonde eyebrows.

"All good, I hope?"

I give her a cracked smile instead of answering.

There are two more monarchs sitting on the far side of the room, silently watching our exchange. From their height and stature, I'm led to believe they're the monarchs of Dwarvenshire, the kingdom of dwarves who rule over both mines and farmland. The woman is wearing a sage green dress with long, flowy sleeves. She has long brown hair with thin braids framing her round face. Her eyes are the brown of rich soil, and her pink lips tilt into a kind smile when she catches me looking. Her husband, the king, has auburn hair and a long beard with several thinner braids throughout. His eyes are narrowed into speculative slits, shading their hazel hue. "I'm Queen Esmelda Stonebeard, and this is my husband, King Gildamere."

I offer them a hesitant smile in return.

Hanson scoots a piece of parchment across the table to me. His look is stern. "If everyone here can pay attention for ten minutes, then I'll care to explain."

Jayden looks over my shoulder at the parchment, his face turns ashen. "You're going to war with Nether?" he asks, dumbfounded.

My blood boils when I read the issuance in red ink at the very top of the parchment. *War.* He's declaring war with Nether.

I *knew* it. Adriene and I *knew* it.

Adriene sweeps from the wall and scoops the declaration up, examining it methodically. Then he glares at Hanson, barring his teeth as he flicks the parchment back at the king. "For what reason?"

Hanson stands up, scooting his chair back. The woman behind him quickly darts forward to spray him with the magical liquid. Hanson curls his lips. "Nether is a defiled kingdom—rotting from its core. It needs to be exterminated, and I have enough cause to do just that." He gestures to Orville and Ella, shaking his head in mock disbelief. "Vampires are banned Unnaturals. They shouldn't even be in this realm, let alone in this sacred place. That's breaking enough laws to call for your execution alone. War, I think we all agree, is the proper response to Nether's insidious actions."

"But Emilia wasn't even a part of creating the vampire army. Everything that's wrong with Nether is Aaron's fault," Jayden says, casting his hands out to the side. "This is preposterous, Hanson. You can't seriously be considering this."

"The declaration has been given, Jayden," Hanson says slowly. "Now it's time to decide whose side you'll fight on." He turns to glide from the room, calling overtly over his shoulder, "I'll see you in one month, Emilia. When I come to eradicate your kingdom."

Chapter Ten

$\mathcal{I}$ glare at the clouds on the horizon for no reason other than them being where they are. My fingernails bite into my palms, leaving crescent marks. *War*. Hanson's wrath is being unleashed on me for nothing more than inheriting this nightmare.

"It will be fine, Emilia," Adriene says, resting his hand on my back. His words from earlier ring through my mind. I should've stood up to Hanson the first time he dared pass judgment on something he knows little about. But I lost my opportunity. Next time I come face to face with the close-minded, I won't stay silent.

"How can you say that? We're going to *war*, Adriene. People are going to *die*." I shove away from his touch. In response, he frowns. "How can this—*any* of this—possibly be *fine*?" I scoff, glancing over the edge of the bridge-like path. The plush clouds roiling beneath look so soft and inviting.

"I may be able to help with that," calls a voice

over my shoulder. *His* voice. The bearer of my sister's crown. The ruler of my blood kingdom. The boy who I thought I loved.

I whip around, eyes wide with the possibility that he may be able to help. That anyone will be able to help in our dire situation. Sky's standing with one hand in the pocket of his navy jacket, the pearl buttons glistening in the blinding sunlight. The red piece of fabric taming his wild hair makes his blue eyes stand out. He's regal and sophisticated in a way he never was before. Before, he was a baker's son, and now he's a king.

"Just listen to my proposition," Sky says, smiling tentatively at me. The gentle breeze catches the end of his crimson hair-tie. Standing with the background of watercolor clouds, he's the definition of exhilarating. Handsome. My heart sputters. Whatever I felt for him in the past threatens to climb to the surface.

I thought my fascination with the youngest Baker brother died when I changed. When I became this cursed queen.

I thought… I glance to my left, where my right-hand man and trusted executioner is standing, brow drawn with curiosity. I thought my feelings may have shifted—that my taste may have changed completely, just as I had. Adriene and I are meant to be together, aren't we? We're meant to fight the

Veiling side by side.

I tilt my chin up, leveling my void-black eyes with Sky's. "Say it then."

His lips thin. He looks quickly around as if checking to make sure no one overhears, then he faces me again. "Kisha, Quicken, and I didn't abandon our quest, Emilia. We retrieved every fragment of Eve… Every piece…except the one that's in Nether." He takes a step forward, extending his hand toward me. "Glaven has always been my home, and I won't stand by and watch it—and my people—suffer. If you give me the last fragment of Eve and allow me to heal Glaven, I will side with you. Glaven's army will fight alongside Nether."

Adriene looks at me, one white eyebrow raised, waiting for me to answer.

I don't know if I should be insulted by Sky's proposal. I was born in Glaven. And, even though I'm the ruler of the fabled Dark kingdom, I don't want to see Glaven destroyed.

I take his hand, and his eyes brighten, lifting from our touch to my face. This time, he doesn't shy away from the Veiling that's pouring from my eyes. "Thank you, Em. I'm glad you're…alive." He swallows and a hint of pink blossoms across his cheeks. "I'll see you in Glaven." He finally acknowledges Adriene's presence, giving him a curt nod. "Tomorrow?"

"Tomorrow," I respond, watching him as he turns on his heel and starts back toward the palace.

"So, Emilia," Adriene says, offering me his arm, "on the cusp of destruction, you're going to save a kingdom?"

"I was always going to save a kingdom, Adriene," I say, patting his arm. "That's what I was brought here for, wasn't it?"

He chuckles, leaning toward me. "You were brought here for more than that, my Emilia."

Thick fog blankets the bog surrounding Nether, and the overcast sky paints the palace and the village below in a silver light. My breath fogs the window in my bedroom, obstructing my view. With a sigh, I cross to the floor-length mirror. I pull the strings of my hunter-green corset, tightening it. I grit my teeth from the sharp pain. The deep-velvet outermost skirt is patterned with glittery spirals of an even darker shade, and my matching sleeves are cinched around my wrists with a ruffled hem.

I lean toward the mirror to fix the crown atop my head. The ivory bones are stark against my outfit. I wonder what Sky would look like wearing Soph's icicle crown. I can only ever picture it on her; paired with her icy-blue eyes and wavy blonde hair, it suited her. Would it also suit Sky, with a head full of shaggy black hair and deep blue eyes?

As soon as we arrived back from the monarchs' meeting, I sent Adriene on a mission to find where Aaron stashed the broken sword. He said he knew exactly who to ask to find out.

I run my hands down the front of my gown, swallowing down my rising anxiety for the day to come. I suppose I'll find out my answer today when I arrive in my birth kingdom to watch it heal, watch Sky accomplish the very thing I couldn't.

There's a knock on the door, and a sigh parts my lips. I spin around, digging my fingers into the fabric of my gown. "Come in," I call, knowing it's Adriene. Hopefully, he's completed his task. Hopefully, in his hands at this very moment is the last fragment of Eve.

The door creaks open, revealing the last face I thought I'd see outlined in my doorway.

"*You*," I growl, narrowing my eyes in utter disdain. "Why are *you* here?"

Garamond's complexion is ashen, and his lips are pursed in a grave line. His black hair is slicked back, leaving a tail to lick down the back of his neck. And his red-tinted eyes are hooded with some emotion I can't quite name. Shame, perhaps? Or guilt? I hope he feels both. I hope he's dragged into the rotting, infernal prison of his conscience. I hope he's so wracked with the ghastly consequences of his traitorous actions that it consumes him, burning his soul. Cursing him as I have been.

Garamond ducks his head, lifting his hands out in front of him to show me what he's brought. "Adriene said you were looking for this. Aaron showed me where it was, hoping that if his palace underwent a raid—I'd be able to protect it." Out of a silvery hilt shoots an intricate, almost lacy blade—the end jagged from where it was broken. *Eve*.

"And where is Adriene now?" I ask, lifting the skirt of my gown and taking a step toward him. My eyes don't stray from Eve.

"He's waiting for us in front of the palace. He said we're heading to Glaven today to repair Eve." He lifts the blade a bit higher to punctuate his words.

I laugh. Well, more like *cackle*. I storm toward him, glaring up at his face in an astonished frenzy. "*You* aren't coming anywhere with us. You don't deserve to walk on the same land my sister did. Not after abandoning her. After playing with her heart, then crushing it." I bite my cheek, enjoying the taste of my blood as it spreads across my tongue. I imagine taking the sword fragment he's holding and thrusting it through his chest, just like I did to Aaron. But Eve won't hurt him—the Sword of Life was made to heal. "You deserve to meet the same fate she did." I tear the blade from his hand and shove past him, stomping down the stairs and into the hallway. Foolish, *stupid*, moronic Adriene. If he weren't the only person who understood me—who related to me on a level no one else can—then I'd beat him into a bloody pulp. I'd watch as he's dragged to the dungeons and tortured, just as so many have been before. How *dare* he insist upon bringing Garamond along with us. How *dare* he send the vampire prince to my room.

Red floods my vision, and it stays like that until I push open the palace doors and see his face.

"You," I spit, tearing down the stairs and shoving him in the chest. He staggers backward but regains his footing too fast for my liking. Adriene watches me, expressionless. He doesn't even look ashamed for what he's done. Adriene is intelligent enough to *know* what he's done, and how it would upset me. "Remember, Adriene," I dig my nail into the soft part of his chin, right at the base of his jaw, "I am the queen here. Not you. I wear the crown. I hold the power. And I am the one who makes the decisions. Go against my direct orders again and you'll be on the chopping block while someone else holds your scythe." I press the sharp part of Eve into him, knowing the Sword of Life can't hurt him; it heals whatever it touches. "Your blood will run down these palace steps before you even know what happened." I back away, trying to calm myself. I am done being trampled over by people. I am done having my wishes pushed aside.

When I look back at Adriene...he's smiling. Grinning from ear to ear as if the most glorious thing just happened. His shark eyes twinkle, and the overcast sun turns his white hair silver. He's decked out in his executioner uniform again, the blade of the scythe glinting in the light. He looks proud... and that disturbs me. But what disturbs me more is the sense of accomplishment swelling in my heart.

"You're breathtaking, Emilia," he says, flashing his pearlescent smile. "That crown was meant for you." He rests his hands on my shoulders, letting his eyes trace every curve and angle of my face. "A crown of bones for a ruthless queen."

I narrow my eyes, forcing myself not to smile. "I *will* kill you if you step out of line, Adriene."

He chuckles, lowering his mouth toward mine. His warm breath parts my lips, leaving my cheeks flushed with a feeling I'm starting to loathe. But he doesn't kiss me. He whispers, sending goosebumps prickling down my body, "I'm counting on it, Emilia." Then he straightens back up, smirking with mischief at the clear state he's forced me into.

"Are we ready to leave now?" he asks, tilting his head toward Samantha as she skips down the palace stairs, Orville and Ella behind her.

Chapter Eleven

*P*ieces of the crystalline palace have fallen and crumbled against the ground, making the garden a minefield of debris and the drive a shimmering battlefield.

"How can it look…so much *worse* after only two months?" I ask, knitting my brows together. My heart stings with the condition of the palace—of my childhood home. If I hadn't been so inaccessible since my sister's passing, maybe I could've helped save it *before* it fell into ruins.

"It isn't any better in the village," Sky says, his voice sounding every bit as devastated as I feel. "My father's bakery had to close. The ceiling collapsed one day, and without hope of reversing the curse, he didn't even try to fix it. That's how most of the residents feel. They're wondering why they should bother to repair anything—their homes, their gardens, their shops—when Aridam's curse is just going to destroy it again the next day." His attention snags on the bundle of cloth in my arms. Hope flickers in his eyes like the embers of a growing fire. "Is that it?"

I nod, my throat suddenly dry. I don't know what I should say—or how I should feel. The Veiling is messing with everything inside me. "Where's the rest of Eve?"

He nods toward the palace. "Your sister's study."

A lump forms in my throat. Grief is a funny thing. I should be devastated, crying, torn apart by the loss. But I've been living in a world that blurs by —every noise muffled, every feeling smothered. Until, suddenly, the world clears a little and the dam restricting my grief breaks.

My eyes glisten with oncoming tears. The door blocking all my memories of Sophia unlocks, releasing them in a tidal wave of despair. When I crumble to the ground, I set the fragment of Eve beside me. My hands are fisted in the layers of my gown, and I sob until my throat is raw and my eyes are puffy and red. No one says anything.

I'm glad they don't. I wouldn't be able to stand a single "I'm sorry for your loss." I can hardly stand their pitiful looks as it is. It feels good to cry—not all of my feelings are truly gone then. I'm still human. I'm just not sure for how long.

Sophia was my little sister—the last remaining member of my family. And she's gone. Does this mean I'm alone now? I peer up at the palace through the tears in my eyes, tracing the glistening stones that construct the crystalline building. The sunlight slides down the stones just as it would a river, creating sparkles of blinding light.

Eventually, when my tears dry and my sniffles stop, Adriene helps me stand, holding me against his side as we enter the palace. I'm not alone. Adriene would never leave me alone. Whatever happens, we're in this together. If we're destined to help each other…then I know I will never leave him, just as he would never leave me.

"Watch your heads," Sky says in warning, gesturing to the ceiling. "I'm not sure how long we have until it crumbles too. Which is why we should do this quickly. I would rather not spend my time and resources rebuilding the palace when the village is in such a poor state."

Adriene holds me back as Sky heads up the stairs, onto the rectangular landing where we found Trelia's body slumped, left there after being drained by Aaron's vampire army. I stare at the spot on the wall, remembering her ravaged neck and the countless vampire bites distributed across her body. I can still hear the gut-wrenching squelch as her slit neck oozed more blood.

I wipe away my tears and push the memory from my mind. A queen doesn't halt in the face of her past—and that is what I am now. A queen. Even if I don't feel like it. Even if I never wanted to be one.

"It's okay, Emilia," Adriene says, turning my face toward his. His eyes flash golden for just a second before flooding to black again. "It's okay to feel what you're feeling. You are no less of a queen for it."

It's almost as if he read my thoughts, plucked them straight from my mind, and told me exactly what I longed to hear.

My lips quiver, and he presses a gentle kiss to them, calming me with the feel of his warmth and his nearness. After he pulls away, a small, grateful smile pulls at the corners of my mouth. This isn't like the time in the shadows of the dungeon. This kiss is innocent, full of comfort and promises for the future.

I turn to glance up at the steps, freezing. Sky didn't continue to my sister's study. He stopped on the landing and saw me and Adriene kiss. I frown, trying to determine how I should feel. I might have hurt a boy I cared for before the Veiling—and that makes my heart pang with guilt. But why should I feel guilty for kissing someone I like?

Sky's nostrils flare, his cheeks flushing slightly. The crown atop his head sparkles as the daylight from the window falls across it. His oceanic eyes flicker from me to Adriene and back again, fitting the last piece in the puzzle of his suspicions. He purses his lips, bites his cheek, then nods toward the stairs. A strand of black hair falls across his forehead, directing my line of sight to his scar. The scar he received because of me. "The curse doesn't wait for anyone." He doesn't sound hostile, nor does he sound happy. Maybe now that my eyes are black and my soul is cursed, he no longer aches for me the way I suspect he did before. I can't blame him. If I were in his shoes, I would feel the same.

I clear my throat before making my way up the stairs, adverting my gaze from the wall where Trelia's body was slumped. I should track down every last vampire that raided this palace and killed my loved ones. I should slit their throats as savagely and heartlessly as Aaron did Sophia's. I know exactly the vampire I would start with: *Garamond*.

The very thought of his blood slicking my hands, of watching his miserable life leave his eyes, swells me with hunger. Adriene would try to stop me, of course. For some unfathomable reason, he wants to keep the vampire prince as an ally.

I follow Sky as he crosses over to Soph's study. I try not to dwell on the familiarity of this palace—of how it felt like home not so long ago—how I won't be able to go back to that time. How this can't be my home now. I no longer belong here. Sky opens the engraved door to Soph's study, running his fingers over the runes etched into the material, almost subconsciously.

When I slip inside the study, followed closely by Adriene, another round of grief hits me. Some part of me suspected that the study would look different —*feel* different. The air is thick with the absence of her. When my eyes land on her desk, outlined by the white light of day, all I see is my little sister. All I'm feeling is her blood pooling beneath my feet, her scream threatening to shatter my eardrums, and Aaron's voice filling the room with contemptuous laughter. I've heard the saying that time heals all wounds—but could it be possible that time only distorts them?

I don't realize I'm shaking until Adriene grips my arms, holding me still against him. I want to curl into the warmth and safety of his chest. I want to vanquish the metallic scent of my memories and replace it with the woodsy smell of my executioner.

But I can't falter, not on a mission as dire and time-sensitive as this. I need to finish what I started. I need to repair Eve, to save the kingdom my sister dedicated herself to rule.

I shake myself from my stupor and take a small, hesitant step closer to the desk, attempting to block all images of Soph's last moments from my mind.

Assembled on the desk, as precariously and carefully as prized jewels, are the four glistening shards of the Sword of Life that were retrieved from the allied kingdoms.

With reverie, I pass the last fragment, bundled safely in cloth, to Sky, who takes it with equal care. He places it at the base of the sword and steps back, glancing at me for permission to complete Eve. "All the history books I've read say in order to repair the swords, they need to be reunited with every piece. Hopefully, if what I've read is true, then this will work." I give him a nod, pinning my eyes to the desk, curious to see what will happen. A nod seems too simple of a gesture for permission to repair this centuries-old sword that united the Solstice Realm.

Sky pieces the fragments together, fitting the jagged edges to each other as easily as placing the last piece into a puzzle. For a moment, nothing happens. Then a blinding white light seeps from the broken edges, like blood from an open wound, winding toward us as Eve stitches itself back together. The light is warm as it slithers across my skin. It feels the same as the light that floods from rune stones.

I want to close my eyes and sink into the comforting light, let it consume me, and sweep away my grief. But just as quickly as it touches me, the light flares and disappears, leaving white spots in my vision. I blink them away and take a step toward the desk, eyebrows knitted together as I behold the fruition of our journey.

Eve is beautiful. Grander and more resplendent than its sibling, Aridam. It's a silver blade that sparkles like the sun against a fresh blanket of snow. Eve's hilt resembles Aridam's, swirling and spiraling with intricate spider-web-thin pieces of metal. They must have been forged by a skilled swordsmith for they look as delicate as spun sugar, though I know from first-hand experience that they're not.

"What now?" I ask, forcing my eyes away from Eve to look at Sky. His mouth has popped open, and a chunk of his raven-feather hair has fallen across his forehead. I want to reach over and sweep it behind his ear, just as I would've before I changed, but I don't. I'm not that Emilia anymore.

"I don't know," he admits quietly, shutting his mouth. His eyes glisten with tears. Tears of joy? Tears of fear that even this won't save Glaven? Or tears for some other reason?

"Well…" I start to say, tilting my head to study the ancient relic, the uniter of kingdoms and the sibling to destruction. "I guess we have to wait—" A shriek from the village catches our attention. Both Sky and I snap our heads up, looking out the window to see what's happening. My first thought is that another chimera swept from the forest and took a child—but this isn't Nether. There aren't any chimeras here. But that doesn't mean it's safe. I used to think it was, but then vampires invaded the palace and pooled blood across the floor.

I suppose it wasn't safe before that. Too many times in my life have I stood in my family's blood.

Sky and I exchange a glance. With a subtle nod, we're both tearing from the room and down the palace steps. I trip over the hem of my gown, but quickly regain my footing, desperate to see what's garnered the attention of the village. More voices carry from down the hill—dozens talking all at once, exclaiming things in hysterical octaves.

Sky shoves open the front doors. He's outlined by the bright sun, throwing his shadow across the palace floor. He jerks to a standstill so fast I nearly jump back, startled. Then he falls to his knees, staring at something in front of him.

I hurry toward him. Adriene is behind me, trying to catch up. His shoes *click-clack* on the marble.

"What is it?" I demand, rushing to Sky's side. I scan his face for any sign of pain, but all I see is awe. Then I turn my attention to the village. From this far away, I can't make out much, just the swarms of villagers flooding the streets, staring at their houses and shops.

I squint. Then I see what's earned everyone's attention.

Eve.

The crumbling houses are fixing themselves, almost as if time is rewinding, reverting everything back to how it was before Aaron broke Aridam. Oak and birch trees rise from the ground surrounding the village, shading buildings from the constant sun. The ground rumbles as more trees, some as thick and towering as Earthen redwoods, border the village. Flowers and berry bushes sprout from the recently infertile ground, and the crops in the little individual gardens are vibrant and flourishing.

Sky's voice breaks as tears flow down his cheeks. "Home. *This* is home."

Envy curls in my heart. *Home. This was my home too.* And now, Glaven is beautiful. More gorgeous and breathtaking than I could've ever imagined.

Chapter Twelve

*M*r. Baker keeps shooting wary glances toward me. I know I must look incredibly different, and I know I must be the most imposing figure in this entire kingdom. Sweat is slick on his brow and he dabs at it with a scrunched-up towel. He tilts his head back and looks up at the roof, a massive grin spreading across his face. His blue eyes sparkle jovially.

The bakery—the one recently destroyed by Aridam's curse—has now reverted to the state it was in before. There are a couple of tables pushed against the wall, underneath the window looking out at the celebrating villagers, and a simple silver candelabra is in the center of each. The front counter now displays a few three-tiered cakes, sporting vibrant pink and dusky blue icing.

Though my memories are still foggy, being suppressed by the Veiling, I distinctly remember a pair of blue eyes and a streak of blue icing. I peer over at Sky. *His* blue eyes. His blue eyes are the ones

I keep seeing, that keep appearing at the most inconvenient times.

No. I am a queen. I have Adriene. Why am I dwelling on Sky?

But…isn't a king more suited? Shouldn't I be after a crown to balance my own?

I shake away the thought. My kingdom is going to war. I should be focusing on *that* and nothing else.

"A deal is a deal," Sky says, coming to stand next to me. He watches his father exit the bakery to talk with a group outside. His eyes dim a bit, knowing the discussion that has to happen.

"What do you mean?" I ask, raising an eyebrow. I tilt my chin up, refusing to let him see my emotions again. I need to be strong. I need to focus. I can't keep getting distracted by trivial things.

"Glaven's army—we will side with you against Hanson." His expression turns grim, and a frown twists his mouth when Adriene steps up to my side. He never liked the executioner, the man who let himself get locked away for two years just so he could guide me. "But I'm not sure how much help we can be…not when we know that most of the kingdoms will side with Hanson. Not that they have anything against you… Nether has always been the outlier, a danger to the perfectly crafted alliance that is the Solstice Realm. Hanson's probably been itching for a reason to decimate it… There's no better time than during the fragile transfer of power. When a new queen is just getting a lay of the battlefield."

"Who will side with us?" I ask, hating the fact that he's right. The majority of the kingdoms will side with Hanson. We'll need to raise an incredible army for even the slightest chance of coming out of this alive.

"King Jayden might. He's your strongest bet." Sky shifts from foot to foot, watching his father outside with a strained look on his face. "Queen Hera is a toss-up. The rest, however, will fight alongside Hanson's merfolk."

"How will Hanson's army even fight us? They can't survive in arid environments for long, especially without someone tending to them, as Hanson demonstrated at the meeting," I ask, crinkling my brow.

Sky nods. "Magic, Em. Trust me…he'll find a way. King Hanson is incredibly smart."

"So then, how will we even stand a chance of winning? How can we grow our army?"

Adriene's shark eyes flit from me to Sky. He flexes his hands, moving them to rest at his sides. "I may have a suggestion."

Sky shoots him a begrudging look. "What is it?"

Adriene sighs, apologetically glancing at me

before saying, "The Banished Realm. We should use our connection through Prince Garamond and recruit the vampire king. He wants to reunite the two realms, so he *will* fight beside us."

"Absolutely not," I hiss, giving Adriene my most *I'll-kill-you-later* glare. "Leave. Garamond. Out. Of. This." I enunciate every word, trying to drill it into his thick skull.

"Think of your people, Emilia," Adriene says. "This may be our only hope."

Sky clears his throat, gesturing to his father outside. "I'll do anything for my family. I say we give the vampire king a visit." He turns to me, resting his hands behind his back. He tilts his chin down, leveling his gaze at me. "You don't have to come with us, Em, but as much as I hate to admit it, Adriene is right. This is our best chance at growing our army and saving both our kingdoms."

I close my mouth, which popped open in dumbfounded shock. "I am *queen*. You're not about to leave me behind."

"Alright. It's settled then." Sky glances between me and Adriene. "When should we leave?"

"Meet us at noon tomorrow in front of the Nether palace. We have to convince Garamond to come with us." Adriene glances over his shoulder as the bakery bell chimes and a crowd of excited patrons buzz inside, encouraged by the hearty laughter of Mr. Baker and the promise of freshly baked scones. "Are you a powerful enough Runespeaker to create a portal between the Solstice Realm and the Banished Realm?"

Sky crosses his arms, a vein in his neck standing out. "I managed to open a portal between the Earthen Realm and here… But it *was* strenuous…" he admits grudgingly. His cheeks tinge pink.

"If Samantha, our resident Runespeaker, assists you…" Adriene suggests, trailing off when Sky picks up.

"I think the two of us will be strong enough to open a portal between the realms," Sky agrees. "Tomorrow then. I'll send out a letter to the other kingdoms to see who's decided on their alliance."

Adriene gives him a curt nod. "Thank you, Sky." He gently rests his hand on my arm, stealing my attention. "Shall we go, Emilia?"

"Yes," I say, pulling my eyes away from Sky's. There's something in his expression that makes my heart constrict. His knitted brow leaves a crease in the center, and the corners of his mouth are pulled down in a contemplative, melancholy frown. I don't know what he's thinking, nor what he's feeling, but I do know that some part of him is disappointed. Disappointed in me. Disappointed that the Emilia he loves is gone. I turn my attention to the dissipating crowd outside, ignoring the light jingle of the silver bell above the door, and the questioning glance Adriene sends my way.

I stop in the middle of the street and stare up the tree-lined path toward the sparkling, crystalline palace. I take a steadying breath of the cold air, filling my lungs. There's one thing I need to do before we leave Glaven. I should've done this months ago. And, after my breakdown this morning, I think it would be unhealthy to put it off any longer.

"Adriene…" I say slowly, turning to look back at him. He's resting his scythe across his shoulder, letting the blade glint forebodingly in the overcast light. The remaining villagers around him give him a wide berth, scared and curious eyes flicking toward the imposing executioner. He lifts an eyebrow, fingers tightening and loosening on the hilt of his scythe. "I need to visit my sister."

Chapter Thirteen

The graveyard is tranquil. I sense that it's alive like spirits are dwelling in another dimension. I don't know how much I believe in spirits, ghosts, or life after death. But I would be stupid to say it's not a possibility after all I've witnessed.

I hope it is true, that my sister is somewhere else, at peace. I hope she's surrounded by joy and laughter. I hope she feels free from the weight of the crown and can finally be a child.

"Adriene," I say, breaking the stillness. A crow caws, perched on the top of the twisting, leafless tree that towers over the graveyard. It's the only tree on the top of this hill, a mile or so away from the village. Adriene's sitting behind me on a stone bench, his scythe resting against his leg. He smiles up at the crow before shifting his focus to me. His eyes glimmer, and his cloud-white hair is windswept from our walk.

"Emilia," he replies. His voice is silky and smooth, a promise of pain and mercy.

I hate how his voice makes me feel. I hate how every time I look at him, I picture us kissing. I picture him in the doorway to my room, looking at me with that cocky, sly grin.

"Do you believe there's life after death?" I ask quietly. I trace the grooves on Soph's headstone. Tears pearl on my waterline when I hover over the words *loving sister*. Engraved on the sides of the headstone are tulips, twisting and spiraling up the side of the marble stone. Sky must've had a say in its construction and design. Tulips... *A crown of flowers for a child queen.*

Adriene's quiet for a while. I assume he's thinking, forming his thoughts into something coherent. Eventually, after the crow caws for a third time, he responds. "I know that there is."

I spin toward him, arcing an eyebrow. "How? How can you be so sure?"

He pats the spot on the bench next to him, so I quickly take a seat, eager to hear what he has to say.

The graveyard is small, surrounded on all four sides by a black iron fence. Tiny budding flowers sprout from the tip of each spike, and iron leaves grow from the posts. There are only about ten headstones here. This plot is reserved for the royal family. It's weird, looking at all these headstones and knowing that I'm related to the skeletons buried beneath them.

Far in the distance, nestled in a valley between hills, is the Glaven village. Glistening on the crest of a hill is the palace. It's a beautiful, sparkling kingdom now that Aridam's curse has been lifted.

A stunning, sparkling kingdom with an entirely new bloodline reigning.

A shift in an era.

"I've seen the dead before, Emilia," Adriene says quietly, gently taking my hand in his. His fingers are chilly, but I tighten my hand in his grip anyway. I study the profile of his face. The pronounced slope of his nose, the bow of his cupid lips, and the shine of sunlight across the dome of his black eyes. I can't believe there was once a time I was afraid of him, deeming him as a monster. Adriene would never hurt me. If there is anyone in this life I can trust, it's him.

"You've seen them?" I urge him to continue, hungry for his confirmation. He's seen a ghost? What do they look like? How did he come across one? I have so many questions, but before I can voice any of them, he's speaking again. I close my mouth and lean against him, resting my cheek against his shoulder.

"Before Aaron took the Nether throne, the previous king gave me a dire task. He told me to deliver his traitorous love directly to the afterlife, to make sure she burned in hellfire and couldn't gain

119

access back to the living world." He wrings his hands in his lap, flicking his eyes over the graves before him. "She was trying to leave him for another man… And he wouldn't let that happen. So, I was told to kill her." He swallows, tightening his lips into a grave line. "The afterlife isn't in *this* realm. It's in a…realm knitted between dimensions. Nearly impossible to gain access to, and it's nearly impossible to escape."

"Do you think Sophia's there?" I ask, shooting up in my spot. He frowns, roving his eyes over my face. His lips part as a sigh escapes.

"I do. But I'm not sure it would be worth it to try to retrieve her."

"Retrieve her?" My mind begins to spin. *Retrieve her?* Is it possible to bring her back? To have my sister at my side again? "What would it take?"

"Emilia—"

I grab his arm, desperation twisting my features. "Adriene. What would it take to bring my little sister back?"

Adriene sighs, relenting. He stares out at the landscape. "Confronting a centuries-old Key Master. There are seven Key Masters appointed by the gods. They're tasked with guarding the portals to sacred dimensions, and only allowing those through who pass a series of trials. The dimension of the afterlife is called Oblivion, and it's guarded by an immortal nymph named Zainey."

My hope starts to wane. "Has anyone ever met her before? Has anyone ever passed the trials?"

He nods solemnly. "One person. I didn't witness it, but I've heard tales of a man from the Banished Realm who found a map that leads to Oblivion. He fought his way through Zainey's trials to retrieve his daughter. He came out with his daughter, who was on the precipice of death... Both of them were missing a hand."

I recoil, crinkling my nose. "Their...hand?"

"There are seven trials, each one led by a different Key Master. Several people have found the sacred portals, but only one person has ever completed them all and came out alive. The trials are designed to break you, to determine who is worthy. If the rumors are to be believed, they challenge every part of you. Your strength. Your mind. Your persistence." His eyes roam over the horizon as the crow in the skeletal tree caws.

"See, Emilia. I can't guarantee that it will be worth it. It may be best if the dead remain that way," Adriene finishes, rubbing a soothing circle across the top of my hand with his thumb. He must know how disappointed and conflicted I feel. How hope flared in my chest moments ago, and now it's replaced with a sickening guilt, a sickening question throbbing through my head: *could I do it? Could I pass all the Key Masters' Trials?*

"What is the name of the man who passed the trials?" I ask.

Adriene sighs, side-eyeing me like he knows what I'm thinking. "His name was Emmett O'hare."

"Do you think…we could visit him? When we're in the Banished Realm?" I try to smother the hope in my voice.

Adriene shakes his head slowly, a line creasing his forehead. "He died a few years ago." His tongue flickers across his bottom lip as his hand slides off mine.

"Oh…" I deflate, sagging against his side. My heart constricts. Hope has a way of doing two things: either shining a light on life or blanketing everything in darkness. "Thank you…for telling me and answering all my questions."

Adriene gets up, tightening his fingers around his scythe. He rests the handle on his shoulder so the blade crosses behind his head, glinting devilishly in the sunlight. "I would do anything for you, Emilia."

I blush, focusing my attention on the headstones scattered in the yard and not on the man standing beside me. I stand up, smoothing my hands down my gown. I fix my crown and turn toward the glistening Glaven palace.

"Let's go home, Adriene," I say, even though the words don't feel true. Nether isn't my home… Not fully. I feel as if I'm divided. Divided between places, between people, between obligations, and between the real me and this formidable curse. I feel myself fighting against the Veiling, having brief moments of clarity before falling deeper into the curse... My thoughts switch to those of evil and Darkness. My eyes flicker between blue and black. My memories become clear and then fog over again.

I'm losing myself, and I hate it. But I don't know how to make it stop.

"Alright, Emilia. Let's go home." Adriene starts toward the creaky graveyard gate, his leather uniform squeaking with each movement.

A headstone near the front of the graveyard catches my attention. It's a white chess piece carved from the same marble as my sister's headstone. I kneel down to read the name at the base of the king-piece and gasp.

In Memory of Igor Strazenfield
King, Father, and Son

I press a kiss to the crown of the chess piece. "I wish I remembered you, Father." A solitary tear crests down my cheek, and I wipe it hastily away. Crying won't do anything...but, sometimes, it's necessary.

Chapter Fourteen

J don't want to think about the upcoming war, Oblivion, or the Key Masters' Trials. I don't want to think about how precarious life is. I don't want to think at *all*.

"Adriene," I call, catching his wrist before he can head toward his room. He must notice the desperation in my voice or feel the desire to not be alone as well, because when he turns around, he's already talking.

"Yes," he says, without hesitation. Without needing to hear what my request is. He steps toward me, ignoring the Shrouds wandering haughtily through the foyer, unconcerned with any responsibilities. "Yes, my Emilia."

"I didn't even say anything yet," I chuckle, raising an eyebrow and smirking.

He reaches up and reverently takes my face in his hand. His eyes land on my lips, and he steps closer. Slowly, he moves his hand down my face and rests the pad of his thumb on my bottom lip, making my mouth pop open. "You don't need to. Remember? I'll do anything for you, Emilia." His expression glows with mirth. He knows the effect he has on me, and he enjoys it a little *too* much.

I roll my eyes. "Will you come with me to the conservatory?" I inquire, offering him my arm. He slips it around his with ease and spins us toward the hallway leading to the conservatory full of our Dark spies. I wonder if any more butterflies have come back.

When we round the last turn in the palace and push open the conservatory doors, a breath of fresh air finally fills my lungs, pushing away my building anxiety. Here, with Adriene, I know I don't have to worry. Life will happen, and I'll find a way, no matter what, to overcome any obstacles.

"So, Sky…" Adriene starts, pursing his lips sourly. The last rays of sunlight fall through the tinted glass of the conservatory ceiling, landing on his snow-white hair and giving it an odd orange gleam.

"Let's not talk about him," I say, shaking my head. A gentle, chilly breeze brushes against my face, nipping at my nose. Winter is around the corner. Well, as *winter* as it can get in the Solstice Realm. "I just want to…be here…with you." The coy smile I give him brings a blush to his pale cheeks. I enjoy toying with him just as much as he enjoys toying with me.

Knowing that a man worships you, will do anything for you, and a smile alone can unravel him is powerful in itself.

I spin around and watch the butterflies above me; the sunlight shining off their wings. An enchanting monarch flutters in front of my face, casting an orange glow across my cheeks.

"Have any more butterflies returned?" I ask Adriene, gaping at the surrounding creatures.

I don't know why I was afraid of them before. Terrified of how they look up close and how they aren't afraid of landing on people. But why, I wonder, did I want them to be afraid of me? Maybe that parallels with who I have become.

Now, I realize how beautiful they are. How trusting of a creature they are. And how foolish I was to be afraid.

Adriene tilts his head toward a small enclosure attached to the side of the conservatory. I hadn't noticed it before, so I follow him with curiosity as he nears it. He flips open a panel, revealing a small enclosure lush with greenery, a bed of flowers scattered across the bottom. Inside, resting among the soft bedding or flying contently along the perimeter of the enclosure, are four butterflies.

I furrow my brow and crane my neck to look farther into the sun-dappled box. It looks inviting and comfortable, and the temperature seems to be controlled by a pale white contraption on the side. But how do they get in? A small round opening near the top of the box catches my attention, leading out into the overcast kingdom of Nether.

"I programmed them to come back here and nestle safely inside until I can retrieve them," Adriene explains, gently offering his hand to the butterflies. A small blue butterfly lands on the bridge of his finger, completely at ease.

It's an astonishing and odd combination: the daunting executioner of a feared kingdom, and a delicate butterfly perched safely on his hand.

My heart warms at the sight, and I feel my eyes start to shift again, changing from black to blue.

The switch must catch Adriene's attention because his head snaps toward me. His eyes widen a fraction, and he swallows. The knot in his throat bobs. "Emilia…"

"I know," I say, surprised at how giddy I sound. "It's just…" I feel a blush bloom across my cheeks. I lick my lips and try again. "You look so…adorable right now." I giggle, grinning from ear to ear. It's been too long since I've grinned. Since a genuine laugh parted my lips.

The sound catches Adriene off guard.

He stills, staring at me as color floods his face. His eyes shift to the golden-honey I've come to love.

"Your laugh…" he mumbles, lifting his hand into the air so the butterfly can flutter into the conservatory. He steps toward me, staring down into my eyes with such an intense passion that my heart begins to gallop. Then his hand finds my face, cupping my cheek as if I'm a prized and precious being. His eyes flicker to my lips, then back.

I want to take the risk, to see his cheeks flush brighter. I take his hand and lift it toward my chest, hovering it above my heart so he can feel how wildly it's beating. How it's beating for him. "Do you want to kiss me?" I ask, shocked at how blunt and taunting my question sounds. There has been something remarkable growing between us for a while now… In the space between our brief kisses, in the feeling of lightning after he takes my hand, and in the intensity of his gaze when he looks at me. I know this isn't the time for romance, considering the declaration of war against my kingdom and my grief for my sister's passing, but it feels destined… It feels *right*. Hardly anything does these days.

He rests his forehead against mine, holding my eyes. His voice is gravelly as he admits, "Yes, Emilia. I really do."

"You really do…*what*?" I tease, lifting my face toward his. I want him to say it.

His eyebrows knit together, and he tightens his

grip on my hand, moving it to his chest this time. Underneath my palm, I can feel his immortally cursed heart beating in sync with mine. "I want to kiss you, Emilia. I want to love you. I want to be with no one but you. For you are the queen of me and my desire." He lowers his lips to mine, and though we've kissed several times before, this one feels different. This one feels like a book when the two characters finally realize they are the end of each other's stories. But…I've read countless books…and I know the treachery that happens afterward. Though my life is no fairy tale, will the treachery of an author's hand still land a final blow to my slowly rebuilding heart?

He pulls away, and I take a moment to regain my composure before glancing up at him. He must've felt it too, because the look he's giving me turns my heart molten. In his golden eyes, I can tell that he would burn the world to keep me safe. Without a second thought, he would chop off the hand of anyone foolish enough to harm me

"The butterflies," I say, gesturing toward the small enclosure beside us. "Our spies. Do they come barring any information?" I need to switch the direction of this moment. Under his gaze, I feel delicate and vulnerable. I am a queen with a crown of bones. *"Vulnerable"* and *"delicate"* shouldn't be in the same sentence as my name.

He flickers the tip of his pink tongue across his bottom lip, then runs a hand through his hair, leaving it disheveled. He glances at the enclosure and takes a deep breath, pushing his shoulders back and attempting to ignore the tension between us. "We'll have to see. I'll take them back to my room with me."

He turns to leave, but I catch his arm. Placing an innocent smile on my lips, I inquire, "About the man in the village... Did you offer him a job as the palace alchemist? I don't want you carrying too many responsibilities, Adriene." I peer through the green glass and toward the village nestled below the palace and before the formidable bog.

"Bartholomew?" Adriene nods. "I extended the invitation, but he declined it. He didn't give me a reason, but he told me to deliver his gratitude to the queen."

I purse my lips. "Shame. I suppose you will have to stay the alchemist until we can find a replacement."

"That's perfectly alright, Emilia. I'm used to balancing quite a lot around here since those useless vampires never lend a hand." He smirks, and his eyes, which shifted back to black after I pulled away from our embrace, twinkle with mischief.

I chuckle. "They *are* quite useless unless they're acting as guards or traitors."

"Speaking of…" Adriene squeezes my hand gently, knowing I'm going to hate what he's going to say next. "We need to inform Garamond of our plan. He's our ticket to Cyprion."

The bubble of solitude from the strains of reality bursts. I scowl at him, but nod in begrudged agreement. "I know we do. But I'm going to hate it. He should get flogged and strung up as food for the chimeras." I cross my arms.

A wicked grin flickers to life across Adriene's face. He drapes an arm around my shoulders. "There's no reason we can't do that later. Now, is there, my Emilia?"

I match his smile. "That *is* true…"

"For now, however," he spins me toward the doors leading into the palace, "go deal with the vampire prince while I capture the butterflies."

I arch an eyebrow and try not to laugh. "Yes, that sounds perfectly accurate. The mean-old executioner jumping around catching butterflies?" I elbow him in the ribs and glance up at him under the canopy of my eyelashes, flashing a teasing smirk. "How adorable you are."

I chuckle to myself as I head back toward the doors, leaving Adriene illuminated by green-tinted, overcast sunlight in his black executioner uniform, flushed an unnatural red.

I find it amusing that the immortal executioner's

undoing is being called adorable.

Chapter Fifteen

$\mathcal{I}$ stall in front of the door to Garamond's room, gnawing on my lip and trying to find any excuse not to raise my fist and knock. Garamond is the last person I want to see. The last person I want to rely on. But we need his father's army if we're going to win this war, so with a disgruntled sigh, I raise my fist and knock.

The door opens rather quickly (much to my dismay) and a groggy, half-asleep vampire prince peers out at me. He's wearing a loose, gray sleeveless shirt and linen pants. His hair is messy and spiked up in places. It's so obvious he just woke up from an evening nap.

How *lovely*. The vampires of this forsaken kingdom have time to nap while we're on the brink of war. People are getting snatched from the village by chimeras, and the other kingdoms are plotting against us.

I'm *so* glad they're not stressed. How unfortunate *that* would be.

I try not to let my irritation show, but I must not be trying hard enough because Garamond's crimson-tinged eyes widen and he takes a calculative step back.

He swallows, offering me a polite yet hesitant bow. "Your Majesty?" He looks to my side. Probably hoping to find a more courteous executioner. "How may I help you?"

"May I come in?" I ask, straining my voice to sound polite. I stretch my mouth open in an attempt of a smile, but it must be grizzly and borderline loony because he just stares at me instead of responding. "Prince Garamond..." I urge, nodding toward his room. "We need to have a little chat... and the contents of which aren't appropriate for a hallway."

That seems to snap him out of his daze. He steps aside, sweeping one arm elegantly toward the sitting area near the window of his room. "I don't have any drinks I can offer you. I was...um...*reading*...when you knocked."

I step into his room and pointedly note the mess of sheets on his bed, no book in sight. "Right... Well, I don't plan to be here long." I slide into a chair at the little wooden table in front of the window, enjoying the remaining sunlight that illuminates my face. His room is on the opposite side of the palace than mine, so it overlooks a section of the dark forest that surrounds Nether and merges into the bog. Garamond takes the seat across from me, leaning forward and tenting his fingers on the table. He raises an eyebrow and quirks his mouth to the side, waiting to hear what I came over here to say. "Yesterday I was in a meeting with the monarchs of the Solstice Realm, during which King Hanson of Aquartia issued a formal declaration of war with Nether," I explain, noting his lack of shock. I suppose everyone—even vampire princes who find the time to nap—were expecting this war. "We're not yet sure which kingdoms are going to side with us, but we know that King Hanson will hold sway over the majority." I tilt my chin up, pinning him with my cursed eyes. I hope my crown of bones and the pure hatred roiling off me in waves intimidate him enough to cooperate. "Do you think your father, the vampire king of Cyprion, will fight alongside us?"

Garamond sits up, a crease forming between his brows, and grimaces. "Father might. He's smart enough to know that winning this war will finally break the laws of the past Glaven king and allow all Unnaturals into the Solstice Realm once again. He's been working toward that goal for years." Garamond peers down at his hands, screwing his mouth to the side as he ponders the inquiry. Then he glances back up at me. The last remaining rays of

135

sunlight drift through the window and highlight the red in his eyes. "Knowing my father, this is the opportunity he's been waiting for, and I don't think he will let it slide on by." He pushes back his chair and stands up. "When are you going to see him?"

I stand up gracefully, smoothing my gown, then level him with my piercing gaze. "We're going to pay him a visit tomorrow at noon."

His mouth pops open. "We?"

I turn to leave, barely refraining from rolling my eyes. "He's your father, Garamond. Of course we're bringing you with us."

"The butterflies pick up on whispers, Emilia," Adriene explains, tapping gently on the top of a glass jar. The same blue butterfly that was perched on his finger earlier is trapped inside. "If they hear the word 'Nether' then they—I suppose the best word would be *record*—the conversation to play back to us."

"How?" I ask, bending down to peer into the jar. The butterfly doesn't look scared, not like I'd assume. If I were trapped in a glass jar with two giants surrounding me, I'd be petrified. "Is it sort of like the message binding spell on the first one?"

136

Adriene gives a brief hum, taking a seat in front of his desk and picking up a quill. "Very close. Though that one was magic. This is alchemy. *Science* mixed with magic." He scrawls something across a pad of paper in front of him, eyes occasionally flickering up to the jar. The sconce on his wall provides enough light to illuminate his desk.

"Do you think you could teach me?" I ask with curiosity.

He stills, pausing mid-sentence. Then his head snaps up as he looks at me, eyebrows drawn together and forming a little crease above the bridge of his nose. His bowed lips pucker in thought. "Teach you...alchemy?"

I nod. "I'd like to learn. It sounds fascinating."

He blinks once. Then twice. Then a third time before letting out a quiet, content snort, as if he can hardly believe his ears. "No one wants to learn alchemy these days. It's a dying profession."

"Well..." I shrug one shoulder. "You're not dead. I'm not dead. And I'd like to learn." I state it matter-of-factly.

The corners of his mouth tilt up in a smile I can only describe as warm. By the gleam in his shark eyes, I'm led to believe it's because we're here together. That I want to learn something he has a fondness for. The light from the sconce mounted on the wall above his desk flickers across his face, casting half of it in utter darkness and the other half in a golden light.

We stare at each other, unblinking, for a long while. I don't know what's going through his head. But the only thought that's bouncing around the cage of my mind is how addicted I am to his company, and how I know—as the queen of a kingdom that everyone wants eradicated—that I should ignore these feelings, this growing passion between us, and let it be nothing more than a short and bittersweet fling. That would be the responsible thing to do. I need to put my people first—my kingdom first.

But as his eyes seem to darken, and his sweet smile turns into something more, I know I'm not strong enough to deny him. Deny whatever is leading me toward my executioner. Maybe it's the curse. The Veiling that's coursing through both our veins, turning us to each other.

A scent reminiscent of decay seeps into the room. I crinkle my nose and jut my chin toward his closed door and the dungeon beyond. "What is that *stench*?"

He lifts his nose into the air as if he can't smell it. "What stench?"

"That," I say, curling my lip. Urine, I realize. It's urine, blood, and vomit. Those are the ingredients of this horrific smell.

"You mean…? The cha klas?" Adriene suggests, studying me as if there's something wrong with me. "It's never seemed to bother you before."

I shrug off his words, trying not to read too deeply into them. He's right, however. The pain of the creatures usually brings a wicked tingle up my spine, and a soft cackle to my lips, but now it's only making me want to throw up. I swallow, trying to keep my lunch down. "*Why* do we torture them anyway? They don't deserve it. They didn't do anything."

He gapes at me. "It's just the way things are. The Shrouds crave them. I can't really explain why."

I turn away from the door, trying to prevent the smell from getting to me. "I want it stopped. Immediately. And I want all the harmed cha klas looked at. I'm sure you can figure out a way to fix them, to give them their eyesight back… Or at least heal them."

"Emilia—"

I shoot him a withering look. "I won't hear any excuses. If you can make butterflies capture conversations as low as a whisper and travel all the way across the realm to return to us, then you can make the creatures better." I soften my gaze…but only by a fraction. "I know you can, Adriene."

He gives me a look. "I'll try, Emilia. That's all I can promise. I'll tell the Shrouds to stop hurting the cha klas on the queen's command."

"Thank you."

He stands up, sets his purple-feathered quill down on his desk, and heads toward his door. He opens it and calls over his shoulder, "I'll be back soon. Who knows how long it will take to get through their thick skulls?" With a wink, he closes the door behind him.

When he's gone, I look about his room. It's disorganized rather neatly, if that makes any sense. I move closer to his bookshelf, squatting down in this insufferable gown—which is incredibly difficult given the restraints of the corset—and study the well-creased spines of his books. Little pieces of paper stick out from nearly every single one, as if he's scanned and pondered every line, annotating all his thoughts in the margins.

I slip a tiny book from his shelf and it almost falls apart in my hands. The faded cover is missing pieces. According to the illustration on the cover, it's a guide on ancient methods of construction. I doubt he's ever read a modern book, or seen a modern building. I smile, knowing that a skyscraper would make him absolutely combust.

I flip open the guide, running my fingertips gently down the margin of the very first page. He's drawn a layout of a house in the upper right corner, marking a kitchen, a bedroom, and a library. His handwriting seems rushed. It's hard to read. I imagine it's only that way because he had to get his idea down on paper, too scared of forgetting even a single element.

Adriene may be the most fascinating person I know. A Shroud. An executioner. But someone who's gentle with butterflies and rushes to rescue a child. A man who the village looks to in times of crisis. An alchemist who devours books, desperate to learn everything he can.

Adriene is a mystery. The more I find out about him, the less the image I first crafted of him fits. He has a wondrous mind and a truly kind soul... He just needs to be freed from the Veiling. To let his golden eyes shine through the black.

He said he'd help me find a way back to my true self.

So, I'm going to help him too.

Chapter Sixteen

*A*driene sits down on his bed, and I slide up next to him. Then he cracks open a dusty book, positioning it in his lap.

It's like the rest on his shelf: aged, worn, and annotated. His handwriting in this one is smoother and more legible. More like notes than the passion-driven desire to describe his inventions. He was studying this... Whatever this book is about.

"You said you wanted to learn alchemy." He smooths the pad of his thumb gently across his writing. "This book is how I learned. You may take it and read it if you truly want to learn."

"I would love to," I say without hesitation, peering at the book and the minuscule font with eyes full of devotion. "The book you gave me before —about the girl—did you want it back? I'm only halfway through." I rest my head against the wall and face him.

A corner of his mouth tilts up, revealing the shadow of a dimple. "No, you go ahead. You can keep it."

"I never took you for a fantasy person," I exclaim, pursing my lips to the side. "How many times did you read the book?"

He tilts his head down toward the guide to alchemy in his lap, then admits, "Not even once, Emilia."

I draw back, biting my cheek with confusion. "But—?" A crease forms between my brows as they lower over my eyes. He didn't even read it once? How can that be when the spine is so broken? The book is falling apart as if it's been held and pored over by countless people. Surely, he must've read it at least once. Why would he recommend a book to me without indulging in its pages? That certainly doesn't make any sense.

"For me, there aren't words in that book. It's full of blank pages." Adriene's hands tighten a fraction on the alchemy book. He eyes me wearily as if he's wondering if he should've said as much.

Shock slaps me in the face like a dead fish. I tilt my head to the side, catching my crown when it starts to slip. "How? Why can *I* read it then?" Endless questions tap at the walls of my mind.

He blows out a calculated breath. "I'm not sure. Tell me, Emilia…when you finish the book. Tell me what it's about." He studies me inquisitively as if he's searching for the answer in my gaze.

"I will," I agree, opening my mouth to say more —to ask the questions that are bouncing about my mind, but he's already tapping a finger on the page before him and issuing a demand.

"Pick one." He pushes the book toward me, flipping through the pages.

"A...what do you call these? They aren't spells, are they? I thought spells were strictly magical."

"An elixir is the proper word, though about anything will work these days." He gestures to the thick, blue leather book. "Pick any recipe, and tonight, we'll make it."

I scan the contents of the book, looking for a title that jumps out at me. I chew on my bottom lip in concentration. There are so many options, so many possibilities.

Love Elixir.

I grin and leave my finger underneath the title, flashing a rather jovial and teasing smirk toward Adriene. "What does this one do?"

Adriene reads the chosen elixir and then gives me a deadpan expression. "Once brewed, slip a drop or two into the tea of the person you're attracted to. It's a rather surface-level recipe. All the elixir does is mess with their hormones."

"I think that's called false advertising then." I continue to scan the contents when Adriene whispers, in a voice so quiet that I'm not sure he even meant for me to hear:

"Trust me, Emilia. You don't need an elixir to make people fall in love with you."

I flush red but continue to search for another recipe, refusing to face him, to confirm that I heard him.

What does he mean by that?

My palms turn slick with sweat, and I have to dig my nails into my hand to stop from reaching up and dabbing away the sweat beaded on my brow.

"This one," I declare, tapping the page, desperate to dissolve the tension in the room.

He leans toward me and smiles when he reads my chosen recipe.

"Memory Metamorphosis," he reads, taking the book from me and locating the specific page. Once he's finished scanning it, he slips it under his arm. Then he stands and grabs two black cloaks from his wardrobe. He tosses one toward me before clasping the second around his neck, concealing the peasant-style shirt and loose linen pants he's wearing. He rests his hand on the doorknob. "Coming?" His eyes study me, waiting for me to follow him. There's a certain twist of his features that leads me to believe that he's excited. I don't blame him. I'm also excited. *What does Memory Metamorphosis exactly mean?*

I pop up from his bed, thankful for the flexible outfit I chose for today. "Definitely."

The night sky outside the palace is breathtaking. The stars sparkle, unobstructed by clouds or fog. They're countless in quantity and breathtaking in beauty.

I've always loved looking at the stars, staring up at the night sky, and imagining what could be out there. The vastness of the universe is terrifying—and knowing how minuscule I am compared to the expanse of space makes me feel invisible, but it also reminds me how my problems are even smaller.

"Wow," I gasp, throwing my head back and spinning in a circle. The black cape Adriene lent me twirls around my feet. The stars dance above me, and I stumble backward, dizzy. I know I shouldn't act so improper—the weight of the crown tells me that much—but I don't care at this moment. Right now, it's just me and Adriene and the vastness of the universe. I grin and turn back to Adriene, wondering if he can see the beauty in the stars as I can. "Aren't they stunning?" I ask.

Adriene isn't looking at the stars. He's looking at me. "Yes, they are. The most beautiful stars I've ever seen." His mouth twists to the side in a teasing smirk as he sits down on the bottom step of the stairs leading to the palace. He opens the alchemy book and removes a few objects from his pockets that he grabbed on the way out of the palace. A chilly breeze drifts over my skin, pushing my hair over my shoulders.

He sets a glass vial down on the step next to him. Then he withdraws a sprig of greenery and a small, collapsible knife.

"Here," he says, gesturing to the spot on his other side. "Sit with me."

I sit down and remove my crown, setting it on the step to my left. I don't want to be queen—I never have—especially not when it's just me and him.

He tracks the movement with his eyes, and then he tilts the vial toward me, propping his arm up on his knee. "Spit."

I raise an eyebrow, ready to object.

"We need liquid for an elixir," he says earnestly.

"Why didn't you put water in it?" I throw a hand toward the palace, scrunching my face in bewilderment. He wants me to spit in a tiny glass vial? That is *so* oddly specific and *so* nasty. "I'm not spitting in that."

"Emilia," he sighs, his black eyes pinning my own. Under his gaze, I'd do almost anything. "Just spit."

I take the vial from him begrudgingly, hiding

behind one hand while I spit into the glass. I pass it back to him while glaring. "Sicko."

His smirk widens, and he bites his cheek, trying not to laugh. He selects the sprig of greenery next, shedding the small buds into the vial, then grabs my hand and pokes the point of the knife into my fingertip before I can protest. I wince, cupping my hand against me.

"Ouch. Why did you do that?" I glare, pressing the cut with my other hand. Thankfully, it's not too deep. Just deep enough to draw a drop of blood.

He scrapes the edge of the knife across the ledge of the vial, watching the drop of blood slip down between the buds.

"What plant is that?" I crinkle my nose when he raises the vial toward the sky and squints into it.

"It's a rare hallucinogenic plant called the Ethereala. It's primarily used in elixirs, best known for expanding the reaches of one's mind. The Ethereala temporarily increases access to more sections of the brain." He flicks the vial once, narrowing his eyes, almost as if he's waiting for something to happen.

I lean forward, trying to see what he's searching for. Faintly, like an aura surrounding a person, blue tendrils of magic flicker around the Ethereala buds. He lets out a content huff and tilts the vial toward me. "Bottoms up."

I cross my arms, being careful to not stain the

148

fabric of my shirt with blood. "Absolutely not."

He sighs, gently shaking the vial from side to side. The blue magic swirls out of the top of the vial like smoke from a chimney. It twirls in the night air before fading. "Drink it, then think of something you want to remember. A moment in your life. A person. Something you lost and want to find. *Anything*."

I straighten my back, my full focus snapping to his face. I lock eyes with him, my mouth popping open and closing without a sound. After swallowing, I try again. "Really…anything? I can have one of my memories back?" Tears pearl on my waterline. Memories—the very aspect of someone's existence—what I came to this realm to find. What I've been longing for…ever since they were stolen from me.

"Drink this and then picture it in your mind… Recall what someone told you about the moment you want to see or think about the person you were with. Anything that will bring that specific memory into focus."

I take the vial from him, staring down at the blue magic entwining itself with the Ethereala buds. I raise it to my lips and tilt my head back, downing the contents. The taste is atrocious, and my stomach clenches in protest, wanting to reject the acrid elixir. I pinch my lips shut. *I need this to work.*

"Think, Emilia…" Adriene commands.

I can hear Sky's voice. He's in front of me, dust surrounding him. Kisha and Quicken are behind him, faces drawn with worry. I'm sitting on a couch, staring straight at the boy with the scar.

"The first time we met, you were sent to the bakery to complete a task for your father. You had to order two-dozen jam-filled pastries for your father's 42nd birthday. We were both eight. I was proving to my father that I could help out at the bakery. My first customer just happened to be Princess Emilia Strazenfield."

A bell rings, and the scent of freshly baked scones surrounds me. I breathe in, my eyes sliding shut, then breathe out, opening my eyes to inspect my surroundings.

I'm at eye level with the counter, peeking at the elaborate cakes behind the glass. I catch sight of my reflection. Piled on top of my head and entwined in a bun with pink ribbon is my brown hair. I'm wearing a pink dress that falls to my ankles, only allowing the tip of my white slip-on shoes to show. White ruffles cuff my neck, and my blue eyes are wide with wonder.

A man moves away from the front counter, so I take a step forward, having to stand on my tippy toes to come face to face with the boy behind it.

We blink at each other for a moment. The boy has deep blue eyes and wild black hair. He's wearing a small beige apron that's dusted with flour. He gives me a warm smile. "Hi. How can I help you?"

I grin back. "My name is Emilia Strazenfield, and I have a request."

My squeaky voice must catch the attention of the patrons behind me in line because hushed declarations of *"The princess is in the village? Is she by herself? Where's the king?"* sound behind me.

The boy's brilliant eyes flicker from the gawking line to me, widening a fraction. "Your Highness—"

I wave a hand at him and giggle. "None of that. I just want some pastries for Daddy."

His cheeks flush slightly, and he runs a hand through his hair, leaving chunks painted across his forehead. "Okay, *Emilia*. What pastries does your father want?" He pulls out a pad of paper from a cabinet on his side of the counter, then follows it with a blue-feathered quill and a pot of ink. He gives me a lopsided smile and urges me to continue.

"Daddy wants two-dozen raspberry jam-filled pastries for his 42nd birthday. Can you have them delivered to the palace that morning?"

He scribbles it down, the tip of his pink tongue poking out from his lips. "Alright. Two-dozen raspberry jam-filled pastries are to be delivered next Friday, with the sun. Did I get that right?"

I beam. "Yes, you did!"

The boy stares at me, transfixed. Then he

blushes and bashfully suggests, "You know, Emilia. I was going to go play with some friends tomorrow... Would you like to join us?"

I tilt my head, arcing an eyebrow. "Friends?" I blink, considering his offer. Would Daddy be fine with me playing in the village? Everyone in the village seems so nice, and it'd do me some good to make friends with people my age and not just the palace staff. I nod enthusiastically. "I'll be there!"

The boy beams as bright as the sun. "I'm Sky, by the way. Skylar Baker."

His name seems so right. So perfectly him. I couldn't imagine him being named anything else. "It's nice to meet you, Sky. I have a feeling we're going to be great friends, don't you?"

Sky rubs the back of his neck, flashing a jovial smile. "I think we will too, Em."

Chapter Seventeen

*C*an I do that again?" I plead, blinking tears from my eyes. When I was under the power of the Memory Metamorphosis Elixir, my eyes turned blue... Slowly, I feel them shift back to the void-black color I'm coming to loathe. I reach up, my fingertips hovering above my cheek as the Veiling reclaims the color of my eyes.

"The Ethereala plant should only be consumed in very small amounts. I'm sorry, Emilia, but digesting anymore right now would do more harm than good." Adriene gives me a sympathetic smile, extending his hand for me to take. "Shall I walk you back to your room? It is late and we should rest for our journey tomorrow."

I take his hand, savoring the feel of his smooth skin against mine. He's warm. I entwine my fingers with his, earning a startled glance from him. We've never held hands before... Not *really*. We've linked arms as he's escorted me places. But holding hands... It seems like a big step. Like I'm committing to this as a relationship, not just a…*fling*.

"When you find out what the butterflies have overheard, tell me." I stand up, pulling him with me. We stand there, on the steps leading to the palace, and stare at each other. The wind gently tousles our hair, chilling my skin. I tug the cloak around me tighter.

He nods dutifully. "Of course. I'll work on that tonight and inform you of the results tomorrow morning. Does that sound satisfactory?"

"It does." I look down at the steps as we walk. The chilly breeze follows us up the palace steps, toying with the hems of our cloaks and the ends of our hair. Above us, the stars continue to dance, unaffected by the turmoil lingering in our outcast kingdom.

"Tomorrow…" I start, letting the beginning of my sentence carry through the deathly silent night. Behind us, far past the treeline, a chimera howls. The sound sends goosebumps up my spine, and I nearly trip on the next step. I steady myself, tightening my grip on Adriene. "Do you think Cyprion's army will fight alongside us?"

We take two more steps before Adriene answers. Another chimera howls, stirring the tranquility of Nether when all the Shrouds are asleep. "I do. They gain more by siding *with* us."

"Do you think…we even have a chance at winning?" I glance over at him, eyebrows lowered slightly and bottom lip jutted out in question.

He stops walking, forcing me to do the same. Taking both my hands, he holds them in the space between us. "I do, Emilia. I think we have a chance at winning, for I know that there are people who will fight for you no matter what. Most, of which, we probably haven't even met yet." He steps closer, his cloak tugging at his collar and whipping in my direction. It floats on a breeze that almost seems intentional like the universe is telling us we're destined to be together by offering us some privacy. He lowers his lips to mine. His kiss is soft and welcoming. But it burns with desire, with passion, with something I'm too afraid to name. His nose bumps into mine, and he smiles against my lips. "My Emilia. *I* will fight for you. I hope that means something."

I rest my forehead against his, holding his vivacious stare. "It means everything."

The sun awakens too early. Before the sun has finished its ascent into the sky, I'm standing in front of the palace, the broken hilt of Aridam strapped to my hip, concealed underneath a lightweight navy cloak. I chose a simple dress today; it's black with sweeping sleeves and a loose, flexible skirt. The bodice is studded with tiny rhinestones, imitating a galaxy entwining up my chest and over one shoulder. As for my shoes, I picked a pair of black leather boots. I don't know what the Banished Realm will be like, but if it's filled with all the violent Unnaturals my ancestors were afraid of, it might be best to have the ability to run.

My eyes latch onto a group of people walking up the path toward the palace. A woman with a blonde bob and a rose-red dress is talking animatedly with her hands to a man beside her. The man has black dreadlocks draped over his shoulders and a regal, rust-colored tailcoat fanned out behind him. Then there's Sky—distinguishable even from this distance. His wild, raven-feather hair is restrained by the same crimson tie that he wore at the meeting. The overcast sunlight makes his scar a ravine of memories. For a brief moment, child Sky takes his place, smiling up at me with those cherub cheeks. But the illusion is gone in a flash.

Garamond, Samantha, and Adriene straighten, preparing themselves for our guests. It takes a moment before their names register.

The blonde woman—Kisha, I remember, pushing past the cursed fog—stops in front of me. Looking me up and down, she flicks her tongue across her red lips, then smiles. "Well, I heard you were scary-looking, Em. But I didn't imagine this." She takes my hair in her hands and pouts. "It's lost its shine. We're going to have to do something about that. Once, you know, this war is over."

"Kisha," Quicken warns, daring a glance at me. He quickly looks away. I purse my lips. I knew someone would be afraid—they usually are. I tilt my chin up higher, refusing to show how much it hurts. Do I truly want to be feared? Especially by the people who claim to be my friends? I pull my attention away from Quicken.

I know something is missing, but I don't pick up on what it is until I catch the glossiness of Sky's oceanic eyes. Jaxon. *Jax*. He should be here. I look away, ashamed that I hadn't thought of visiting his grave when I was in Glaven. I don't even know where he's buried.

"Are we ready to go?" Sky asks, clearing the emotion from his throat. He chances a look at me, which leaves his lips tugged down in a frown. "Is this all the people we're bringing?"

Adriene gives the group a once-over before nodding. "I figured we should keep it small since I didn't want to deplete your energy reserves more than necessary."

Sky's eyes flicker over the executioner skeptically. "That's very...considerate of you."

Adriene tries to suppress a wicked smile. "Don't worry. I won't make a habit of it."

Sky swallows back his retort, extending a hand for Samantha to take. "I don't think we've properly met. I'm Sky Baker from Glaven. And you are?"

Backstabbing imbecile.

Samantha smiles coyly, tucking a blonde strand of her hair behind her ear. Draped across her back is the embroidered navy cloak she wore when she, the Shrouds, and her hellish king stormed my palace. "I'm Samantha Kelligan from Nether."

I watch them stare at each other, protest and repulsion roiling in my stomach. Once upon a time, he stared at me like that. How odd that only a couple of months can make that change. Maybe I'm reading too much into their exchange. Maybe he isn't moving on from me, as I assume, but reveling in the presence of someone just like him. Someone who can understand the intricate swirls and jagged lines that make the language of the runes.

"It's exciting to meet another Runespeaker," Sky admits as they step in front of the group. Sky pulls a smooth, white stone from the pocket of his tunic, running his thumb across the subtle blue symbol engraved on the surface. "Runespeakers are pretty uncommon these days."

Samantha chuckles, bashfully looking down at her knee-high brown boots. She pulls a slightly smaller stone from the pocket of her burgundy dress. "That is true. I've only ever met one other, I be-lieve."

I dig my nails into my palm, half-tempted to shout *kiss already!* Watching these two fawns flirt over magic is making me want to mutilate myself like the cha klas in the dungeon.

Adriene must feel the same, because when I glance over my shoulder at him, he's rolling his eyes to the back of his head. That pulls a smile from me. I reach back and take his hand, giving it a gentle squeeze. We're in this together.

Sky and Samantha step closer, linking their hands. With their free hands, they lean down and skid their stones across the ground, toward the group. As soon as the rune stones clink together, white magic licks toward us.

It slithers, hunting for flesh to envelop. It's blindingly bright, and I instantly regret not closing my eyes. Kisha and Quicken exchange a weary glance as they're swallowed by the magic, teleport-ing to a realm of monsters and madness. When it reaches us, I tighten my grip on Adriene's hand. No matter what, I won't let go.

Chapter Eighteen

irty water slicks the soles of my shoes and hot air burns the nape of my neck. When my vision finally stops swimming, I make out the dark, dismal atmosphere of the Banished Realm. No wonder they're trying to leave. Steam lifts from the ground to swirl around our feet like mini cyclones. Through the material of my boots, the heat licks my skin.

The palace standing before us is monstrous, and the walls must be some kind of molten metal. If I so much as touch it, I fear I'll burn the skin right off my hand.

"This is where your father lives?" I ask Garamond, gaping at the behemoth of a building. The palace walls flare red and bright orange in some places, while in others it's the cool tone of steel. Barred with black wrought iron, the windows stretch up the side of the palace, and the daunting entrance stands three times as tall as Adriene.

The doors are as black as obsidian, with handles

in the shape of matching fangs. Above us, the sky is the color of ash and the sun burns like a freshly forged sword. I tug at the collar of my dress, the back of which is sticking to my skin with sweat.

Garamond doesn't tear his eyes away from the front doors. He gulps and nods. "Yep… This is home."

Lined with gothic lampposts and barren, craggy tar-black trees, is the path that winds into the village. Houses hide behind tall hedges, enveloping themselves in shadows. Golden torchlight outlines a silhouette in the house closest to us. It's a young woman with long hair. She's just standing there, facing us with a speculative tilt of her head.

The buildings here are cobblestone or brick and constructed in a style that reminds me of townhouses in the UK. At least, what I recall seeing on a TV show when I was in the Earthen Realm.

I flatten my lips into a line of determination and curl my hands into fists at my sides, taking a step toward the brutish entrance to the Cyprion palace. Before I can take another step, however, the doors open, revealing a tall man in a sleeveless tunic and a molten metal crown on a head of neatly combed black hair. There's no doubt who he is. His skin is as pale as moonlight, and his cheekbones are high, casting shadows over his jaw and making his face appear long and slender. His nose is thin and straight, narrowing into a slightly rounded point. Under a pair of thick, black eyebrows are crimson eyes—the trait of a vampire.

"Queen Emilia, we've been expecting your arrival." His voice is gravely and hoarse as if he just finished commanding an army—which, he might have, he looks as much a general as he does a king. His eerie red eyes land on Garamond, and he allows a corner of his mouth to lift. "Garamond, my son. I'm glad to see you doing well."

Garamond grimaces. "Yes, well... Father, we have something very important to ask you."

"Is it about the war?" He raises a thick black eyebrow and smirks at our dumbstruck expressions. "We may be ostracized from the rest of you, but such an era-ending event will always find its way to our ears." He steps toward me and extends a hand that's easily twice as big as my own. "King Cassius Quinn of Cyprion. It's a pleasure to meet the fabled Emilia Strazenfield. Please, come inside. I assure you, it'll be a lot cooler." He rolls his eyes to the glaring sun before heading back inside the palace.

"The walls..." I mumble, following him inside, unsure if it's a stupid question. I don't want to ruin my reputation within three seconds of meeting Cassius.

He chuckles, raising the hair on my neck. These *dang vampires* and their unnerving Veils. "No. It's not hot, if that's what you were going to ask."

I wonder what material it's made of, but I think I reached my *not-actually-important* question quota for right now—not when I have a grave favor to ask of him.

He turns to the right of the foyer, where a chandelier with flickering candles dangles at least six feet above our heads. The walls are slick and glisten as if they're wet. An absolutely absurd thought occurs to me: what if the palace is *sweating*?

I mean…I don't blame it.

Cassius eventually stops in front of a tall oak-colored door, there doesn't seem to be a doorknob, so he pushes it open with the palm of his hand. I'm sure the door is made from some fantastical metal, just like the rest of the palace. Swinging inward, the narrow door reveals his study.

A grandiose throne-like chair made from the same obsidian material as the doors to the entrance sits behind an equally large desk. Neatly arranged on either side of the desk are piles of parchment and a burgundy-feathered quill sitting ready in a bottle of crimson ink.

There are three smaller, less elaborate chairs lined up in front of the desk and six more distributed evenly against the wall on either side of the door-way. Almost like a waiting room.

Thin, black-metal shelves perched on the wall in

uneven positions house thick tomes. And a window overlooking another section of the Cyprion village takes up most of the wall behind his desk, along with obnoxiously thick, red velvet curtains.

"Have a seat," Cassius says, gesturing to the chairs. He takes his place behind his desk, resting his hands on the arms of the throne chair. On his left hand sparkles a brilliant ruby embedded in a silver ring. I squint. The ruby appears to be carved into the likeness of a rose.

If I remember correctly, vampires can't be near roses. So why does he wear one so lavishly on his hand? I tilt my head speculatively at the vampire king, wondering if there's a story behind it.

Once we're all seated, a tall woman with whorls of black hair plastered to her cheeks in an elegant design appears—slipping under the door in a purple mist and solidifying in her vampire form before our eyes. She's balancing a silver tray in one hand. She sets it down on a clean spot on Cassius's desk before re-misting herself and leaving the way she came.

Cassius casually pours tea from the simple, unadorned teapot into tiny porcelain cups before distributing them to us. I take the porcelain cup gently, trying to mask my surprise at the woman's entrance. From my studies, I discovered vampires can turn into mist to fit through narrow places, but I've never seen it before.

The tea isn't actually hot as I expected. It's slightly chilly as if it's been sitting out, waiting for us for a couple of hours already. I'm rather grateful. I don't think I can handle more heat right now, not with the sweltering sun blaring down on the metal palace.

"So, Queen Emilia, did you come to ask for our alliance in the Solstice War?" Cassius stirs his cup of tea gently with a small spoon, clinking it against the sides before adding another scoop of sugar from the bowl the vampire woman brought with her. His crimson-tinted eyes study me so intensely it's like he's searching my soul for the answer.

The Solstice War? Is *that* what it's being called?

I take a sip of the tea, not wanting to appear eager. "Yes, Your Majesty. I think an alliance will benefit us both."

Cassius watches me, sipping quaintly on his tea. It's an odd image; this behemoth of a vampire king, sipping from the tiniest teacup known to man. It makes my brain itch. "I agree."

I blink. That was too easy. "But...?"

He chuckles, setting his teacup down on his desk. When he looks back up at me, his eyes flame with power. "But the majority of my army was born after the Great War. They don't have experience with regular humans, mages, or the creatures in the Solstice Realm. If we're to fight alongside you, then

I request that you stay here and help train my army." He reclines, letting his deal hang unwaveringly in the air.

"You want *us* to train *your* army?" Sky asks, piping up from a chair in the corner. A bead of sweat slips down his temple. I'm not sure if it's from the warmth of this realm or from the intimidation of the vampire king.

Cassius glares at the accusation in Sky's voice. "I won't send my people into a realm without knowledge of what they're going up against. They're skilled warriors—but they're also parents and spouses. I refuse to tear apart a family. The destruction of war, even when we know our enemies, is enough to haunt me." He turns back to me. "Do we have a deal, Queen Emilia?"

I tilt my chin. "We do." My voice sounds steady and determined, and for that I am thankful. I am a queen, but I am also only eighteen.

Cassius pushes back his chair and thrusts his hand toward me. I stand up, praying to whatever god there is that my legs don't shake. His hand dwarfs mine as I shake it, and the look he gives me over our locked grip sends ice shooting through my veins. "We start tomorrow. For today, you may do as you like. Ulinda will show you to your rooms so you can get situated. Dinner is at sundown. Summon Ulinda and she'll show you the way to the dining hall."

The woman from earlier vaporizes herself under the door again, making me almost pee myself. I don't think I could ever get used to that. I knot my hands in the thin fabric of my skirt to stop myself from jumping out of my skin. Vampires will always freak me out—but I don't have the luxury of showing my genuine emotions, not when I have so many people looking at me. With the crown comes the responsibility of maintaining the air of a regal queen.

Ulinda's skin glows ethereally as if she's wearing layers of foundation and has never gotten a pimple in her life. In fact, Garamond and Cassius both have that same effect. I suppose it's a vampire thing. How *unfair*.

"Please, come with me," she says, sounding as prim as her complexion. I'm about to comment on how we can't vaporize ourselves under doors when she reaches over and pushes it open with her palm.

As we follow Ulinda down a hall and up a flight of metal stairs that *clank* beneath our feet, a growing sense of anxiety builds in my chest. I don't know what will happen tomorrow, the next day, or even tonight. But I know what will happen at this moment. And right now, I'm going to choose to not let the fear of the coming war stop me from living.

Chapter Nineteen

The room Ulinda brings me to is astounding. The ceiling doesn't leak like it does back in Nether, and the windows don't overlook a daunting bog. I'm standing in the doorway as Ulinda shows the rest of the group to rooms situated evenly down the long hallway. The walls are made from that same dark stone that accents the palace. They appear slick with moisture. Mounted on the walls between the rooms are torches, illuminating the eerie hallway. Adriene flashes me a smile as he disappears into the room beside mine.

I don't wait to see where everyone else gets placed. I step into my room and close the door, pressing my back against it and letting out a sigh. My heart is beating irregularly, the start of a panic attack I'm so accustomed to. I rest my hand on my chest and breathe, knowing nothing is wrong. Everything will be fine. *It has to be.*

The bed is massive with four midnight-black posts that jut from the corners like the teeth in a chimera's maw. Red transparent curtains drape from the bed on all sides. I push some aside to inspect the bed further, running my hand along the intricate engravings on the headboard. They're runes, I realize, though I don't know what they mean. I wonder if Sky does. I might have to ask him the next time I see him. The wood is splintered in some places, leaving the runes sharp and jagged; a sign that they're engraved by hand. The headboard is elaborate, reminding me of a crown. It dips low before spiking in the center. Carved into the point of the headboard is a rose. I frown. Why would King Cassius have a rose ring and roses engraved into his furniture? Do roses affect vampires the way I thought, or is the book I read wrong?

Draped across the bed is a gray wolf's pelt and situated against the headboard is a series of six small black pillows. I'm all for multiple pillows on a bed (a controversial opinion, apparently) but six is excessive. I let the curtain fall back into place and move to the end of the bed, taking note of the wall directly across from me. Eerie red sunlight drifts through the window, highlighting motes of dust that float in the air, and casting menacing shadows on the surfaces behind me.

There's a seat built into the base of the narrow window that overlooks a forest of dark, barren trees. If I could see through the shadows of the Banished

Realm, I bet I could make out the slinking form of creatures skulking within the forest. But for all the rust-red, ghoulish light the sun expels, it doesn't seem to be any good at dispelling the shadows within this realm.

I shudder and turn away from the window. The door to my left is as tall and narrow as the one to King Cassius's study. Just like that door, this one doesn't have a handle. I push it open with my palm, revealing a personal bathroom with black tiles flecked with drops of white, like snow on the back of a raven.

A simple red curtain—nearly as translucent as the one surrounding the bed—divides the shower section from the rest of the bathroom. I'm very glad these are personal rooms—I'd hate to walk in when someone's showering and get an eyeful of something I'd rather not see.

I spin back around and put my hands on my hips. There's a desk to my left, resting against the same wall the entrance is on, and a bookshelf to my right, filled with tomes like those in the king's study.

I'm not sure what I should do now. I guess I could wait until dinner—but that would be incredibly boring. Just as I'm about to turn to the bookshelf, there's a knock on the door.

With my eyebrows lowered in curiosity, I open it, sighing in relief when it's Adriene. Part of me was expecting it to be Cassius, with an additional cost for their alliance.

"Want to go on a walk with me?" Adriene asks, leaning against my door frame and giving me one of those coy smirks that makes my heart thunder.

"In this heat?" I grimace.

He pushes off the door frame and steps toward me, unclasping my cloak and tossing it to the floor. He's missing his cloak as well. "Now you'll be cooler." He turns around, calling over his shoulder, "Coming?"

I give my room a once-over before closing the door and trailing after him. I don't know what he has in mind, but I'm positive it'll be a lot more fun than sitting in my room all alone.

The Cyprion village is quiet even though it's the middle of the day. It's nearly as dark as night, with the red sun now blocked by a mass of ugly gray clouds. Maybe that has something to do with the unnaturally still kingdom.

Clutched in Adriene's hand is a tiny version of his scythe. Just like me, he didn't want to come to a realm full of vampires without a weapon. An easily concealed weapon is more advantageous than a

171

weapon the size of his scythe—especially since we're trying to get these vampires to trust us, and openly carrying around a weapon isn't the best way to achieve that. Even *I* pushed past my resistance to the cursed sword and brought along the jagged blade of Aridam. My hand reflexively hovers at my waist, where an old sheath I found in Aaron's wardrobe hangs. I haven't found the courage to hold the blade since I plunged it into Aaron's chest, concealing it in my dresser until this morning. Maybe the creatures in this realm have heard of the Sword of Death. If they have, maybe that'll stop them from attacking me. I don't think my title alone will protect me—not out here.

"What's that called?" I ask, walking beside Adriene. With each footstep, I splash puddles and kick up droplets onto the toes of my boots. The flames from the glass-domed street lights lining the way to the village reflect off the puddle-speckled path.

"This?" Adriene lifts the mini-scythe, catching flame light on the clean blade. "It's a sickle. I figured it would be easier to conceal." Strips of black leather are wrapped around the hilt. There aren't any indentations from use, so it must be a new weapon.

"Hmm…" I hum, scanning the still streets of the Cyprion village. "So, where are we going to go?" If it weren't a hundred degrees and as dark as evening,

Cyprion would seem like a pretty peaceful place to live. There are little shops farther down from the houses, with candles flickering on the windowsills to illuminate displays.

Voices lift from a particular storefront on the corner of the main street, overlooking numerous other streets that branch off from this one. It's the brightest shop in the area, with lit candelabras on every available surface that glows through the clean windows.

Adriene stops in front of the bright red door. A window in the shape of two fangs is at eye level with him. "How about here?" He turns to me, flashing a mischievous smile. "Shall we see what these vampires get up to?"

I peek into the large window next to the door, straightening my crown in the reflection. Inside what appears to be a bar is a mass of vampires smiling, drinking from tall, clear glasses full of red liquid, and leaning over a table playing pool. Laughter and easy conversations drift alongside subtle, centuries-old music that derives from a man holding a guitar in the very back of the bar. Lowered over the man's eyes is a black fedora, and he has one long leg stretched in front of him. He slouches on the wooden stool tucked into the corner as if he's meant to only be heard and not seen.

This would totally be a *what the heck* moment.

This place seems too human to be operated by vampires. How different are vampires compared to humans then?

Before I can stop him from walking into the vampires' den, Adriene opens the door and steps right in. A tiny silver bell tinkles joyously. Instantly, all the vampires freeze, snapping their attention to us and pinning us with their unsettling crimson eyes.

I gulp, knowing I shouldn't be afraid. I'm a queen, for heaven's sake...but I've never seen so many monsters in one place before. Every vampire in the bar focuses their attention on me and Adriene.

"Well, who do we have here?" a man asks, leaning his elbows on the bar top. He has a black mustache that swirls on either end and thin, slicked eyebrows to match. He's wearing an unbuttoned black shirt, exposing his pale chest, and slicked back into a cow-tail is his midnight-colored hair. His eyes are a strange mix between blue and red, like his vampirism got layered over sky-blue irises. They're almost purple...and entirely too enchanting. His intimidating stare moves from Adriene to the crown atop my head, then he straightens up, and his eyes widen a fraction. He's only a couple inches shorter than Adriene, but the way he stands—with his chest extended and his shoulders back—makes him just as intimidating. When his lips twitch back in a curious smile, his sharp fangs glint in the candlelight.

Taking the cue from the bartender, the other vampires all notice my crown, falling eerily silent and still. The regard of dozens of vampires prickle over my skin, and I straighten up, wanting to be rid of their scrutinizing gaze.

"I am Queen Emilia of Nether and this is my executioner—*that* is who you have here," I announce, flashing a wicked smile. Even though I don't have fangs, nor do I have magic, by their reactions I think I unsettled them just enough. Maybe it is my void-colored eyes or the crown of human finger bones situated elegantly on my head.

The bartender with the purple-tinted eyes swallows, then lifts two tall glasses onto the bar top. "Welcome, Your Majesty. Care to join us for some drinks?" He quirks a thin eyebrow at the invitation.

Chapter Twenty

The bartender—who introduced himself as Percival—claps Adriene on the back. The vampires surrounding the pool table throw their heads back in laughter, exchanging jingling pouches of coins. "Good game, Adriene." He sighs. "A bet is a bet." He tosses a pouch from his trousers pocket onto the pool table and nods toward it. "I wonder if you're as skilled with a sword as you are with a stick." To emphasize his point, he clinks the side of his pool stick on the table.

Adriene shakes his head, grinning from ear to ear. He picks up the pouch of coins and weighs it, eyebrows lifted in consideration, before dropping it back to the pool table. "I'm terrible with a sword, actually. My weapon of choice is a scythe."

"Is that what you'll be bringing to the battle-field?" Percival hops up onto the pool table, waving off the vampires clamoring for him to get back to the bar and pour them drinks. After a round of curses in his direction, he reclaims the bag of coins and nods at Adriene in thanks. "How does a scythe compare to a sword? Maybe I'll have to get myself one soon." He looks between Adriene and me, raising one eyebrow. The corner of his blush-colored lips tilts wryly. "The only reason you both are here is to ask King Cassius if he'll ally with Nether in the Solstice War, right?"

I give him a brief nod.

"I figured." He drops his head, something flashing in his eyes. When he pockets the coin pouch, he pushes himself off the pool table and gestures to the men and women at the bar, glaring at him with empty glasses clutched in their hands. "If we're all going to war, then let's drink!" His declaration is punctuated by a flurry of pale fists pounding the bar top. Percival leads us through the eager crowd, returning to his station behind the bar. Adriene and I slide up on two empty bar stools that creak under our weight. Percival pulls out two bottles and two glasses, setting them before us. He adds a splash of light, caramel-colored liquid to the glasses before topping them with a generous pour of something clear.

The rest of the vampires all raise their glasses in the air, tipping back brown concoctions and suspicious blood-colored drinks.

The environment is rich with celebration—just like it is around the holidays. Everyone united, laughing, focusing on the same obstacle: the upcoming Solstice War.

So far, I haven't seen any vampires that resemble the Shrouds back at the Nether palace; those disgustingly lazy, incompetent buffoons. These vampires—dancing, flirting, enjoying their day—remind me more of people back in the Earthen Realm. Spirited people who just want to live life. At least—what I *can* remember of them.

The music from the fedora-clad man in the back pairs amiably with the lighthearted atmosphere. I smile and tilt back my glass, downing the drink, which immediately sends a hot burning sensation to my stomach. I've never tried alcohol before—and to be honest, I don't think I like it. My face scrunches up in disgust, which makes Percival beam. He flashes me his long, white fangs with jest, resting his forearms on the bar top and leaning toward Adriene and me.

The cuff of his shirt shifts, revealing the end of a black and red tattoo. I can't quite make out what it is, but it spirals and appears to have leaves and thorns. "So—the Veiling, is what ya'll call it—is that what the creepy eyes are from?" He points to his own eye, snickering at my bemused expression.

"We aren't the only ones with creepy eyes, Percival," I say, giving him a look which has him tossing his head back and barking laughter.

"Fair enough, Your Majesty."

Percival moves to make drinks for the vampires at the other end of the bar, but before he can get out of earshot, I add, "Emilia, please. *Just* Emilia."

Adriene gives me a look, eyebrows drawn low, mouth opened a little in consideration. It doesn't dawn on me until the corner of his lips twitch up in the semblance of a smile. Emilia *before* the curse used to say that, Emilia *after* the curse...not so much. Maybe I'm successfully fighting the Veiling. Maybe Adriene and I can make it out of this and find our true selves, after all.

Percival returns to us, wiping his hands off on a white rag. "Tonight, some of us are going down to The Tracks. I know you're a queen and probably want nothing to do with those below you... But I think you might enjoy it," Percival offers, setting the rag aside. "When the moon is highest in the sky, follow the Troll Steps at the edge of the forest surrounding the village. You can't miss them." He taps the counter with two knuckles. With a wink, he adds, "Consider it an open-ended invitation."

I bite my cheek, considering his invitation. I don't know what The Tracks are, or what exactly this vampire bartender does in the middle of the night, but King Cassius said that in order for the vampires to fight beside us to the best of their ability, they'll need to know more about us. What better

179

way to do that than to join in their endeavors? "I will think about it," I respond, dipping my head in gratitude.

He doesn't look too hopeful, but he smiles at me nonetheless.

At sundown, Adriene and I enter the dining room, inhaling the thick scent of charred meat and the metallic stench of fresh blood. Bile rises in my throat when I notice the crystalline decanter in the center of the long obsidian table. Crimson liquid glistens within.

Maids drift along the edges of the dining room, preparing it for this evening. I've heard word that Cassius and Garamond are going to hold a meeting with their generals after dinner. A few maids push through a pair of gigantic doors to lay platters of intoxicatingly delicious food on the red, lacy table runner that falls elegantly off either end of the table; the fabric cuts into a drastic point.

My eyes flick from the food up to the doors behind the head of the table as they open with a grand flourish. Cassius enters with his hands behind his back, head tilted high and lips twisted in a rather content smile. His son, Garamond, enters behind him, hidden by the imposing shadow of his father.

Cassius gives Adriene and me a cordial nod before taking his seat and pouring himself a drink from the decanter. When we don't move, he glances back up at us with one thick black brow lifted in inquiry. "Were you not going to sit?" he asks, a demure edge tinting his voice.

I bite my cheek and find an empty spot at the center of the table. Adriene sits across from me and we exchange an unsure look. *Are we going to attend Percival's party—or whatever it is—tonight?*

Light laughter floats from the front hall, and I immediately know who it is, even though it's been months since I've spent any quality time with her.

Kisha.

The front doors that Adriene and I came through moments ago open, revealing a group of four, smiling among themselves and sharing a quiet conversation. They don't halt their conversation even as the vampire king's gaze settles upon them. I admire that... Their willingness to look in the face of their adversary and decide that they—like anything else—won't stop them from being themselves.

Kisha and Quicken claim the last two seats on my side of the table; Quicken sits next to Garamond, who is opposite the king, while Kisha sits on my right, next to the king. Samantha, who I avoid looking in the direction of, sits down next to

Adriene. Adriene stiffens when Sky reluctantly pulls out the remaining chair next to him and sits down. Adriene shoots me a slightly perturbed glare that has me biting my cheek to stop from smiling. It's strange to see such a disturbed expression on the ever daunting executioner's face.

I don't know why Sky and Adriene don't like each other—but I can only guess that it has something to do with *me*.

"Please…do dig in," Cassius declares, waving toward the spread of freshly prepared food before us.

My mouth waters when I take in the crispy, golden skin of some kind of enormous bird. It looks like a turkey…but with longer legs and wings twice as large that lay sprawled out from its sides, across the table, as if the bird just got shot from the air and this is where it fell.

Relief fills me when I note the absence of bugs. Adriene must feel the same because his shoulders relax and a smile twitches at the corner of his mouth, but when Sky spares him a glance, it instantly disappears, a bitter grimace taking its place.

I'll need to find out what's going on between those two if we're going to work together—and fight alongside each other.

Adriene reaches toward a plate of steaming vegetables… At least…that's what I think they are… But they're all varying shades of purple. The aroma permeating the vegetables is sweet, like hot maple syrup beneath a stack of pancakes.

Sky goes in for the vegetables at the same time and their hands touch. They both retract them back to their sides in an instant, the temperature in the room chilling about ten degrees as they shoot irritated glares at each other. Tension roils around them, earning the attention of everyone else at the table. Kisha leans back in her chair to share a look with Quicken. I dig my nails into my palms, trying to convey a message to Adriene by only using my eyes: *don't you dare start a fight over purple vegetables!*

I don't think he understands because he turns toward Sky and bares his teeth wickedly. "What is your problem, *Baker*?" Turmoil spills from his shark eyes.

Sky sits up, clenching his fists on the table. "*My* problem? Trust me, *Death*, you don't want to get into it right now." He glances around the room, clicking his tongue. "This *definitely* isn't the place."

"Where is 'the place' then?" Adriene challenges, arcing a lightning-white eyebrow. He tilts his thin, regal nose into the air, pushing Sky toward a fight. I want to strangle him and sit and watch at the same time.

But Sky is right. This is definitely *not* the place to rip each other's throats out. I glance toward King Cassius, afraid that he'll be rallying his guards to remove Sky and Adriene from the palace, but frankly, he's looking a little too happy about the drama unfolding before him. Like he's been starved for entertainment for far too long.

Sky pushes back his chair, furrowing his brow and curling his lip. He glares menacingly at Adriene, unspoken threats churning around him in impenetrable waves. His hands tighten into white-knuckled fists at his sides, and he takes a step closer to Adriene. Adriene simply casts a pitiful look toward the rest of the table before standing up and towering over the newly named Glaven king.

"Are you threatening me, Baker?"

"It is *King* Skylar to you," Sky declares, his anger increasing. The force of his rage washes over the table and across my skin. I shiver, rubbing a hand down my arm, my appetite suddenly lost.

I wish I could read the tension between them to figure out what it's all about. The only common denominator is me—which is unsettling. Adriene is my right hand, my executioner, and a cursed man who's wiggled his way into my heart. I don't think threatening a king—no matter how recently crowned he is—is going to help him any.

The corner of Adriene's eyes crinkle as his lips pull back to flash a skeletal, undeterred grin. Sky pales, but he holds his ground, staring into the executioner's pitch-black eyes. "And it is Adriene the Executioner, Death Himself, and Your Worst Nightmare. I think they're all fitting titles, don't you?" Adriene tilts his head coyly, pushing and prodding to get a rise out of Sky. I'm half surprised he doesn't pull out his weapon to see Sky's fear reflected on the blade.

"We'll finish this—" Sky starts, trying to calm himself down enough to return to dinner. I'm surprised he has an appetite left after their display of testosterone.

"Tonight. Meet us at the Troll Steps at the edge of the village." Adriene smooths a hand over his chest, feeling the edges and ripples of his leather uniform. The taut leather shines in the flickering light from the torches mounted along the perimeter of the dining room.

I gawk at him. *The Troll Steps?* Did Adriene extend Percival's invitation as a challenge to Sky?

"Name a time and we'll be there," Sky insists, sweeping his hand toward Kisha and Quicken, who don't look too thrilled to be involved.

"Midnight."

When Adriene sits back down, I can tell he's thrilled with himself. I don't know what tonight will hold, but I do know that I won't easily forget it—and by morning, I'll finally get to the bottom of the boys' rivalry.

Chapter Twenty-One

The Troll Steps are exactly what they sound like. Giant footprints are embedded in the ground from constant use. They're at least a foot deep. Each footstep is paced at least three yards away from each other. I can picture the monster that created them, sluggishly maneuvering through the eerie forest, searching for something—or *someone*—to devour. Scanning the group beside me, I'm thankful Samantha didn't come. She muttered some excuse, claiming she's going to spend the night researching runes she found engraved in the walls of the palace.

The moon that now replaces the sun in the cloud-filled sky shines dully through the branches of barren trees, jutting from the ground like the fingers of a rising corpse, and across the uneven terrain.

The unnerving forest casts long, dark shadows over the Troll Steps. I can almost hear the invitation whispered on the gentle breeze that drifts through the dusky forest: *come, take the path. Come find us.*

186

Come, let's have fun.

Fun? I don't know what Percival and his vampire friends do in such an unsettling place in the dead of night. It could be anything—from a party, to a ritual, to a sacrifice.

I certainly hope it isn't the last one, though only for the sake that it could be *me*. The thought of another person getting their intestines pulled from their stomach like yarn doesn't disturb me—instead, it brings a pleasurable smirk to my lips; a result of the Veiling... I now thrive in the presence of someone's agony, even if I don't want to.

"*I'm* not going first," Kisha declares, breaking the silence. She tugs a fox-fur shawl around her shoulders and leans into Quicken, whose hand comes up to wrap around her waist. Kisha smiles faintly, and her cheeks tinge pink—a change I can see even in the gloomy lighting. They seem comforted by each other's touch. I glance at Adriene, who's standing beside me.

"Sky? Do you want the honors?" Adriene offers, sweeping a hand toward the creepy path that stretches before us, pock-marked by the troll's footsteps. An owl hoots somewhere in the depths of the forest, making goosebumps flicker across my skin. I rub my hands down my arms and take a step closer to Adriene.

I can tell that Adriene hopes Sky accepts his offer

—and that perhaps a ghoulish monster is waiting to see who will take the first step and become its meal. A hint of a malevolent smirk tugs at Adriene's mouth.

"I'll go," I say, not wanting either boy to win this stupid stand-off. I don't turn back to gauge their reactions. The moon has already peaked in the sky, which means we should be at The Tracks already. Being late doesn't sit well with me, no matter the occasion.

I hop down into the first crater created by the troll's footsteps. It's not that deep, but it still brings a wave of goosebumps across my skin. I've never encountered a creature whose foot alone is as big as me. I'm used to being short—just not *that* short.

When I make it to the next Troll Step, I can hear the others following along behind me. I glance back to see who decided to go second. Sky meets my eyes and scowls. He's irritated, but I'm not sure it's directed at me. Knowing Adriene, Sky's irritation is at him.

Walking alongside the Troll Steps would probably be easier since we wouldn't have to keep climbing in and out of them—but the forest is too close on either side—so the only way to stay on the path is to walk in the footprints. It's arduous, even though they aren't too deep, but the constant movement on the uneven ground makes a thin sheen of sweat slick my skin. I'm increasingly glad that I chose a loose dress with a flexible skirt, knowing I would need to be agile while visiting the Banished Realm.

I snap my attention toward the forest again, climbing out of the crater and hopping down into the next one. My mind fills with questions, wondering what Percival is up to, how tomorrow will fare with the vampire warriors, and what the rivalry between Adriene and Sky is about. If I had my journal, I'd be making a list of all my questions. But that journal is a part of my past. A past where Jax and Soph were alive. I don't want to taint my past with my dreary present.

We must've only been walking for ten minutes when the ground quakes, sending me falling into the side of the Troll Step. My fingernails dig into the packed dirt, and I squint into the forest, wondering what in the world is happening. Is this an earthquake? I glare down at my dress in disdain; it's now streaked with dirt.

"Oh no," Sky mutters from behind me. Suddenly, he's gripping my arm and attempting to pull me from the crater. A root from the nearby tree that leached down into the footprint snags on my skirt, refusing to let go. Sky tugs on me harder, desperation pinching his face and forming creases of concentration around his mouth.

I reach down and fumble with my skirt, trying

to tear the fabric to free myself. My attention stays on the sprawling path before us. Another quake sends Sky falling backward, freeing his grip from my arm. Kisha yelps somewhere in the tree line. A hushed whisper from Quicken follows.

From the darkness, I can see a pair of glowing amber eyes, hovering fifteen feet in the air. Then the monster takes another step, shaking the ground.

"The trolls in the Banished Realm have a terrible knack for eating humans. If it sees us, we're as good as dead," Adriene exclaims, kneeling on the edge of the crater to take my skirt in his hands. He tears the fabric away, leaving a gap that exposes my thigh. I take one last glance at the wide, glowing eyes before scrambling from the crater, cutting my leg on the exposed root. Adriene grabs the nape of Sky's shirt and intertwines his fingers with mine, hauling us into the looming forest. The troll takes another step, shaking the ground. I stumble into Adriene's chest, digging my nails into the leather of his uniform. Adriene pushes Sky toward a tree, then twists to the right and leans against one, holding me to his chest as if his life depends on it. "Be still and absolutely quiet."

I relax into Adriene's embrace, knowing he'll protect me. That no harm will come to me—or any of my friends—when he's near. He may be a daunting executioner—but, just as the woman in the

Nether village said, he's also a protector.

Hiding behind the thick trunk of the tree to our left is Kisha and Quicken. Quicken has Kisha pinned against the trunk as she cowers into his suit jacket. One of his hands is holding her head to him as he rubs soothing circles across the back of her head with his thumb. His eyes are pinned on the path we just bolted from, and his gaze is unwavering.

The ground shakes again, and I dig my fingers deeper into Adriene's leather. We hold each other's eyes as the troll stomps closer and closer. With every shake of the earth, I can tell that the monster is going to be upon us in no time. A half-choked sound comes from our left, and I glance over to see Kisha smothering her face in Quicken's jacket, trying to quiet her terrified sobs.

Adriene leans toward me, pressing a kiss to my cheek while I'm still observing Kisha. It takes me off guard that I almost say something, almost ask why he felt the need to kiss me right now. But then, as my attention shifts from the beautiful executioner holding me to a large amber eye peering toward us, the temptation to speak abandons me.

I bite my cheek, refusing to move in fear that I'll draw its attention. I don't know if it can sense me, or even see me, but I don't want to die in its meaty fist.

Chapter Twenty-Two

What are we going to do?" I whisper, keeping my eyes trained on the troll. It's massive—bigger than I originally thought. Bigger than I read about in the book back in Glaven. Its swollen skin is purple, marked with warts and stray strands of swamp-green hair. Large hands with cracked, yellow nails press into the ground, leaving indents beside the footprints. A grimy, cream-colored cloth hangs loosely over its giant frame, barely hiding its bloated body from view. Its colossal feet destroy the caved footprints that line the path through the forest, decked in stained sandals that are held together with large, white threads. Are we supposed to defeat this beast? Or is the best—and safest—decision to stay still and hope it goes away? We're already late for whatever Percival has planned. But how long does this troll plan on staying?

Did Percival know there would be trolls out here when he invited us? Did he want us—the outsiders—to be eaten by this beast, preventing him and his friends from being drafted for the Solstice War?

He had to have known. This place is called the Troll Steps, after all. I just didn't think I would run into one.

I bite my cheek and force myself to stop cowering away from the monster. A queen shouldn't be afraid and shouldn't be hiding behind her executioner in the shadows of a tree. A queen should be comforting her people and her friends. So, that's what I will do.

I force myself to step away from Adriene's embrace and turn to face Kisha, refusing to be terrified of the monster peering into the darkness in which we're hidden.

"It's going to be alright, Kisha," I whisper, taking in her weary state. She meets my gaze—my black coal eyes—and her lips thin into a line. I know my appearance unsettles her, as it does anyone who knows what I looked like before and has something to compare it to.

But she smiles and nods her head, pushing past the unease, deciding to see her friend behind the Veiling. I'm not sure how I feel about that… I don't know how I feel about anything. I'm battling with who I am now, who people expect me to be, and who I was before. It's fragmenting my mind. Splintering my soul into millions of pieces.

A twig snaps behind us, and I shoot around, drawing Aridam's broken blade from where it's sheathed at my waist. I hold it out in front of me, preparing to attack whoever is sneaking up on us. Adriene steps to my side, brandishing his sickle—it glints wickedly in the moonlight.

Percival melts from the shadows, smirking. With his shirt sleeves rolled up, I can decipher the tattoo wrapping around his arm: a series of blood-red roses with sharp, thorny vines that twist across his skin like barbed wire. "We were wondering what got the troll's attention. Trolls are sluggish creatures, except for when it comes to food. And, since the only people who intentionally lurk in these forests are vampires with dead, congealed blood, we figured he must've been hunting a fresher snack." Another man steps out behind Percival. He's bald, with a matching tattoo of a thorny rose curving over the dome of his head. His eyes flash that unnatural red when he scans us; fear pricks at my spine.

"Cut it out, Reuben," Percival demands, shooting his friend an annoyed glare. "They're here to join us, not hurt us." He turns his attention back to me, grinning as he extends his hand. "You *are* here to join us, aren't you?"

I don't bother acknowledging my friends around me. Instead, I take his hand, allowing him to pull me deeper into the forest and away from my group. Percival's eyes glint with mischief, though I can sense that he doesn't mean us any harm. My Soul Sight allows me to sense deception...but does it even work? I couldn't sense Garamond's deception, nor could I sense Samantha's.

"How big of a threat is...*he*?" I ask, gesturing toward the troll that's still gazing into the trees, squat nose protruding squarely from its pudgy face.

Percival shrugs, extending his bottom lip in consideration. "Eh, he's not bad. Poor creatures have terrible eyesight and hearing. The only thing trolls are good at is sniffing out a meal." He nods toward the forest. "Coming? The game's about to start."

"Reuben and I will be the captains, so we'll pick our teams. Huddle up," Percival declares, crossing his arms and standing in front of rusting train tracks that disappear into the forest on either side. Thirty vampires surround him, eyeing us contemplatively.

The vampires form a cluster in front of the captains. We hesitantly join them. What kind of game are we going to play? I thought this was going to be some sort of twisted vampire party... But they're just out here, in the middle of the forest in the middle of the night...playing *games*?

Reuben chooses first, standing on the edge of the train tracks to gain a slight height advantage over the onlooking crowd. The moonlight streaming down from the coal-colored sky reflects off his bald head and highlights the rose tattoo, which directs attention to his piercing crimson eyes. Expressionless, he points to a blonde woman with corded muscles near the front of the group. She pumps her fist in the air in excitement and joins him near the tracks. Reuben doesn't share her enthusiasm. Instead, he crosses his arms and glares at the vampires beneath him. His gaze doesn't seem to intimidate the vampires, but as soon as it swerves to our small group on the outskirts of the crowd, an uneasy tingle travels up my spine. Beside me, Kisha steps closer to Quicken, gripping his arm.

Percival studies the group, his eyes settling on Adriene. He raises a thin black eyebrow. "Adriene, come join me."

Adriene doesn't seem that surprised at being chosen by Percival first. He gives me a calculating look before making his way past the vampires that push their way in front of us. He positions himself next to Percival, resting one hand casually on the base of his sickle as if he thinks this could be some elaborate ploy to kill us.

I should be skeptical too. It would be *smart* to be skeptical, to look at all the angles this situation presents. But my Soul Sight is silent, which means I'm not being deceived. Now is as good a time as any to trust myself. Or, at least, *learn* to trust myself again.

Reuben selects a shorter man with tattoos running up both his arms next. Then Percival locks eyes with me, the corner of his mouth pulling into a playful smile. "Emilia."

I purse my lips and push past the people in front of me, stepping up beside Adriene. Adriene glances down at me, his black eyes warming slightly. I want to elbow him and tell him now is not the time for anything of that sort, but I refrain. Instead, I focus back on the game—on Reuben as he watches the crowd, searching for his next teammate.

The crowd dwindles, and soon we're lining up horizontally on either side of the train tracks, our hands locked with the people beside us, facing the other team. My fingers are intertwined with Adriene's and a female vampire with long blonde hair. Kisha is on my team, while Quicken and Sky are on the opposing team. Sky and Adriene glare at each other, locked in a battle of ticking jaws and fiery gazes. I dig my thumbnail into Adriene's palm to make him stop. All he does is side-eye me, which does not help matters.

Tonight, I'm going to get to the bottom of the boys' stupid vendetta.

"I'll explain the rules of the game *once* for every-one new," Percival declares, his voice loud over the din of excited vampires. A tree somewhere in the forest behind us falls, shaking the ground. I peer over my shoulder, searching for danger between the dark, skeletal trees. A gust of wind glides through the forest, carrying a peculiar stench of rotting flesh and metallic blood. I grimace, turning my face away from the wind. Percival laughs off the felled tree—as if an approaching troll is something to laugh at! I doubt it happened naturally, not with the behemoth-sized monsters tromping through the forest. Percival doesn't even seem scared about potentially being eaten alive. Maybe when he said that trolls prefer fresh blood, not dead, congealed vampire blood, he was also saying that the trolls don't come after them. That would explain why all these vampires deem it safe to venture into the forest to play games. "I don't recall the Earthen name of this game, but we came up with our own. We call this Choose Your Sacrifice. Each team member will have a chance to call out the name of a person on the opposing team. That person will then have to run across the tracks and try to break our hold on each other by using their body weight and speed alone. If they successfully break our hold, they'll join our chain. However, if they don't, they'll need to hunt down one of the dozens of pool balls hidden in the forest to earn their ticket back into the game. Forfeiting isn't an option here—cowardice marks you as fair game for our vampires. Death isn't the goal—but there's a lot of blood you can lose before you achieve that." He claps his hands together in anticipation. "Now, who's ready to play?"

The vampires around me erupt in cheers, scaring birds from the trees. A branch snaps off from a section of the forest behind me that's too close for comfort. All this noise is drawing the trolls here; they may not be interested in the vampires, but Kisha, Quicken, Sky, Adriene, and I are still alive and pumped full of fresh blood that I'm sure they'd find well worth the intrusion. I exchange a weary look with Adriene, trying to convey all my worries through my eyes alone. I think he understands because he frowns slightly and glances back at the forest, examining the shadows in search of the encroaching man-eating troll.

"Reuben, you go first," Percival declares, nodding to his friend directly across the tracks from him.

Reuben grunts in response, scanning the line of fifteen or so people. He lands on a small, blonde girl near the end of the line. "I choose Katie." His smirk is as sharp as a dagger, malevolently challenging her to break their chain. By the dangerous glee glinting in his crimson-tinted eyes, I wonder if he has a grudge against Katie—or if he just likes to see people smaller than him squirm.

Katie bites her lip, staring at the pair of six-foot-tall guys across from her. There's no way a girl of her stature will get through them, which she must already have concluded based on her withering expression. I'm not sure if there are creatures in these forests that would hunt down vampires, but I don't think finding that out by sending in a petite girl to search for her ticket back in is wise. Nonetheless, Katie tilts her chin up, steps over the first rail to stand on one of the beams in the tracks, and fists her hands. With a determined breath in, she takes off at superhuman speed toward the boys' interlocked hands. In the blink of an eye, she's thrown back onto the tracks as the boys snicker. Katie winces, rising to her feet. She glares at the boys before trudging into the forest in search of a pool ball.

Now it's Percival's turn. Percival narrows his eyes, a daring smirk flitting across his narrow face. "Send Reuben on over."

Reuben flashes Percival a wicked smile, cracking his knuckles and his neck before squeezing his hands into fists and charging toward our line. There's a teenage boy and girl holding hands in front of him, and as soon as his muscular body makes contact, their arms fly apart and they grunt in dismay. Reuben grins triumphantly and joins our side, shooting a mischievous glare toward his former team. I admit, Reuben's competitive spirit and burly frame will definitely help our team win, but there *is* such a thing as being *too* competitive. Reuben thrives off violence, and I can't help but compare his eagerness for bloodshed with the tingle of satisfaction that shoots down my spine when I'm in the presence of pain… All thanks to this stupid curse.

Next, it's Sky's turn. He glares over at Adriene, his blue eyes piercing in the darkness. "I choose Adriene." He practically spits out his name as if it burns his tongue.

Adriene smirks, and without hesitating, charges toward Sky and the woman whose hand he's holding. I sigh, taking the hand of the tall man who now takes Adriene's spot. I know that Sky's strength isn't a match for Adriene. And, just as I predicted, Adriene breaks Sky's hold and grins. But then his smile falls as he realizes what he has to do next. I don't think Sky thought it through when he called Adriene over.

Adriene looks down at Sky's hand as if it's poison ivy. Then fear enters his eyes, and he opens and closes his mouth, speechless. "Do we—" Adriene starts.

Percival interrupts him. "Just get on with it, *Death*. He's not going to bite." Sky gives Percival an *are-you-sure-about-that* look.

With a dramatic sigh, Adriene takes Sky's hand, flushing with anger. I have to admit, it's a strange visual to see them *holding hands*, especially after their spitting contest that's lasted the entire day.

Adriene meets my eyes and scowls. I flash him a teasing smirk, which makes his scowl deepen. Maybe I don't have to get myself involved in their fight. Maybe they'll sort it out by themselves. *That would be preferable.*

"Your turn, Adriene," Percival says, nodding toward him.

My skin prickles as Adriene's attention shifts to me. Is he going to call on me for revenge for laughing at him? Or is he going to call on me because he'd prefer to hold my hand instead of Sky's? I narrow my eyes at him, even though my lips tilt up in the corners traitorously. "Send Emilia over."

I tilt my head, studying their hands, wondering if I can separate them. I doubt they'd lock their hands tightly, just tight enough to give the appearance of playing the game.

I don't doubt my ability to break their grip. Stepping over the railing and onto the tracks, my confidence leaks from my coal-black eyes. I pump my arms and take off across the train tracks; my speed isn't nearly comparable to that of a vampire, but I wouldn't say I'm slow either, not with the thrill of the game surging through me. What I don't expect, however, is tripping over the last rail instead of hopping over it like I planned. I slam into their connected hands, my crown slipping forward. I barely catch it before it falls off, scooting it back onto my head, and then I blink at their hands in bewilderment. How in all the realms did I fail at *that*? Even Adriene is staring at me in shock. His white eyebrows inch higher on his face, and his shark eyes twinkle with mirth.

"*Your Majesty*—you're out," Percival exclaims, amusement twisting his roguish features.

"Emilia," Adriene whispers as I duck under his arm. When I stand back up and peer at him over my shoulder, he's biting his lip, trying so hard not to laugh. I tilt my chin up, not giving him the satisfaction of a smile. Then I face the forest and the trees that stand like ominous soldiers. Fog settles among the sharp branches and thorny bushes, cloaking the forest floor and hiding whatever beasts lurk within. I'm the queen, controller of the Shrouds, and Wielder of the Sword of Death. I shouldn't be afraid of a forest. But that doesn't mean I'm not. I gulp as a branch slams down somewhere ahead of me, shaking the ground. I'm not scared of the *forest*. I'm just terrified of what's *inside it*.

I don't allow myself a second thought, stepping between two tall, gangly trees that stretch into the dark sky. The fog quickly cloaks me, hiding the train tracks and the rest of the forest from view. I'm standing enveloped in a fog that mists my skin and leaves a faint feeling of water behind. I don't know which way is forward or back. I don't know where Percival hid the pool balls, and I certainly don't know where to start looking.

I bite my cheek and take a hesitant step in the direction I'm facing. A sickening thought occurs to me after I've wondered a few yards into the white, leeching fog: *how will I find my way back?*

I can barely see the trees on either side of me. Their thick, black, and gray trunks break into the fog before slowly disappearing like the top of a mountain disappearing in a cloud. I lose track of how many paces I've traveled away from the others when a scream reverberates around the forest, scaring a few birds—at least I hope they're birds—from the trees on either side of me. I can't see them, but I hear the branches shake and startled squawks.

I turn toward the direction I think the scream came from. It sounded human—or vampire—or whatever is the proper term to use. It must've come from Katie since she's the only one who's been kicked from the game besides me. Unless someone else ventured into this dismal place.

What kind of danger is Katie in? I thought she'd be safe from the trolls since she's a vampire, but maybe that's not true. Or maybe there's something worse lurking behind the sentinel trees.

With cautious footsteps, I head in her direction, hoping that she's okay. At least, hoping that I can get to her fast enough to help.

The path I'm on narrows and sharp branches reach out for me, snagging on my clothes and tearing my skirt. I rest my hand protectively against my crown, having lost it once already in the bog back home. I don't particularly care for it and all the responsibilities that follow—but it might grant me some protection in the Banished Realm.

There's a sudden cry to my left and my head snaps there accordingly. Submerged in the wall of fog is a face. I think it's Katie, though it's hard to tell since it's so dark and she's cloaked with thick fog. I wave my hand, trying to banish the fog before me, and squint toward the disembodied face. I hope it's her. I really would prefer not to run into something else out here, all by myself. My hand inches toward the jagged fragment of Aridam I have dangling from my waist.

The face is pale with crescent eyes that appear silver, though that could be a trick of the moon. It *could* be Katie. It looks like a young girl, with a thin face and long, blonde hair.

"Katie?" I whisper, taking a step toward her. "Is that you?" As soon as my words leave my mouth, the face falls back into the encroaching wall of fog, and I lose sight of her immediately. If that isn't Katie, and it's some monster using her face, then I've gotten myself into a rather sticky situation. I can't see *whoever* that is, but as the hair along my neck stands on end, I have a sinking suspicion that she can see *me*. I tug Aridam from my belt and brandish the jagged sword in front of me, falling into a defensive stance and peering into the suffocating fog.

Something rustles to my right, and I whip around, refusing to be caught off guard or attacked from behind. My feet crunch the brittle grass beneath me as the air seems to drop ten degrees. I can't see anything except the thick, roiling fog. But I hear whatever is scampering around, only feet away from me, concealed by this admonishing fog. Then the sound is coming from directly behind me. I jump, slashing Aridam through the air automatically, refusing to take any chances. But the blade doesn't hit anything...because nothing is there.

My hand starts to shake as primal fear grips me. Whatever creatures are surrounding me must have an even stronger Veil than the vampires, because *I*, Queen of the Shrouds, am *petrified*. I shouldn't be, for I know that I am capable of horrible, violent things...and that I can defend myself... But King Cassius wasn't wrong earlier when he said that knowing your enemy can give you an upper hand.

"Reveal yourself," I call, straightening back up and stepping in a tense circle, trying to keep my eyes in every direction, even though I know that is a fruitless endeavor. Even as I demand that they reveal themselves—since I'm sure it has to be more than one with how much scampering and rustling is going on—I don't want them to. I don't want to see the monsters stalking me right now.

A hiss slithers across the base of my neck, and my eyes widen. I feel hot breath on my skin, and the acrid smell reminds me of a spider... I can't place exactly why a spider shoots to the forefront of my mind, but I know the Veiling and its tampering with my memories is to blame.

"*Hello, tasty girl*," says the creature behind me. Its voice is raspy and shrill. *Definitely* not a human. *Definitely* not a vampire. And *definitely* not a mage. Whatever monster this is—it is completely different. "*Don't be afraid...*" A sadistic cackle parts the air. "You *asked to see me.*"

"I did," I say, pushing past my fear, trying to be stronger than its Veil. I turn in a circle toward it, very slowly, scared of what I'll see.

Then I have to tilt my head down to meet its overly-large, silver eyes. It's the girl that I thought was Katie. Though looking at her up close, I see the differences. Her eyes are too big, her mouth too large, and her clothes fall on too supple of shoulders. Almost as if this creature tried to wear her as a mask, to carve the visual of her from clay, but didn't put enough effort into the details.

I know exactly what I'm staring at right now.

A *shapeshifter*. One of the most dangerous Unnaturals.

"*Hellooooo*," it coos, tilting its head. It's strange watching this creature try to imitate the actions of a person since it is anything but. Its movements are too stiff, almost as if it watched a human and practiced imitating them in a mirror. It reaches a finger with five joints toward my face, caressing the skin that papers over my cheekbone. "*I like your skin. I think I want to wear it.*"

I step away from its touch, which seems to bring the shapeshifter even more glee. Its silver eyes bulge before shifting into a darker tone, eliminating the whites of its eyes. Its face begins to thicken, its cheekbones shifting upward. The blonde hair that falls around its sickly figure darkens into a brown, then it peers up at me with a face similar to my own.

"*Helloooo*," it croons again in its scratchy warble. "*I like your skin.*" It tilts its head. "*But I wonder what you'd taste like.*" A black tongue flickers from its mouth between rows of pointed teeth.

"*Don't we all,*" comes a series of voices behind me. Silent feet pad across the ground and cold, disproportionate hands grab at my clothes. I spin around, slashing my blade wildly at the creatures surrounding me. They all look the same. They're all wearing slightly disfigured versions of me. Aridam's blade nicks one on the arm and it screeches, falling backward and throwing an enraged glare at me.

"*Witch,*" it declares, pointing a five-jointed finger at me in accusation. The red slash across its arm turns black, spreading across its pale skin like a virus. The cut draws the shapeshifter's attention away from me. It stares at its arm as it turns completely black, pieces flaking away like dust. "*What did you do? What did you do to me, witch?*"

"Queen," I say, leveling the jagged point of Aridam at the monster's throat. Its silver eyes narrow at me in disgust, but before it can lash out, the entire creature turns to ash and scatters on a supple breeze.

The rest of the shapeshifters blink at the spot where their friend was, then at me, then at the blade I'm holding. Aridam, the cursed Sword of Death. Just as everything Eve touches heals, everything Aridam cuts dies.

I tilt my chin up and shift the sword in my grip, raising it out in front of me. "Who's next?" I ask, challengingly.

They don't like that, and before I can swipe my blade at them again, something hits me over the head, and my crown of bones tumbles to the ground. I fall, my vision swimming black. I feel the cold, prickly grass beneath me, and their Unnatural fingers grasping and tugging at my arms.

Then everything fades away.

Chapter Twenty-Three

The walls are slick and dripping with red liquid. I blink, trying to clear the fog from my brain. Where am I? Something clicks against the stone floor behind me, but I don't react. I blink again. My vision swims with black dots. Then I make the mistake of rolling onto my back, crinkling my nose at the putrid, metallic scent that permeates the air. Stalagmites hang from the ceiling, and splashes of that same red liquid paint the ceiling and pool on the ground.

"*She's awake*," something hisses from an area beyond my vision. Dark chuckles fill the air, echoing off the stone walls. I don't know how many creatures are in here, but I know there is more than one. They outnumber me. My vision clears, and I squint, focusing on the stalagmite above me as a vein of red drips down the side of it and beads at the end of the stalagmite. It splatters on my cheek and that all-too-familiar smell washes over me again. *Blood.* Blood coats the walls, the ceiling, and the ground.

"*Helloooo, tastyyyy,*" the shapeshifter hisses, leering over me. It doesn't look like me anymore. Its skin is gray and as thin as paper, coating the fragile bones that make up its supple body. Its silver eyes are large and bulging from its narrow face, and there's no pupil; just silver disks set into yellow-tinted eyes. It snaps its jaw above my face, hitting me with its acidic breath and showcasing its mouth full of sharp teeth. I have no way of telling them apart, but I think it's the same one as before. It drags a spindly finger down my face. "*I'm so hungry still. You'll help me with that, won't you?*"

I reach for Aridam, crinkling my brow when I can't find it.

The shapeshifter *tsks*, twitching its head from side to side. "*Looking for your blade, witch?*"

"Queen," I correct again, scooting away from the creature and pressing my back to the bloody wall.

"*But where's your crown?*" it taunts.

I survey the area, confirming my suspicions that it's a cave. There's a gaping entrance about twenty yards away, leading to the fog-filled forest. Hunched in the corner at the farthest part of the cave are the rest of the shapeshifters. There are five of them, and they all look alike, with silver eyes and pale skin. They're wearing nothing but a fraying cloth over their private regions. I can't tell if they're male or female, but I'm sure their gender doesn't matter. They're going to eat me anyway.

In the space between the first shapeshifter and its pack is a circle of smooth rocks and a dimly burning fire. Black smoke drifts up from the fire as something burns.

The shapeshifter in front of me sniffs the air, expanding the nostrils of its sunken nose into the size of quarters. "*We don't waste… We eat every last… piece.*" As if that were a command, one of the creatures from the corner lurches forward, its legs buckled like it's permanently squatting, and snatches the hunk of meat from the fire. It makes direct eye contact with me as it tears into the meat with its endless rows of teeth.

A trail of blood leads to the fire from the corner where the pack is huddled.

"*Tasty, tasty, tasty… What should we do with you?*" the first creature asks, stepping toward me, pressing its palms into the cold stone floor, and bringing its ghoulish face up to mine. It breathes in, relishing whatever it smells. "*Fresh blood. So much tastier than vampire blood.*"

My eyes betray me, flicking over to the corner. That scream… Could it be?

The monster titters excitedly, bringing its fingers together in an unusual clap. "*Oh… Was she*

213

your friend?" It tilts its head. "*We don't normally eat vampires... But, you see, we're so hungry... We'll eat anything.*" Its black tongue snakes from its mouth, skimming my cheek. The shapeshifter shudders with satisfaction. "*Soooo taaaasty,*" it sings. The pack in the corner surges forward in anticipation.

If I don't get out of this, then I'm going to end up just like Katie. I scan the cave for Aridam. The cursed sword is my only hope now. The shapeshifter studies me with unflinching, humored eyes. "*Looking for your blade? Your cursed blade that turned our sister to ash?*"

I don't give it the satisfaction of answering, gritting my teeth in determination instead. *I'm going to get out of this.* I just don't know *how.*

"*Tell me about the blade, witch. Then I might consider giving it to you,*" it teases, pressing its nose against mine. Its skin feels wet, almost greasy.

My Soul Sight flares. *Lies, lies, lies. Deceit.* There's no way this monster will return Aridam, not after seeing its sister turn to ash with a single swipe.

So, I lie as well.

"Do you promise?" I will my voice to sound earnest.

The creature beams. "*I promise.*"

Lie.

I press my lips into a line, trying to seem hesitant. "Fine. The blade is called Eve. I'm sure you've

214

heard of it. It answers to the intentions of the person wielding it. I wished your sister harm, so when the blade cut her, she died."

The shapeshifter's eyes sparkle with interest. Its mouth tilts up in a grin. "*We can wish for anything? And what do we need to do to receive it?*"

"It only works with blood."

The shapeshifter slithers away from me, back toward its pack in the corner, flashing me a promising look over its bony shoulder. I realize too late what I said. *Blood.* I didn't specify *whose* blood.

The dim moonlight that reflects off the white fog outside and slides through the cave catches on the jagged blade as the shapeshifter thrusts it into the air.

It prowls back to me, brandishing the sword like a trophy. "*Blood, blood, blood.*" Its voice snakes over my skin, raising goosebumps.

"It can't be mine," I say levelly, refusing to give away the panic I'm feeling as the blade hovers so close to me. "Not yet. To fully enact a wish, you need a drop of your blood to touch the blade first. It has to be that way or it won't work."

The shapeshifter's eyes dim. It believes me. Then it narrows its eyes and glares at me. "*But I didn't see you prick yourself…*" Its slimy voice drips with accusation.

"I did," I insist. "You must've not seen me do it.

215

I'm quite accustomed to using that blade, so I can activate the magic rather quickly."

Its eyes flicker to the blood-stained floor, then it nods its head. "*I see.*" It peers back up at me with a mischievous smirk that pulls on its thin, gray lips. "*If you're telling the truth, then you do it. I'm not going to cut myself and be fooled by a* human." It offers Aridam to me, face poised as if it's so clever.

These creatures sure are dumb.

I take the hilt of Aridam in my hand, tightening my fingers around it until my knuckles turn white. I try to force my features to convey guilt or shame, but my pride must shine through because the shapeshifter realizes too late what it has done.

It returned the sword to me, after all.

I plunge Aridam deep into its chest. Its silver eyes bulge, and it stretches a finger toward me before falling limp on the end of my jagged blade. I remove Aridam from the shapeshifter's corpse, stealing enough time to confirm that the skin around its wound is turning into black ash and floating to the ground, consuming the shapeshifter in Aridam's curse, before sparing a glance at the raging pack now coming to their senses and targeting me with beady silver eyes.

I head toward the mouth of the cave, not even caring what is hiding behind the cloak of white fog. Whatever is out there is certainly better than in here.

I'd rather not be eaten today, thank you.

My feet pound on the blood-slick cave floor. I enter the fog of the forest just as a spindly finger reaches out to draw me back in.

I dodge the shapeshifter's reaching hand and tumble to the right, pushing myself to run as fast as I can, not caring in which direction that is. All I need to do is get away from them, then I can figure out the rest.

The shapeshifter's enraged cries fade behind me as I zig-zag through the forest, crashing into tree trunks that uproot themselves in my path and snapping fallen twigs that litter the ground. I need distance more than I need stealth.

At least, that's what I think, right before a hand grabs me and drags me behind a thick black trunk. I raise Aridam, preparing to strike my attacker and turn it to ash. But it's not a shapeshifter. I breathe out in relief, slipping the blade back into its sheath and collapsing my face to his chest.

"Adriene, you scared me," I admit. Then I jolt back, scanning his face to make sure it's *really* him. It looks like him... He doesn't have silver, bulging eyes, and his narrow face has all the correct angles.

"*You* scared *me*," he says, shoving something against my chest. I glimpse his teeth. His flat, humanoid teeth. I relax against the trunk. It really is him. "Emilia. What happened? Why did you drop this?"

I look down at what he's trying to give me. My crown. I take it from him and pick a bit of moss off one of the finger bones, flicking it to the ground. "Let's get out of here, Adriene."

"Alright, Em—"

"What in Eve?" Sky huffs, glaring at Adriene and me. He's holding a dagger at his side. "You could've let me know you found her."

"I *literally* just did," Adriene replies, scoffing. "You think I want you wandering this forest by yourself, *Skylar*? You'd probably end up dead and somehow it would be *my* fault." He rolls his eyes, muttering, "Pathetic."

Sky's face flames. "Excuse me?" he demands, storming toward the executioner. He lifts the point of his dagger toward Adriene's chest and bares his teeth, looking more frightening than I've ever seen him. "I hated you since the moment King Hanson mentioned your name. You are nothing but a coward. A selfish, simpering, *pathetic* coward." He presses the tip to his chest, leaving a little indent in Adriene's leather. "I should kill you right now."

Adriene steps toward him, inviting the dagger to dig deeper. "I would like to see you try."

I huff. So, they *can't* deal with this themselves. Looks like I need to get involved, after all. Especially since this is not the place to have their battle of testosterone. I glance in the direction I came from, swallowing the lump that forms in my throat once I confirm that there's no face peeking out from the fog and no scampering noises headed in our direction.

"What is going on with you two? We are on the precipice of war. We don't have time for pointless rivalries." I shoulder past them, heading in the direction Sky emerged from, assuming it's the way back to the train tracks.

But the boys continue their little brawl. I turn around, digging my heel into the ground. I situate the crown back atop my head and cross my arms. We need to get out of this forest as soon as possible. I don't want the shapeshifters to find us again. I've outsmarted them once, but the likelihood of doing that twice seems rather low. They may be stupid creatures—but they're fueled by hunger. And hunger is a powerful motivator.

"You're doing that on purpose, aren't you?" Sky demands, gripping his dagger so tightly I swear he's going to cut off circulation to his fingers. "You don't even have genuine feelings. You're just an immortal monster. Hanson said that a past Nether king created you. You weren't born—which means you're not real. Not like Emilia and I."

Adriene falters, creasing his brow. But then pure, animalistic rage fills his face, and he backs Sky

219

up against a tree, plucking the dagger from his hand as easily as taking candy from a whining child. "What feelings are you referencing, Skylar? Because I have plenty of them." He lifts the dagger to Sky's cheek, studying the depth of his scar. "Are you talking about the annoyance I feel when I look at you? The glee I feel when I draw blood from another living being? Or the feelings I have for Emilia?" His lips turn up in a taunting smirk. "Which feelings are you talking about, Skylar?" He rests one hand on the tree trunk, blocking Sky from escaping, while he holds the dagger perfectly still above his scar. "If you're going to throw around accusations, then at least be prepared to answer my questions."

Sky glares up at him, masking any fear he may feel. A moment of clarity hits me, leaving a gap for my memories to swim through the Veiling. *That* is Sky. Brave, determined, and unrelenting Sky. I remember back when we were in the carriage, talking about giving up because Aaron was too strong. Then the apothecary in Kase, when Sky gave some of his blood to save his brother. Then the moment in the flower field, when he was so close to kissing me. The Veiling folds back around my memories, and my eyes shift back from blue to black. Whenever the Veiling fades, even for a moment, my eyes change back to the color they used to be…but the curse can't be held back for long. Not yet. I need to find a cure for the Veiling. If I can access the memories being blocked by this curse, would that lift the Veiling from me?

"We need to go *now*," I insist. "I don't want to be out here any longer." The forest seems to close in around us like a predator hunting its prey. An owl hoots somewhere in the distance, sending a spike of electricity jutting up my spine. I rub my hands down my arms, trying to keep away the eerie chill from this haunted land. But it seems the boys are still bickering. I roll my eyes. I'm the *queen* of Nether. Why am I being ignored?

"Sounds like you just admitted your feelings for her," Sky insists, pushing Adriene away from him and claiming back his personal space. His blue eyes shine with anger…and something else. *Jealousy*.

Adriene *tsks*, looking to the sky as if some god will help him. "Yes, I like her, Sky. I like her quite a lot." His demeanor shifts, turning from rage to something soft. Understanding? "And I know you do too."

I purse my lips and tilt my head speculatively. I figured Sky was harboring feelings for me, but I don't have the time or the energy to deal with two boys fighting over me, especially since the Veiling distorts my memories of one of them. There is a war on the horizon, growing closer and closer with

221

every passing minute. I should be focusing on my subjects and my kingdom instead of romance.

Sky's gaze softens, and his anger seems to evaporate. He sighs. "I do. But that was before the curse..." He grunts in frustration and shakes his head. "Do you think... How does the Veiling work?"

"She's still Emilia," Adriene explains. Both their tones have turned melancholy. Almost sympathetic with each other, as if they're bonding over their mutual interest in me. "The Veiling brings out the Darkness in a person, amplifying it. Her memories are being forced back as well. She's losing bits and pieces of her past. The Veiling doesn't normally affect a person's memories this strongly, but I think because of Emilia's previous affliction, her brain is sensitive to change—especially of the magical kind."

Sky pales, glancing at me. "She doesn't remember me?"

Adriene follows his gaze, offering me a shadow of a smile when he catches my confused expression; the Veiling doesn't normally mess with people's memories like this? I thought everything I was going through was normal for someone cursed with the Veiling?

"We've been trying to find a way to break the curse and push back the Darkness," Adriene says, hope lacing his tone. "So far... We've managed to switch our eyes back to their original state. But it only lasts a moment."

Sky crosses his arms after sheathing his dagger at his waist. "If there's a way to stop the Veiling then we need to find it. If you come up with any ideas, please let me know. I'd be eager to help."

"Thank you, Sky," Adriene responds.

Sky frowns. "I'm sorry about what I said earlier. You're...not so bad. Maybe we could...get along..." He shrugs, not entirely committed to the idea.

Adriene chuckles. "We'll see, Skylar. We'll see."

The palace is creepy this late at night. The moon is high in the dark red sky and black clouds are smattered around it, creating an eerie pattern of silver light that washes across the kingdom.

Adriene and Sky haven't talked since we left the forest and the vampires, but the tension that was taut between them all day is noticeably absent.

"Em, can I talk to you before we head back in?" Sky asks, stopping at the palace doors, which creak open as if they sensed our arrival. Adriene nods to the maid inside and exchanges a quick, calculating look with me before slipping into the stone-walled palace. His posture is stiff, and he turns his cheek toward me, trying to catch a sliver of our conversation before the doors close.

"What is it?" I tilt my chin up. The silver moonlight can't reach me here, hidden in the shadows of the daunting palace.

Sky's expression falters, and a disheartened smile finds its way to his face. "I'm sorry if I treated you any differently because of...your curse. I know you're still in there, and I know that we'll find a way to free you from the Veiling." Hesitantly, he reaches across the space between us and pats my shoulder. His mouth pops open as if he wants to say more, but his thought dies on his tongue. With a last apologetic look, he slips into the palace as well, hanging his head.

I stare up at the sky, at the black clouds etched with silver and red, and the sleeping village lining the ominous streets of Cyprion. I want my memories back. I want *all* my memories back. And I want this formidable curse to go away. Whoever I was before the Veiling claimed me is who I am supposed to be... Right? Or am I supposed to carve a path for myself with these black eyes and this violent heart?

A chilly breeze brushes across my arms, and I shiver, stealing one last glance at the sleeping vampire kingdom before turning to walk inside.

Adriene's story plays through my mind: *the trials are designed to break you, to determine who is worthy. If the rumors are to be believed, they challenge every part of you. Your strength. Your mind. Your persistence.*

Emmet O'Hare.

As I close the door behind me, I watch the sliver of Cyprion disappear. Torchlight flickers across my pale skin, and I rest my forehead against the door.

Chapter Twenty-Four

The palace library is beautiful, shimmering with ruby fixtures and decadent, blood-red armchairs sprinkled in clusters at the end of each wide aisle. Every book is bound in black-dyed leather and has crimson deckled edges. The librarian —a stout, pale vampire woman with long, golden hair and narrow red eyes—lifts her finger to point at the thickest book in the sixth aisle. The text on the spine reads *Banished Realm—Citizen Registry*; it's dusted with flakes of silver. Her dark navy dress is cuffed with thick ruffles, and her black ankle boots have small metal spikes attached to the toe part. I wonder if all the citizens of Cyprion are dressed for a fight, or if this vampire librarian's style is just unique.

"Thank you. This is exactly what I'm looking for," I say, giving her a genuine smile. She blinks at me, then dips into a polite curtsy before scurrying back to the front desk. I touch the crown that stands regale on the top of my head. Sometimes the weight of it, the expectations, and the displays of submission make me loathe it. I shake my head, stamping down that traitorous thought. *I am queen.* It's only proper that people bow to me. I bite my cheek and reach up to claim the heavy book, pulling it down to land with a *smack* across my arms. Dust billows into my face, and I cough, blowing it away. I carry the tome to the end of the aisle, where an elegant armchair is waiting to be occupied. A sconce in the shape of smiling lips with a pair of dripping fangs houses a torch that flickers light across the space, letting me read the tiny words scrawled throughout the book.

I settle into the chair and tuck my feet under my dark navy dress, positioning the book comfortably on my lap and turning to the contents page.

King Cassius said we would reconvene after lunch to teach his army about the Solstice Realm and the enemies they'll face. Until then, I've given myself another task.

I want to find out more about Emmet O'Hare and Oblivion. Even though Adriene said he's dead, I still feel the desire to learn as much as I can.

I don't know what kingdom in the Banished Realm he lived in, so I start with the first kingdom at the beginning of the book, shifting through its list of past and present residents.

Sendoria.

I raise my eyebrows at the heading: *Sendoria,*

Kingdom of the Yetis. I didn't even know yetis existed, let alone that they had a kingdom.

I skim down to the O-section for last names and begin my search. After each name, it lists if they're alive or not. I frown, flipping to the next kingdom, concluding that Emmet didn't live in Sendoria.

Kwael is the next kingdom listed. And the heading again makes my eyebrows shoot into my hairline. Dragon-kin? What does that mean? People who turn into dragons, or dragon-like people? I bite my lip, shoving my face deeper into the book as I scoot back in the chair. No Emmet O'Hare in Kwael either.

Next is Tarene, Kingdom of the Werewolves. Which doesn't have any O'Hares, living or dead, listed.

Irritatingly, I slam that section shut and switch my search to Tartarus, Kingdom of the Orcs.

No such luck there either. They have an O'Hare living there, but it's an Affelynda O'Hare. Definitely not an *Emmet*.

The second-to-last kingdom, Orion, Kingdom of the Elves, doesn't have any O'Hares either.

I furiously flip to the last kingdom in the book, Cyprion, and glance down at the O-section doubtfully. Hope withers in my heart, believing that this is a fruitless mission, after all.

Emmet O'Hare.

I sit up in excitement. So, he was a vampire? It'll be so much easier to research Emmet since I'm already in the kingdom he lived in. My mouth falls open when my eyes snag at the end of the line containing his name.

Emmet O'Hare (Alive)

He's alive? But Adriene said he died? Why would Adriene lie to me about such a thing, unless he was trying to stop me from searching for answers on Oblivion?

I slam the book closed as the desire to visit him grows. I need to find out more about Oblivion, and who better to ask than someone who's gone there, and come back? If there's a possibility of saving my sister and bringing her back to life, then I owe it to her to try. Don't I? Isn't that what I would've done before the Veiling? Wouldn't I have tried to save my family? And I'm sure I could face the Key Masters' Trials. *I'm sure I could . . .* But what do they entail?

I drop my face into my hands, rubbing the creases from my forehead. I feel a headache start to loom behind my eyes. Maybe I should rest before joining King Cassius and his army. I can't work with a headache hindering me. But first, I stop at the front desk, tapping my fingers impatiently against the sleek red counter while the librarian fiddles with a notebook and a raven-feather quill. She glances up, eyes flaring with annoyance.

"What else do you want?" she asks, trying to rein in her temper. Probably because I'm a queen.

"Can you get an address for me?" I try to give her my most genuine smile, but it must come off a bit creepy because she winces.

"I can try. Whose address are you trying to find?" she asks, setting her notebook and quill aside. She steps up to the section of the counter I'm standing at and ducks down, rummaging around for a second before popping back up and plopping a heavy book on the counter between us. She looks at me, waiting for a response with one finger curled around the deckled paper.

"Emmet O'Hare," I say.

She stares at me another moment before flipping the book open and trailing her fingertip down the page.

I wonder how many people know about Emmet O'Hare and his quest for Oblivion. Since he lives in Cyprion, I'm sure they, out of everyone, know the most. I hope it's not suspicious that I'm searching for Emmet. If she mentions it to anyone and it gets back to Adriene... I don't want to think about that.

"88 Excalibur Drive." She shuts the book with a *thwa-omp*. "Will that be all, Your Majesty?"

I don't bother smiling this time. "How far away is that from the palace?"

"Approximately a ten-minute walk, Your

Majesty." She smiles, but it doesn't reach her eyes.

"That'll be all." I don't add a thank you either, not finding it in me to thank someone who clearly is annoyed by my presence. What is *with* these vampires?

I leave the library, my hands lifting the long navy skirt of my dress while I walk, my mind elsewhere. The stone walls are dark, reflecting my mood. Adriene lied to me. Either he lied or he didn't know better. Why would he lie? Especially to me? Especially when it involves my sister?

I briskly return to my room, the headache pounding against my temples now. Thankfully, I didn't run into anyone. I don't want to explain where I've been or what I've been doing, nor do I want to tell them about the return of my headaches —the result, alongside my memory loss, of a portal jump gone wrong.

I shut the door and sigh. I barely make it three steps into my room before my headache increases, leaving my vision speckled with white spots. I stagger to my bed and lay down, pinching my eyes closed and drifting off into a much-needed slumber.

"This is General Andromeda Faree," Cassius introduces, gesturing to a woman with long blonde hair and dark brown eyes flecked with crimson. She's taller than me—which isn't difficult—standing at a staggering 5'11, I estimate. She's wearing a silver chest plate and matching armor strapped to her thighs and calves. A broadsword hangs at her waist, glinting against the red sun in the training field beside the palace. Lined up behind her are three dozen vampires; faces neutrally poised and pale hands clasping the broadswords at their sides. "She'll be working alongside you and commanding the troops that will join the Solstice War. She was at the top of her class during training. The best general our kingdom has ever had."

Andromeda shoots a hand out to me, offering a wisp of a smile, showing the points of her pearly fangs. "It's nice to meet you, Queen Emilia. We've heard lots about the former heiress of the Golden Kingdom."

"The Golden Kingdom?" I raise an eyebrow. I've never heard of Glaven referred to as the *Golden Kingdom*, but it seems pretty accurate if my last visit is any indication. Glaven is breathtaking, sparkling with country sunshine. And if I remember correctly, odd everyday objects such as plates and books are encrusted in gold.

"Sorry," she chuckles, waving it away as if it

were an insult. "That's what we call it around here."

I return her smile, though I'm not sure if it reaches my eyes. Instead of continuing this small talk, I jut my chin toward the army amassed behind her. "So, how should we begin?"

Andromeda seems happy to be done with the small talk, as well. She gets right to the matter at hand. Her lips tilt up in the corners, exposing a pair of deep, identical dimples. Her red-flecked eyes flick across the army. "We need you to tell us about the enemy; their strengths, weaknesses, and their weapons. Anything you think would be beneficial to us." She purses her lips. "We need to keep our loss small, Your Majesty. Which means if it gets too risky, we'll have to retreat. Cyprion's people won't be happy if their families die fighting a war some of them may have never even heard of. You understand." She gives me a sympathetic look that makes my expression wither. I want to keep their loss small too. Asking Cyprion to join in on our war and then letting their people get slaughtered on the battlefield won't reflect well on Nether. Not like much reflects well on Nether anyway.

Andromeda claps her hands together. "Let's begin."

Chapter Twenty-Five

The kingdom that officially waged war against us was Aquartia. It's a kingdom completely submerged underwater and made up of merfolk. I'm not sure about their strengths, besides their excellent craftmanship of boats and other water-faring mechanisms. But they could be hiding potentially dangerous things from us. Aquartia regularly receives visitors to trade, which means they could be in possession of objects from any corner of the Solstice Realm, or perhaps even from realms besides ours." I walk up and down in front of the soldiers, trying to project my voice as much as possible so everyone can hear it. I don't want to have to repeat myself. "However, they have a very limiting weakness. Merfolk can't survive out of water by themselves. They need someone to spray them with a magical substance that keeps them from dying. I witnessed that firsthand. I'm sure they've found a way to merge that magic with their armor or impregnate themselves with a temporary solution… Merfolk are clever and creative. Never underestimate what they'll do."

A few of the soldiers snicker at the thought of a war started by a species that can't survive out of water. I shoot them a glare at the same time as Andromeda, and they immediately go silent, their faces paling even more—if that's possible.

"We aren't sure of who will fight on their side," I admit. "But our best guess is that Olympus will fight with them since their queen, Hera, has known King Hanson longer. What I do know, though, is that Glaven and Eirae will fight alongside us. The Glaven army, though a bit sparse, is strong. The same can be said for the Eirae army, especially combined with your forces, and my army of Shrouds back in Nether." I try to imbue my voice with a level of confidence I'm not exactly feeling. "With our numbers and our varying species and skills, I'm sure we will dominate the battlefield."

Andromeda smiles at that, violence flashing in her vampiric eyes. She claps her hands again before resting one of her hands on the hilt of her sword. "Alright. You heard her. Now get into position. Find a partner and let's show Queen Emilia what we can do." She spurs her army into action, and they immediately turn to the person next to them, faces stoic, and unsheathe their swords, raising them in the space between each other and bending their knees.

I stand back, watching what the vampire soldiers can do. I focus primarily on a pair to the right of the front row. It's a broad-shouldered woman with short black hair and a slender man with moon-white hair like Adriene's. Their faces are emotionless and their bodies are stiff, the sense of war flooding their systems.

I don't know what I expected from vampire soldiers, but as their swords clash against each other and they dance around one another, I don't expect what happens next.

The male vampire with the white hair turns into a dark gray mist that flits around the woman's ankles like a tiny tornado before he materializes on the other side, his sword snapping forward and dropping hers to the ground. I gawk. I knew they turned into mist, as the lady from King Cassius's study proved, but using it as a technique in battle is brilliant. It makes them harder to hit and gives them a level of stealth no other species has. My confidence in us winning this war increases as I scan the rest of the army, watching in awe as more and more vampires shift into varying colors of mist and disorient their competitors.

Andromeda grins at me, gesturing one hand toward her army. "What do you think, Your Majesty?"

I snap my mouth closed and tilt my chin up, tucking a lock of my dark brown hair behind my ear. I cross my arms and nod toward the army. "I think our chances of winning this war just got a lot higher."

Andromeda nods in agreement. "You are welcome to stay and watch as we practice, Your Majesty. We'll take what you said and try to incorporate that into our drills. King Cassius wants you to win this war, so we'll try our very best to make it happen. Besides, many of us have longed to see the Solstice Realm, and we're told that if we win, that will happen."

The corners of my lips twist into a small smile. "Thank you, General Faree."

"Andromeda—or Meda—is fine," she says, flashing me a bemused look. Someone in her army catches her attention and her expression sours. "It was nice meeting you, Queen Emilia. I have to go correct someone's stance for the umpteenth time." She moves toward her army and they part for her without breaking stride in their paired battles. Andromeda stops at a pair near the center of the army, bending her neck to talk down to a short male vampire. I take this as my cue to leave. If they're going to be practicing all day, I don't feel the need to stay and watch. I'm confident in Andromeda's ability to train and prepare her army. I have something else I need to do.

The street sign is made of weathered wood with bold, black letters burned into it. The street itself is lined with scraggly gray trees that reach toward the reddish sky. Quaint thatched houses line either side of the street, and it ends in an inconspicuous cul-de-sac. I wouldn't guess that a survivor of Oblivion lives here, yet as my eyes skim the hand-engraved letters on the street sign again, I'm proven wrong.

Excalibur Drive.

I cross the invisible threshold and pass into the cozy neighborhood. It's quiet, save for the fluttering of bird wings in the forest and the lone barking of a dog in the yard of one of these houses. I wasn't aware vampires cared for dogs—let alone that there are dogs in the Banished Realm.

Vibrant green lawns sprawl down the slight incline the houses are built on, ending at a hard-packed dirt path that encircles the cul-de-sac. Lantern light flickers from the open windows of the small homes I pass and humanoid figures cross in front of the windows, setting their table for lunch or working inside their home study. Whatever these vampires are doing—it's so homely, so human, that I start to doubt that I'm even in the Banished Realm. That these are even *vampires*.

I stop in front of a house near the end of the first row, right before the cul-de-sac curves, and stare at the black metal *88* nailed to the white-painted wood beside the matching front door. There's a picket fence that branches off from the side of the house to enclose a tiny garden. A dog with scruffy cream fur and soft brown eyes presses its face against the wooden slats, barking at me. When my black eyes latch onto it, it starts to cower away from the fence, drawing my attention farther into the garden, where an older man is dusting his knees off and turning his attention from his garden to me.

His eyes widen before narrowing into inquisitive slits. Hesitantly, he steps in front of his dog and closes the distance between us, halting when he reaches the fence. I watch him take in my regal outfit and my crown of bones. His Adam's apple bobs before he's finally able to find words.

"For what do I owe the pleasure of your company, Your Majesty?" His voice is scratchy like he smoked every day of his life, or he just finished screaming for hours on end. He's a strange-looking vampire. He isn't at all intimidating. His pale skin glistens with sweat, a thick brown mustache sits on his upper lip, and his head is scarcely covered with matching hair. He's pudgy, stretching the cotton of his button-up shirt, and he's wearing a pair of brown shorts made from a material resembling denim. His feet are strapped into a pair of cork sandals, and his red-flecked gray eyes are clouded behind a veil of worry.

"I'm looking for Emmet O'Hare. I was told he lives at this address," I say, raising an eyebrow.

The man's face shutters, and he takes a calculated step back. "He doesn't live here anymore."

Lies, lies, lies.

"Are you sure?" I ask, since I know he's lying. I press up to the small gate that matches the picket fence around it. I rest one hand on the gate like I'm about to open it and tilt my head speculatively. "I checked with the palace and they assured me he still lives here."

The man rubs his sweaty palm down his shirt, leaving behind streaks of dirt from his garden. I notice his other sleeve covers his missing hand. "What does the palace want with me?" he relents, his brow pinched in concern.

"Nothing," I insist. "I have a few questions…of a private matter I was hoping you would answer."

Emmet dips his head, his eyes flicking up to the crown perched atop my head before responding, "I'd like to know who I'm talking to. Your name?"

I give him a genuine smile—though, admittedly —it's still ghoulish. "I'm Queen Emilia Strazenfield of Nether. I have a series of questions relating to your venture to Oblivion."

His thin eyebrows shoot up and in a disbelieving tone, he inquires, "You came here all the way from the Solstice Realm to ask about a fairy tale?"

My heart plummets to the pit of my stomach, and my voice comes out squeaky. "A fairy tale?"

He nods gravely.

Chapter Twenty-Six

*I*f I were allowed to reach across this dining room table and strangle Emmet, I would without hesitation.

"Tell me the truth, Emmet," I hiss between gritted teeth. A *fairy tale*, that's what he called it, when in actuality he meant a *mistake*; an admission I only received after showing him the glint of Aridam and telling him about the cursed Sword of Death and whose blood has slicked its blade. "Why was saving your daughter a mistake?"

Emmet shakes his head, staring at the wooden table as if the pattern of the grain is the most fascinating thing in the world. "She's different. She came back *different*."

"Different how?" I persist, needing to know exactly what he means. How did his daughter come back from Oblivion...*different*? Is he talking about the hand she—and Emmet—lost in the Key Masters' Trials? I would've pegged that as *obvious*.

He finally looks up, fear masking his face,

pulling his lips down in a grimace. He meets my eyes, holding them, searching for something in the darkness. "She looks just like you."

I sit up straighter, lowering my eyebrows. "How so?" His expression is haunted as he stares at me, raising the hair on the back of my neck and along my arms. *How is she just like me?*

He points to his eye with his shaking hand and gulps. "She has your eyes. The Darkness. The Veiling. As soon as she came out of the portal to Oblivion, I noticed it."

He starts to shake his head as the door to the front of the house creaks open and a cheery voice calls out, "Dad! I'm home. I grabbed most of the items on your list at the market over on Spinster Avenue." A girl rounds the corner into the dining room, a slip of parchment fluttering in one hand and a bag of groceries hanging from her arm. I can see the resemblance between her and Emmet. She has shoulder-length brown hair and pale skin, a petite nose that turns up at the end, and a pudgier frame. The smile drops from her face when she sees the state of her father, and her black eyes twinkle when she discovers me…and the similarities marking us as *different*. "What's going on?" Her voice quivers slightly, though I don't think it's out of fear. It seems she's more curious and excited to see someone who shares her cursed trait.

"Vivienne," Emmet mutters, appearing on the edge of utter despair. "This is Queen Emilia Strazenfield of Nether. She has some questions about Oblivion." He drops his head into his hand, pinching the bridge of his nose with his thumb and pointer finger. His plump body is hunched over the table, appearing older than he is. "Vivienne, please leave us."

Vivienne's eyes flash, and she protests, "Dad, if this is about Oblivion, I should stay. You only know one side of what happened that day. Let me tell her *my* side of the story."

Emmet lifts his head to command her to leave when I interrupt. "I'd like to hear your story, Vivienne." Emmet huffs in response, but doesn't say anything further.

She offers me a half-smile, setting the bag of groceries on the dining table and dropping the list in the bag. "Can we take this into the living room? It's a lot comfier in there." She eyes the wicker dining chairs pointedly.

I stand up and follow her out without sparing Emmet a glance. I have a feeling Vivienne will be more help than her father.

I follow her to the living room that looks out at the front lawn and the side garden. Vivienne plops down in a beige armchair that faces a matching couch and watches me expectantly. "Are you *really* a queen?"

I sit down on the couch, gesturing to my crown. "Of course." I don't have time for idle chit-chat. I need information—not friends. "Do you remember what it was like in Oblivion?" What were the Key Masters' Trials like? What was *Zainey*, the Key Master of Oblivion, like?

Her face falls slack, and her skin seems to pale even more. "It was cold. And dark, except for the stars. Thousands of stars all twinkling in unison. An endless expanse of time spent in a vast pocket of the universe. A black hole but for the souls of the diseased." She shudders, pressing her hand between her thighs and resting her stump on her leg. "I only remember the feeling of losing myself. Kind of like I wasn't whole, in a way. Like I was fragmented. I didn't have any control over my movements, but I was...*aware*. I had my thoughts, but I could never dream. It was like..."

"Being trapped in your own mind?" I suggest, leaning forward. "Sometimes the cage of your mind is far worse than one with four walls." I remember saying that to Adriene...before the Veiling took control. I don't remember where we were at, nor the context it was in. But I remember it was a moment between me and him. I think it was our first.

Vivienne startles, nodding. "Yes, exactly that. For a brief moment, a blinding white portal started opening up, and that's when my dad reached in and *plucked* me out."

"Were there other people—*souls*—there with you?"

Vivienne shrugs. "I couldn't tell. I didn't see anyone. Just the endless stars."

Endless stars… I can't imagine looking out at a sea of stars for a space of time that feels frozen. "Was it worth it? Are you glad you're back?"

"Worth it?" she looks down at her arm, where her hand looks like it was burned off. The stump is scarred and pink. She purses her lips to the side, her shark eyes flicking back up to meet mine. I wonder why the Veiling took her. Is it because she died? To be resurrected, she had to race back through the seven Key Masters' Trials to be free from the grasp of death, only to end up being cursed with the Veiling? Does she have the same tingle of satisfaction that shoots up her spine when something horrific happens? Does she revel in violence, just as I seem to? Does she remember her life before the Veiling, before Oblivion? I have so many questions, but before I can ask another and bombard her, she's speaking. "I'm alive, aren't I?" She seems to be questioning it herself. Her eyes stare off into the distance, and her bottom lip quivers. She digs her nails into her thigh before blinking out of her daze and rubbing the sore spot lightly. She glances down

246

at her leg and shakes her head. "Sometimes, I need to make sure I'm really here. That must sound crazy." She chuckles humorlessly.

Crazy. I know a thing or two about being called crazy. Sympathy for this lost girl surges inside of me, but I tamp it down. Now is not the time to feel sympathetic. I came here for answers, so answers I will get.

I purse my lips. "What about your father? He had to charge through the Key Masters' Trials by himself? Do you know what hardships he endured? Did he ever recover from them?" I ask, watching as Emmet shuffles back and forth across the hallway, rubbing his hand through his thinning hair in a frantic motion. He's muttering something to himself, but I can't hear what he's saying.

At this, Vivienne's expression seems to darken even more. She watches her father, her brow creased as she chews on her lip. "I'm not sure. I think he regrets bringing me back. I think...maybe...facing the Key Masters made him...go *mad*. I think he lost himself the day he saved me, and for that, he despises me." She frowns. "I am grateful to be back. I *obviously* wish I had my hand, but if a hand is the price for a second chance at life, who wouldn't pay it?" Both our eyes flash over to Emmet. "I just... don't know if it was worth it. If this second chance at life for me was worth throwing away my father's.

If I had to choose…I think I'd remain in Oblivion, just so my father would be okay."

I sit up, taken aback. She'd throw away her second chance to make sure her father lived a full life? She doesn't…*like* seeing him go mad? She doesn't revel at the slightest twinge of pain—as I seem to? Is it really the Veiling that forces me to delight in people's agony…or is it just *me*? Am I truly crazy?

What would be the price of bringing my sister back? What *are* the seven Key Masters' Trials?

"What were the trials like? Are they the same for everyone?" I ask Vivienne, desperation lacing my tone. What would I need to do to bring Soph back?

Vivienne gives me a sorrowful smile. "I have a way to find out. I hunted it down after my father saved me. I'm not sure why. I just knew I should have it." She stands up and heads toward the hallway, casting a look over her shoulder. "Maybe you're the reason why."

Intrigued, I follow her down the hallway, past her bumbling father, and to a little room near the back of the house that looks out at the forest surrounding the cul-de-sac. Lacy black curtains hang gently by the square window, letting sunlight spill across a short-legged, round table with a crystal ball mounted on a glittery purple platform. There's another cream couch pushed against the wall and piled on the floor are colorful pillows with tassels sprouting from the corners.

Vivienne takes a seat on a pink and blue pillow, crossing her legs underneath the short table. Her lips thin as she stares at the crystal ball as if it's going to spring up and bite her on the nose.

I sit down across from her, folding my legs under my dress. The crystal ball swirls with gray smoke, almost as if it's dormant, awaiting instructions. The smoke reminds me of dark gray clouds right before a storm. "What is that?" I ask, nodding toward the ball.

Vivienne responds, almost giddily, "This is a scrying crystal. There are only a few of them in existence, mined by an ancient elvan race that supposedly lives on the highest mountain peaks. Of course, that's just a rumor. There's no evidence that they're still alive." She places her arms on either side of the scrying crystal, leaving a few inches of space between her skin and the crystal's surface. "It looks into the deepest part of a person's soul. It can unbury the deepest of secrets, of wishes, and can help discover what people crave and what they fear. It supposedly works by connecting with the electricity in your body. Here, give me your hands." She places my hands on either side of the scrying crystal. "Now, think of whoever you're trying to save. Think of Oblivion." Her lips twitch up in a macabre smirk. "Think of the *stars*, Your Majesty."

I close my eyes, picturing what little I can remember of my sister. First, I see her gravestone. The cool stone and the freshly carved letters that form her name. The lone spiked tree protruding from the cemetery like a beacon, and the feel of the grass beneath me. I picture Adriene sitting on the bench, then my hot tears sliding down my cheeks as my memories of my sister briefly slip through the Veiling.

Finally, I see her. Her long blonde hair frames her petite face and her ice-blue eyes. I see her pink lips tilt into a confident smile and the spikes of her crown that look like icicles dripping upward. The crown that now resides on Sky's head.

Then I see a field of tulips and a beautiful boy with oceanic blue eyes and a sheepish smile. A creek burbles beside me as the birds sing in the trees. Following that is a flower crown—not just any flower crown though. It's a cake decorated with candied tulips and light blue icing. *A flower crown for a child queen.*

Suddenly, I hear Vivienne screaming my name, begging me to respond. A headache looms behind my eyes, throbbing at my temples, and my head falls forward.

"Your Majesty!" Vivienne shrieks, catching me before my head can hit the table. She pushes me back up, her eyes frantically scanning my face. "Are you alright? What happened?"

I blink away the spots dancing across my vision. My headaches are coming back… What happened two years ago must have affected me more than I thought. Right now, that doesn't matter. The only thing that does matter is getting the answers I came here for. "Did it work? Did you find what you were searching for?"

Vivienne studies me for a second longer before turning to squint into the scrying crystal. Her eyebrows pinch together and she chews on her cheek, shaking her head in disbelief. She glances back at me as if she's seeing into my soul. "Impossible."

My heart thunders in my chest. "What's impossible?" I grip the skirt of my dress tightly.

"It's telling me that you've already faced your greatest fear… That you don't have one, not anymore." She cocks her head, narrowing her eyes at the swirling fog in the scrying crystal. "At least…not a fully intact fear."

"What does that mean—for Oblivion?" I hate the way desperation leeches from each syllable.

She sighs. "The Key Masters' Trials are formed from the participant's greatest fears. If you've already faced your greatest fear, then it won't work because you'd have nothing to go through. It's like a monster…it feeds on your soul, and in return, it gives you a slightly altered version of what you paid for." She waves her hand to her eyes. "What have you lost, Your Majesty?"

I know without a doubt what my greatest fear is now—what the Key Masters' Trials would have been constructed from...

Losing myself.

Losing my memories.

Chapter Twenty-Seven

Vivienne's confirmation is still ringing through my mind—even hours later, when I'm strolling through the palace beside Adriene and Andromeda, discussing battle tactics and where we should meet when the war begins. I recommend bringing the war to their doorstep since they wouldn't be anticipating that and it would give us the upper hand, but Andromeda brings up a good point: how would we fight underwater? Battling in Aquartia would give *them* the upper hand, if nothing else.

Andromeda's hand perpetually rests on her broadsword, ready to draw it at any moment. We turn a corner, the lantern light flickering over our faces as we pass by, and head toward the soldiers' barracks. Most of Cyprion's top soldiers live on the palace grounds, in a wing designated for their barracks—closely resembling dorm rooms.

The black rock wall looks slick as the lantern light bounces off it. I feel the change in the atmosphere before I see it. The ground rumbles, and the walls shake, debris falling around us. The flames on the torches flicker.

"What is that?" I ask, stopping to peer up at the ceiling. A crack spreads across it, spider-webbing outward to snake down the walls. Instinctually, I duck, my eyes following the fracture as it fragments the palace above us.

Andromeda scrunches her face, withdrawing her sword to hold it in front of us. She pushes us back the way we came, shouting, "Get out of the palace! Quickly. We can't have it coming down on your heads." The quaking of the palace rumbles in my ears, fueling my fear. *What is happening? Is this normal for Cyprion?*

"Where are we going?" I demand as Adriene takes my hand. I weave my fingers between his, my other hand moving to the blade strapped to my waist.

Andromeda juts her chin toward the barracks, where her soldiers are resting after a long day of training. "I have to get them out." The ground shakes again and the cracks widen. Without another glance, Andromeda charges down the hall, toward the barracks, shouting, "GET OUT! GET OUT NOW." Panic sears into each word, and I can tell how deeply she cares for her soldiers.

Adriene whisks me back down the hallway,

heading toward the entrance, where maids and butlers are converging. Pieces of the stone ceiling are crumbling around us. The cracks leach across the floor.

The maids and butlers shout in alarm, grabbing the hands of anyone they can see and pulling them out of the palace to safety.

Adriene pushes me ahead of him, and we both stumble out the doors, staggering to a stop, gawking as the red sky splits open and a blanket of brilliant stars sprawls into the beyond.

Stars… *Think of the stars…* Vivienne's voice floods my mind again. Could Oblivion be the universe? Or could the stars be other souls, just too far away to see, but bright enough to notice?

"What's going on?" a maid in the group behind me asks, fear evident in her tone. A man says something in response, but it gets lost as an ear-splitting boom reverberates across the realm. Adriene withdraws his sickle from its sheath, tightening his hand around the handle.

A white portal opens up like the gaping maw of a great beast, and suddenly, hundreds of people are plummeting from the sky and landing on the streets of Cyprion. Their tridents are raised toward the patchwork sky, and their swords glint with danger.

At the front of the army is a man I've come to loathe. A man I used to think I could be friends with. A man whose green scales and dark skin shimmers with some kind of cloaking magic, protecting him from dying in the arid environment.

King Hanson.

So, the war has begun.

The ground quakes as the portal opens wider, tearing the realm open as easily as removing a wayward stitch from cotton. The palace rumbles as stones break across the ground and windows shatter, spraying glass splinters onto the grass and people below.

Adriene tucks me against him, using his back and shoulders to catch the projectile glass. I crush my cheek against his chest, rage simmering deep within me.

I should've known King Hanson would do this —but *how* he did it is the question. Does he have an entire legion of Runespeakers at his disposal? Or did he create a new form of magic strong enough to break open the divide between the two realms?

Whatever he did, I'll have to figure it out later. Right now, I need to focus on saving a kingdom.

"Run, get away from here as fast as you can! Go as far as you can. Arm yourselves and stay together," Adriene commands, pointing to the road that leads into the Cyprion village. The palace staff, after a brief cursory glance at Hanson's awaiting army, turn and charge down the streets, drawing onlookers from their homes and shops, who quickly retreat back inside or join the fleeing fray.

Adriene turns his shrewd gaze on the merfolk king, whose head is encircled in a thin film of magic that resembles an iridescent bubble. I wonder what would happen if someone popped it.

"What do you want?" Adriene demands, pushing me behind him and stepping toward the growing divide between us and the enemy. "Why are you here?"

Hanson's lips twist into a smug smile. "Did you think we wouldn't find out about your plans to involve Cyprion? To have the vampire army join ranks with your own?" He *tsks*, shaking his head in disgust. "That's cheating. The war is in the Solstice Realm. You're directly going against what the Solstice Realm stands for."

My blood boils. Soph's entire goal was to bring the realms together, to open a free path between them, and to have as many Unnaturals live in the Solstice Realm as long as they wanted. Soph died trying to complete her wish. Maybe now it's my time to take her place. To stand up for what my sister believed in.

I step up next to Adriene, leveling my glare at Hanson. "There's no law in war, *Hanson*. If you're going to attack us and uproot our homes, then we're going to do everything in our power to stop you, even if that means recruiting the enemies of our ancestors."

Hanson sneers, raising his gold trident in the air. The red sunlight and the silver starlight bounce off the prongs in a myriad of colors. His dark, two-pupil gaze lands squarely on me, and I can see his hatred for me brewing inside him. "You'll die in this war, *Emilia*. If I have to risk my life to thrust my trident through your black heart, then so be it. But you *will* die. Mark my words."

Adriene growls, "Leave, Hanson. Before you do something you'll regret." Anger laces his words. I imagine he wants to rip Hanson's head clean from his shoulders and mount it on a spike to warn anyone else who dares threaten his queen.

Hanson scoffs. "There's no law in war, Adriene. We're here to kill—and kill we must." He raises his voice, clashing it against the crumbling palace. "Bring out King Cassius. No one is going anywhere until I see him kneeling before me."

The doors part as more stone fragments crumble, breaking across the steps. Andromeda and her slightly beat-up army close ranks in front of us, blocking us from Hanson. Andromeda stands in front of her army, her broadsword raised before her. There's a cut on her forehead that's dripping blood down the side of her face, and her hands are already slick with crimson from helping her soldiers.

"You'll never get your hands on our king," Andromeda exclaims, barring her fangs. She lifts her sword, looking down the blade at the merfolk king. "You'll have to go through us." The vampires behind her raise their weapons as well, slipping easily into fighting stances, barring their fangs in preparation to rip out tracheas...or something equally macabre.

Hanson stomps the end of his trident on the ground once and the merfolk army behind him shifts, pointing their tridents and swords toward the vampires. I notice, speckled throughout the merfolk ranks, are humans and mages. By their tall statures and unearthly complexions, I'd say they're from Olympus.

Hanson narrows his eyes, tightening his grip on his gold trident, before screaming across the distance between us, "CHARGE!"

His army starts forward, hovering a few feet above the ground or stampeding across it, heading directly for us.

Andromeda's army surges forward as well. The silence before the two armies collide is deafening. And then, the realm is filled with the grunts of wounded soldiers and the clash of blades. Rage and determination simmer across the kingdom-turned-battlefield. Goosebumps erupt across my skin as blades cut through flesh and blood trickles onto the ground. I try to shake myself free from the Veiling's grip, to not fall victim to the Dark curse, to not be compelled to deal in fear. Though try as I might, I'm not stronger than this curse.

"We should get out of here," Adriene suggests, tightening his grip on my hand. "There's not much we can do, Emilia."

I know he's right. What *can* we do? He only has his sickle and all I have is Aridam. I don't have magic... But Adriene does. He can alter realities. King Hanson knows that, since Adriene made the chest they kept Aquartia's fragment of Eve in. Maybe, if Adriene can get close enough to Hanson, he can scare him into retreating. Or alter his vision to make it seem like he is somewhere else. It would be disorienting, if nothing else.

"Emilia," Adriene says, already knowing what I'm going to say.

"We need to help them, Adriene," I insist. I feel as my eyes shift back to blue. I reach up to touch my face, transfixed in the way I switch from this cursed Dark queen to the girl I was before.

Adriene stares into my eyes, memorizing the icy pigment, and how it darkens around the pupil. He sighs, but a smile fixes itself on his features. He lifts his sickle and the crescent-moon-shaped blade winks in the myriad light.

I unsheathe Aridam and grin, the thirst for blood

flooding my veins. Adriene taps his sickle against my broken sword, and with a wink, he says, "Cheers!" before thundering into the battle. His sickle slices through the air, and his leather armor creaks with his movements.

Blood sprays across the grass as his blade finds its targets.

I watch him in awe. Then, as my eyes shift back to black, I fling myself into the battle as well, getting lost in the rhythm. *Swipe, swish, slash, stab.* Blood squirts as muscles tear and eyes lose their luster. A gleeful cackle leaves my lips, startling a vampire fighting beside me. The bloodshed jolts through my body as if I've been struck by lightning. And it feels *good*.

I meet Adriene's eyes through the crowd. He's grinning, completely at ease, even *happy* as his sickle cuts down his enemies. I smile back...but just as quickly, his smile fades and he's lunging through the battle toward me, a scream leaving his lips and getting lost in the commotion.

I turn, frantically trying to see what has him so concerned. Hanson glares down at me, his trident already arcing through the air, directed toward my heart. I'm too late to raise my sword to block him. Pain sears through my body at the same time as someone crashes into me. I can't make out what anyone is saying. All I can see is white, and someone's hands pressing against my wound, trying to staunch the blood from Hanson's trident.

Everything is warm.

Chapter Twenty-Eight

The sky is blue, the sun is golden, and the white clouds look like splotches of watercolor. I blink, biting my cheek through the excruciating pain.

I groan, lifting my hand to tentatively check my wound. My fingertips come back covered in red and my shoulder throbs in protest.

"You're going to need stitches. But, thankfully, it didn't hit anything *super* important." A pair of arms come out of nowhere, wrapping around me and trying to help me up. I blink again, clearing the remaining white spots from my vision. For a brief moment, I don't know who's holding me. Should I pull away? My shoulder does *really* hurt.

Finally, he comes into view. A head of black hair and striking blue eyes. "Sky? I ask, pressing my hand to my shoulder and wanting to bellow in agony. Instead, I bite my cheek, blood swathing my tongue, and check my surroundings.

There is a fenced-in playground across the street

and a brick building that says *Jefferson Middle School* in bold white letters.

"Where are we?" I ask groggily, scooting back on the bench I'm sitting on. I peer behind me. Bare trees spot the park. "A park? Why are we at a *park?*" I scrunch my brow, a headache looming behind my eyes again. I shake my head to force it away. "Sky. Be straightforward. What...*happened?*"

Sky sits down next to me. His cheek is freckled with blood, but I don't think it's his own. To be honest, it's probably *mine.* "King Hanson was going to kill you. I should've been there sooner. I'm so sorry I wasn't. If I went outside as soon as the palace started crumbling, I could've gotten to you before you got hurt." He scowls, inspecting my wound again. He gently moves my sleeve off my shoulder to get a better look at the gash.

"Don't do that," I hiss in annoyance, tugging my sleeve back up. I glare at him.

His head snaps up. "Did I hurt you? I was trying to estimate how many stitches you'll need. I didn't mean to—"

"*That.* Don't do that." I roll my eyes, leaning against the park bench and looking up at the brilliant blue sky. For being a winter day, it's oddly sunny. "You saved me. *Again.* Don't downplay that."

He doesn't say anything, but he does relax

against the back of the bench and look up at the sky as well. He bites his lip, and his oceanic eyes glaze over as if he's lost in thought.

I force my attention away from the boy beside me and toward the school across the street. There are kids bundled in puffy sweaters with beanies covering their heads exiting the brick building. Excited chatter lifts through the slightly chilly air toward us, over the rumble of a yellow bus parked in front of the school.

We went from the midst of a battle to a peaceful winter day who-knows-where. I tilt my head to look at him. "*Where* did you take us?"

Sky blushes. "I didn't have an opportunity to create a new rune, so I used the same one I did months ago. This is the Earthen Realm. The town you used to live in. And this," he pats the bench we're sitting on, "is the same bench you were found on two years ago. When I first sent you here." He frowns. "I wasn't going to leave you again."

I watch him. Studying the way the winter sunlight explores the ravine of his scar and plays with the shades of blue in his irises. This is Sky. He doesn't know how magnificent he is. Flashes of him standing over me in the bathroom of Roosevelt High School all those months ago push through the Veiling. That was the first time I *remember* meeting him.

"Thank you, Sky," I say. I can feel my eyes shift back to their original ice-blue color as I stare at this boy I used to have so many feelings for. But…are those feelings *really* gone? Or were they directed at Adriene because of the Veiling? Is there even a way to know?

Sky bashfully glances at me, then his eyes widen and he shoots up from his seat. "Oh my! Your eyes— they *do* switch!" He beams. "Em?" He leans closer to me, a blush already starting to paint his cheeks. He's so coy now… I imagine this is what he was like before the Veiling.

I smile at him out of instinct. "Sky?"

His cheeks warm, and he tilts his head, refusing to take his eyes off me. I bet we must look out of place to passerby; a girl in an elaborate gown with a crown of finger bones adorning her head, and a roguish boy with a deep scar and a crown of icicles.

Then the moment—if that's even what you can call it—is broken when my wound starts stinging again. I wince. Sky jumps into action, helping me off the bench. "Let's go get you fixed up."

"Where? It's not like we can go to a hospital. They'll ask too many questions," I grunt as we walk, leaning heavily on Sky. The three-pronged gash in my shoulder coats both of us in hot, slick blood. I don't think losing this much blood is healthy. Shouldn't it have stopped bleeding by now? I suppose I *wouldn't* know.

We look like we just murdered someone. Hopefully, there's no police nearby. I don't want to have to explain…all of *this*.

Sky gives me a look. "The only place we can go is your house."

Gnomes are scattered across the frosty grass that sprawls before the white house with blue trim. There's a winter-themed wreath on the door, and the cream curtains in the living room shift before falling back into place.

I nervously adjust the crown on my head, knowing I should feel happy about seeing these people again, but I have to fight with the Veiling to even remember *why*. This is my Mom and my brother—*that's why*. Even if I can't remember them fully, I still have to trust that they'll help me.

My hand goes to shield my eyes from view once again, but Sky knocks it out of the way.

"You can't hide your eyes the entire time we're in there, you know," he insists. "The sooner they see them, the sooner they can start to process… *everything*."

Everything? We're going to tell them who I

truly am, and what has happened? That I killed a man and took his throne? That I revel in *hurting* people? That there's a war going on in another *realm*? Would they even be able to process everything, or will it splinter their minds?

I peer at the house, trying to feign determination when all I feel like doing is crumbling. But I am a *queen*. If I can't face my family and tell them the truth, then what am I truly capable of?

"Ready?" Sky asks, watching me.

I give him one curt nod, not wanting to risk my voice wavering as I answer.

He accepts it—probably knowing the internal battle I'm fighting—and we walk up the path toward my Earthen home. Making our way through the conglomeration of gnomes, we step onto the doorstep. Before we can even knock, the door flies open and Sandy's wide brown eyes meet mine.

"Come in, quickly," she says, stepping aside to allow us in. She scans the street, completely ignoring the crown of bones perched atop my head and my obsidian-black eyes. I glance toward the street, wondering what she's searching for. Why is she acting so...*normal*? Why is she acting like her daughter showing up on her doorstep months after disappearing, with cursed eyes and a fantastical appearance, isn't surprising?

Sky steps through the door, and I follow him.

I'm immediately hit with a burst of warm, garlic-scented air drifting from the kitchen. She was probably making soup when we arrived—so who was peeking out of the curtains when we came up? I turn to look and find a familiar face staring at me with his brown eyes wide and his mouth twisting into a sad frown. *Ricky.*

Sandy studies me and the three-pronged wound on my shoulder. I hold my breath, waiting for her to comment about my eyes, or back up in shock… When she looks at them and doesn't say anything, I wonder if they have switched back to blue. Maybe being back here, in this home and around these people, triggered them to change. I didn't feel them change… But why isn't Sandy reacting?

"So, the Veiling got to you." She shakes her head knowingly, and I reel back, stricken.

"You—know?" I glance between Sky and Sandy, demanding to know what's going on. "How? *Why?*"

Sandy nods toward the living room, where a pair of navy armchairs face a matching couch. "Please, take a seat. We have a lot to talk about, my darling."

Sky and I claim the couch while Sandy and Ricky take the armchairs; Sandy perches on an arm, wiping her hands down the front of her apron and nervously fixing her blonde hair, pushing a strand behind her ear as she finds what she wants to say.

She gets up, wanders down the hallway toward the bedrooms and the bathroom, and comes back with a first aid kit and a bottle of alcohol in her hand. "I'll explain while you let me stitch you up. It's not too bad, but the sooner it's closed, the less chance you'll get an infection." She helps me lie back on the couch, resting my head on the arm and poking my knees up in the air. Sky moves to give me room. Sandy snaps open the first aid kit and removes a needle and a bit of dissolvable thread, then she assists me while I slip my arm out of my gown, exposing my shoulder. The movement causes a jolt of pain to course through my body.

Sandy sighs, pressing her lips together as she forms her words. She shares a look with Ricky across the room and nods, coming to a conclusion. "Ricky and I are mages from Glaven. We worked with the king, your father, on his Kingdom Relations Council," she starts, dripping some of the alcohol on my wound. I pinch my eyes closed, biting my lip. My lip splits and blood coats my tongue. Sandy winces, pressing a hand to my cheek. "Oh, my darling. Just stay still, okay? I'll be done soon and then you can have some soup I made."

I don't respond—not because I don't have a million questions and clarifications running through my mind—but because the waves of agony crashing through me are stealing my energy. I just want to

270

rest, but I know I need to hear her story. I pin her with my inquisitive, black-eyed stare. She doesn't flinch, nor does she look scared. It's as if she still sees the girl she took in, the girl she calls her daughter. Is that why she seemed hesitant to let me go to Victoria Johnson's party? Because she knew it would change the course of my life, that it would whisk me away from her...? But she still let me because she knew that's what needed to happen. I needed to set out on a course to save our kingdom and discover who I truly am. That last part still hasn't happened. We did save Glaven, but who knows for how long with Hanson's war looming at our doorsteps?

"When Aaron first threatened your father, saying he'd kill the Nether king and take Aridam as his own, and that your father would be forced to give him his blessing... Your father formed a secret council to watch over you, wherever you ended up going. It included Ricky, myself, and—"

There's a harsh knock on the door, followed by it flying open and a red-headed girl stomping into the living room. She's impressively tall, and her green eyes land on me.

"Victoria," Sandy finishes, scowling at the ginger. "The three of us were tasked with watching you, protecting you, and preparing you for the day that you'd return to Glaven and fix what Aaron did." She finishes stitching my wound closed and ties off

271

the thread. She gives it a closer inspection to make sure everything is good before disappearing into the kitchen and coming back with a bowl of garlic and potato soup, a silver spoon resting against the edge.

I cannot believe *Victoria* was tasked with watching me and making sure I was *okay*. I don't remember much thanks to the Veiling, but I do remember Victoria's incessant bullying.

"Did you know?" I ask Sky, already glaring at him. What is with everyone keeping secrets from me? Earning my trust and then destroying it. But even as I look up at Sandy's serene face and know that she lied to me for years, it doesn't make me love her any less. She took me in, gave me a home, and loved me like her own. I don't have any family left besides these two.

"I swear, I had no idea," Sky exclaims, shaking his head in bewilderment.

True.

"You said you're a mage," I say, studying Ricky and Sandy. "What abilities do you have?"

Ricky lifts his hand up and little flames flicker to life across his fingertips like they're fleshy candlesticks. "I figured glass welding was an excellent opportunity to practice my magic."

I watch the tiny red flames die out as he closes his hand into a fist. So, he was only going to the glass welding class at the local community college to practice his fire magic...?

"And you?" I ask Sandy.

Sandy sits back down on the arm of the armchair and gestures to the bowl of soup in my hand. "I can heal people through the food that I cook. Eat up, your shoulder will stop aching soon."

I peer into the bowl of soup, seeing a vague outline of my face on the creamy surface. I suppose that's why she always tried to get me to eat when I complained about my headaches.

I sip the soup, relishing the taste and the thick, creamy texture. Almost as soon as it hits my stomach, my body feels warm and the pain in my shoulder slowly ebbs away. I drink every drop and discard the bowl on the coffee table in front of the couch.

"What about *her*?" Sky asks, jutting his chin toward Victoria. "What's her ability?"

Victoria's scowl deepens, and she outright glares at Sky.

"She doesn't have one," Sandy answers, earning an *I'm-going-to-kill-you-later* look from Victoria. Sandy looks over at me again, scanning my dark gown and my crown of bones. Her expression is guarded, so I can't tell what she's thinking. "Let me help you to your bed, Emilia, and you can tell me what's happening in the Solstice Realm and why you're here now." She helps me sit up, draping my arm around her shoulders as Ricky takes my other side. It's…nice…to be surrounded by my family. By people who love me regardless of my curse.

Ricky pushes open my bedroom door and the chilly breeze drifting in from the half-cracked window brings with it reminders of my home, of my life before I left. Small snippets of memories return, bringing tears to my eyes. I blink them away. I won't let them see me cry.

I am a queen. I *don't* cry.

They give me a moment to myself to climb into a pair of clean, soft pajamas before rejoining me in my room. I set my crown of bones on the night-stand beside my bed, glad to have a brief break from wearing it.

Sandy helps me settle into my bed, tucking me under the covers and pressing her warm palm to my cheek. I can see in her eyes how much she loves me, and it makes my heart melt in my chest.

Ricky sits down on the end of my bed and gives me a small smile, quirking one corner of his mouth up. "How's Jaxon?" he asks.

I raise my eyebrows. "You knew Jaxon?"

Movement in the doorway draws my attention away from my brother, and I glance over to see Sky standing in the doorway. His eyes are clouded over with sorrow, and his bottom lip trembles. He sucks his bottom lip into his mouth and sinks his teeth into it to stop it from quivering.

Ricky nods. "We went to the Solstice Academy for Unnaturals together for a short period."

"He wasn't a mage. Why did he go to an academy for people with magic?" I ask, furrowing my brows. I tuck myself deeper into the covers and sink into the stack of pillows behind me. If I were to close my eyes right now, I'd fall asleep in an instant.

Ricky catches on to my use of past tense and his jaw ticks. He looks down at his shoes and then up at Sky, who's leaning against the door frame, looking out the window of my bedroom. His face is stoic, his chin tilted up, and his arms are crossed. But I can still sense the sorrow emanating from him.

"He got a scholarship that allowed him to apprentice in the academy's newspaper as an investigative journalist. He only stayed there for a term, but his writing was...spirited." He smirks, chuckling. "He got kicked out for an article he wrote about *The Woman of the Woods* and a murder that supposedly happened years before."

"Jinx?" Sky asks, cocking his head. "We've met her. She worked with the king. Jaxon never shared his writing with me before. He just came back home one day and told me he decided the academy wasn't for him."

"That sounds like Jax," Ricky agrees. "I'm sorry. I hope, however he went, it was quick and painless.

He was a great guy."

Sky nods, fixated on the window and the gray-blue sky outside again. "It *was* quick. Aaron made sure of that." His voice is gruff, and he coughs to clear the rising emotions from his throat.

Sandy and Ricky exchange a sympathetic look. Sandy turns back to me. "And Sophia?"

I hold her eyes and slowly shake my head, dropping my gaze away at the same time as her. She sighs. "I'm sorry… She was too young, too innocent." After a pause, she asks, "Was it Aaron?"

I nod, not finding it in myself to look at her. Soph was loved by many. Sandy spares a knowing glance at the icicle crown perched atop Sky's black waves, a newfound understanding dawning on her; the crown passed on to the ruling monarch of Glaven. The crown that used to sit upon my sister's head, her blonde hair waterfalling down her slender form.

"There's a war going on. King Hanson of Aquartia just ripped apart the barrier of the Banished Realm and attacked Cyprion. He's going to destroy any kingdom that stands against him." I adjust in the bed. The pain in my shoulder has completely subsided. Sandy's magic is more powerful than one would think. "We need to get back to the Solstice Realm. We can't leave our people to fight alone."

Sandy finds my hand in the folds of the blankets

and pats it reassuringly. "Don't worry, Emilia. We'll figure out a way to get you back. You rest up. There's nothing you can do until your strength returns."

Chapter Twenty-Nine

*V*ictoria pops a chip into her mouth, sitting on one of the dining room chairs with her feet propped up on another. She's glaring at Sky, Sandy, Ricky, and me as we take up the rest of the table. Clutched in our hands are bowls of leftover soup from the day before and glasses of orange juice. I reluctantly changed from the comfort of my pajamas to a pair of khakis and a loose t-shirt. Books are spread open and piled across the table.

Sandy had a stash of books in her closet, covering topics such as magic, Glaven, and portals. Earlier this morning, she told Sky and me we should retrieve them and see if they hold any information to help us return to the Solstice Realm. Sky seems particularly fascinated with *Portals, Crafting, Traveling, and More*. Etched on the spine of the thick blue book are runes. I can't decipher what they mean, but I know Sky can. I've noticed how excited he gets when he spies a rune, like it's a part of his history, ancestry, and a secret talent all rolled into one.

I lean back in the dining room chair, the sunlight falling through the window behind me and casting a soft glow on the table, and watch Sky as he absorbs the information in the books. Strands of black hair are flopped across his forehead, and his pale scar leads invitingly up to his sun-kissed, ocean-blue eyes.

Sky flips another page in the book, enchanted by the information stored within. I've been studying a book on healing magic; Sandy dog-eared and bookmarked several of the passages already. But I can't quite seem to focus on the text before me. My attention, instead, is riveted on Sky, trying to place him in my foggy memories.

"It says there are other ways to create a portal besides using a rune stone," Sky exclaims, setting the book in the center of the table and tapping on a particular line. "I think we can create an energy portal to return to the Solstice realm." His face is aglow as if the knowledge he's discovered is as precious as buried treasure.

"Why don't you just use one of your special rocks?" Victoria drawls, setting her bag of chips aside and glancing at the text he's pointing to. There's an image of a circle of clouds against a light blue sky. Her lips tilt down in boredom, and her green eyes flick from the book to Sky.

Sky glares at her. "Because I don't *have* any of my *special rocks*. To create a portal with a rune stone, it needs to be a particular stone—those only found in the Solstice Realm. I can't just engrave *any* stone."

Victoria sits back in her chair and crosses her arms, smacking on a piece of gum obnoxiously loud. "So, your gift is pretty useless then."

Sky's lip curls. "Says you."

Rage radiates off of Victoria so I stand up and draw their attention away from each other. "What did you learn about energy portals?"

Sky taps the page again, the tension lessening by a mere fraction, just enough to focus on the task at hand. Though by the stiffness of his shoulders and his ticking jaw, I can tell he's still angry. "If mages find a conductor to connect their energy, they can open a portal as long as their energy storage doesn't dry up. If it does, it'll have deadly consequences," Sky finishes reading the section and turns to us. "We have three mages. Do you think that would be enough to open an energy portal?"

Sandy shrugs, examining the text. "I'm sure it will be. The hard part is finding a conduit that's strong enough."

"Well, what does it say will work as a conduit?" I ask Sky, crossing my arms. If we can create an energy portal quickly enough, we can return back to the Solstice Realm today. I wonder how Adriene is doing... If he got hurt in the battle that Sky saved me from... I pinch my eyes shut, refusing to acknowledge that as a possibility. Adriene, the immortal executioner, couldn't have gotten hurt—I know that. But knowing it and seeing it are two very different things, and my anxious heart can't handle not seeing him and being positive that he's fine. I want to slap myself silly—when does a queen have time for *anxiety*, *caring* about others, or being *saved* by someone else? A queen should be strong in mind and will, care for only her crown and her kingdom, and save *herself*.

Shouldn't she? Isn't that what a queen is supposed to be like? What if I don't want to be that... What if I want to be *past* Emilia? What if I want my eyes to permanently shift back to blue, smile at people without having them shiver, and frolic under the perpetual spring sun? And what if I don't want to wear this terrible crown of bones and live in a kingdom surrounded by mutants?

"It says a Ring of Nature can draw out and unite the energy of the mages standing in the circle, if they have their hands connected and truly want to create the portal," Sky reads, thumbing to the next page. He holds the book up and shows us the page where a drawing of tall trees is shooting into the sky and a stick-figure "mage" is standing beneath them. There are little green squiggly lines coming from

281

the trees and surrounding the mage—supposedly the energy that the Ring of Nature is connecting. "Don't humans believe in the energy of nature and all that hippie voodoo stuff?" Sky inquires, raising an eyebrow.

Ricky snickers, nodding his head. "Yeah, they sure do. And I think I know exactly the place that we can go. There's this nature preserve about a two hour drive away. If we leave now, we can get there right before it closes."

"But what's so special about that place? Why can't we go into the backyard and find a tree to stand under?" I ask. It seems silly to have to drive two hours to accomplish something we could do in ten minutes.

Ricky laughs again, screwing his mouth up with an amused smile. "Trust me. You'll understand when we get there. I went there once on a date— with a *hippie voodoo girl*—and it truly was magical."

Sandy claps her hands together and offers the group a sweet smile. "We should get going then. I have my minivan out front, and I can pack some sandwiches real quick. Should I drive?" Sandy moves to the kitchen that's open to the dining room. She opens the fridge and removes a pre-sliced block of cheddar cheese, a package of deli ham, a bag of lettuce, and a container of Miracle Whip. After removing a bag of seed bread from the corner cabinet and a small blue cooler from the closet near the kitchen, she sets to work making a cooler full of sandwiches for our road trip.

Ricky takes another look at the book Sky so proudly presented. "Yeah, I think you should drive, Mom."

"I call shotgun," Victoria declares, sneering at me.

"I think Ricky should have it," Sandy responds. "He's the one who knows where we're going."

Victoria rolls her eyes to the ceiling, knowing she's going to be stuck in the back either by herself, with Sky, or with me. I'm pretty sure she'd rather be alone. I wonder…since Victoria was sent as part of my father's team to watch over me, was her relationship with Kevin ever real? Or was she using him as a cover?

How did I not notice Victoria, Sandy, and Ricky deceiving me? What is the point of my gift if I can't sense deception—only straightforward, direct *lies*?

Once we are all ready, we head to Sandy's purple minivan resting at the curb in front of the house. Sandy unlocks the doors and sets the cooler of sandwiches in the back of the minivan before hopping into the driver's seat. Ricky takes shotgun, bringing up the route to the nature preserve on his phone. Sandy pulls out a pair of dark-lensed sunglasses from her glove compartment and passes it to me. I put it on, knowing it's probably best that I don't draw anymore attention to myself. I already look like a woman who likes to collect bones and turn them into jewelry—as evident by my bone crown. But in this day and age? I doubt anyone would look twice.

Victoria slides the side door open and scowls at the two rows of gray-colored seats. She eyes the middle section in consideration, then bends almost in half to find a place in the very back. She lays back in the seat, buckles herself in, and props her legs up, jamming another stick of gum into her mouth and a wireless earbud into her ear. I can hear a whisper of the rap she's listening to.

Sky claims the spot closer to Ricky while I sit behind Sandy. My shoulder only aches now when it's bumped; Sandy's magical soup healed it almost completely overnight. With the gentle purr of the van's engine and the background hum of rap music, we set off on a mini road trip to find a Ring of Nature to summon an energy portal that'll return us to the Solstice Realm. I wonder how far the war has waged since we fell through the portal. I wonder if I'll have to count the corpses of my fallen soldiers or if the Nether Shrouds have prepared themselves for Hanson's abrupt attack. As soon as he's through with Cyprion, I know where he'll head next. He's going to eradicate the troublesome kingdom he's loathed for eons.

I lean back in the seat, watching the town I struggle to remember roll by, as Ricky's phone squawks directions about when and where to turn. Tortuous possibilities lurk in the depths of my mind, haunting me with a horrid reality to which I could return. Adriene could be dying right now. Kisha and Quicken… All of them could be gone. And I'm unable to help them. Does that make me a failure? I failed to save my father and Sophia from Aaron's cruel hands. I failed to save Jaxon. Who have I saved? I can't think of a single name. I pinch my eyes shut in anguish, needing to return to my people —my kingdom—as soon as possible.

A half-hour into the trip, something hits the back of my head. I glare at Victoria, who is munching on a sandwich she retrieved from the cooler, then notice the crumpled baggy it was in, balled up on the floor after bouncing off my head.

I roll my eyes—a total Victoria move—and return to the quiet landscape of the Earthen Realm.

It's still light when we arrive at the nature preserve. The big wooden sign in front of the chain-link fence declares it: *Mount Alayna Nature Preservation.*

There's a large parking lot that stretches down the side of the chain-link fence. Most of the parking spaces are already taken, leaving us a spot near the very end between a Ford truck and a white SUV. A mom is pulling her baby out of the back seat of the SUV; the baby is screaming its bald head off like the mom is ripping its arms from its tiny body.

We pile out of the minivan, Sandy carries the cooler and Ricky double-checks the address on his phone to make sure this *is* the place with the acceptable Ring of Nature. A cold gust of wind travels through the surrounding forest. My hair blows over my shoulder, and I rest my hand against my crown to keep it in place. Sky does the same. I'm sure we're going to earn some strange looks from families who've come to enjoy this winter day surrounded by beautiful, massive trees and birdsong. But I don't care. The quicker we find the Ring of Nature and create the energy portal, the quicker we can get back to the Solstice Realm and finish this war King Hanson began.

My blood boils just thinking of the merfolk king. I clench my hands into fists, my nails digging little crescent marks into my palms. *Hanson*—that meddlesome, demanding king—is going to die by my hand, and my hand alone. I will gut him with Aridam, just as I slid the cursed Sword of Death into Aaron's Dark heart.

Sandy beams at us as if she doesn't recall any mention of war, and that we're just out on a family picnic. "Ready to go? Does anyone need anything? There's a porta-potty up by the gate in case anyone has to take a tinkle."

Victoria smacks her hand to her forehead and storms off down the long strip of parking spaces, toward the entrance to the nature preserve.

"Did I say something?" Sandy squeaks, pursing her lips to the side and squinting her eyes against the winter sun shining down on the narrow lane of parking spaces in the middle of the Alayna Forest, which is on the base of a great mountain, half of which is cultivated and protected by the nature preserve.

Ricky and I exchange a look before leaving her and heading to the gate. *I have…no words.* Sky follows soon after, his cheeks tinged pink from holding in a laugh.

A metal building is beside the creaking gate. A couple of employees in dark green shirts with yellow text spelling out their names and the name of the nature preserve are waiting patiently near the small building. A man with short brown hair is accepting money from the line forming in front of the gate while a blonde woman hands out time-stamped tickets. The gate is already partially open, but the woman takes a break from handing out tickets to open it further. A white sign plastered on the front of the gate declares that the preserve visiting hours close at 6 pm on Thursdays—which happens to be today. We have two hours to find the Ring of Nature and open the portal. Hopefully, Ricky is right and the Ring of Nature isn't too far into the forest.

Sandy finally catches up with us, eyeing the growing line behind where we're already standing and a couple of people in front of us before holding her finger up and announcing, "I'm going to go to the loo real quick. Can someone hold the cooler?" She passes the cooler to a reluctant Victoria, who seems as if she would rather be anywhere else.

Sandy disappears into the blue porta-potty beside the guardhouse and pops back out two minutes later, washing her hands in the gray hand-washing station they have set up beside the porta-potty, and then she rejoins us in the line. There's only one person in front of us now. A man with a black goatee and a polo shirt. He takes his ticket from the girl and dips his head in gratitude before slinking through the gate.

I watch the forest through the open gate. It's beautiful. Tall pine trees stretch up to the gray winter sky spotted with white watercolor clouds. The scent of pine and rich soil drifts on the chilly wind. Birdsong plays through the trees as bluebirds and robins flutter between the pines. The forest floor is scattered with pine needles and pinecones, layered on top of dark, rich dirt that looks as if it's never been touched by humans, regardless of the everyday foot traffic. The nature preserve is stunning; I wouldn't mind living here, surrounded by the peace of the trees and the scampering of creatures in the underbrush. The entire place is shrouded in tranquility. Immediately, a weight lifts off my shoulders. I breathe in the scent of untainted earth, absolutely gob-smacked at the wonders hidden in the valleys of the planet.

We move to the front of the line and Sandy pulls a fifty-dollar bill from the back of her phone case and passes it to the man, receiving a ticket that tells us the closing time, the time we checked in, and the number of people in our party.

The blonde woman, who appears to be twenty, smiles at us, her brown eyes twinkling with mirth. "Are you guys ready for a magical adventure?"

I smile at her. "Yes, I think we are."

Chapter Thirty

I sense the energy shift even before we see the Ring of Nature. The air is thick with magic, and I know, without a doubt, that Ricky is correct. This is the most effective place for opening an energy portal. Birds sing in the forest, squirrels scamper across the branches above us, and the whisper of peoples' treading footsteps drifts on the winter breeze, carrying it toward us even though we can't see anyone around.

Ricky stops in the center of the forest, where the tallest pine trees in the preserve are shooting toward the sky in a circular pattern. Their sparse branches stretch toward each other to connect the ring. He spreads his hands wide and grins at the trees. "Will this work, Sky?"

Sky turns in a circle, examining the magic of nature surrounding us. There's nothing like being surrounded by the gentle sway of trees and the crisp scent of rich soil, clean streams, and fresh air. My eyes clear again, switching to blue, and the blockade of my memories releases a single one: *camping*. I see Sandy standing above a fire pit, coals hot with flames that lick toward the black sky, and a stick with a marshmallow on the end drooping toward the fire, threatening to fall off. Ricky and I are laughing our heads off, clutching our stomachs as Crumbs the beagle licks up scattered pieces of food from around the campsite. We almost fall off the back of the log we're sitting on. Sandy just beams at us, and the marshmallow slides completely off the end of the stick and burns in the fire pit, sending Ricky and me into another fit of hysterical laughter. We tumble off the back of the log and clutch each other's hands, struggling to breathe. The stars blanket the dark sky. We just lay in the grass, admiring the universe above us, and feeling gratitude for the people around us. At some point, Sandy lies down beside me.

When I glance around, my eyes returning to black, Sandy and Ricky are both smiling, their eyes clouded as if they were recalling that exact camping trip as well.

Ricky suddenly clears his throat, checks the forest surrounding us for anyone walking by, and asks, "Who's ready to open a portal?"

Ricky, Sandy, and Sky all link hands, positioning themselves in a sort of triangular shape. Victoria and I stand off to the side, waiting and watching for anyone to get within eyesight. How would you explain away a group of five people opening a portal in the middle of a forest?

Sky instructs the other two mages to close their eyes and try to connect to the energy of the trees surrounding them. I study the ring of trees, noting the cracked bark and the rivulets of sap trickling down the trees. A thick cloak settles over my skin, as I would imagine a layer of mist doing, and I wonder if that's the energy of the forest.

The air intensifies with electricity, making the fine hair along my body stand on end. Sky's eyes shoot open, widening as they land on something in the sky above them. My gaze follows his at the same time as Victoria's. We both stumble backward, barely catching ourselves from falling on our butts by grabbing onto each other's arms.

The clouds roiling in the sky right above us are black. A crack of thunder parts across the forest, followed shortly by an alarm, and a woman on a speaker system demanding that everyone head to the gift shop and information lobby immediately. A bolt of lightning as thick as I am wide slashes across the sky and strikes the ground in the center of the mages, searing the ground where it landed. We're thrown backward. My vision swims with brilliant white spots, and the crackle of electricity fills my head.

Everything is *hot*.

When my vision finally regains color, and my head stops pulsing with pain, I blink up at the sky, searching for the black clouds that were there moments ago.

Instead, there's a giant crack in the sky, breaking apart the tranquility of the Solstice Realm's ever-constant spring sun and blending it with the harsh contrast of gray winter clouds and snow. The edges of the crack are blindingly bright as they expand to encompass the entire realm, destroying whatever layer there is between the Solstice Realm and everything else out there.

A snowflake lands on my face and immediately melts. I wipe away the spot of water and sit up, feeling the cold, snow-dusted ground around me. Sky's already up and helping Victoria stand. Ricky is still unconscious, so Sandy is tending to him and checking if the energy portal had any ill effects.

I rub my head where I hit it against the ground, and push myself to standing. The world around me is as I've never seen it. I've returned to Nether, and the ground is dusted white, with huge snowflakes plummeting from the broken sky. And, roaring all around us, is war.

Mages from Glaven are decked out in iron armor and wielding swords of mismatched design. They are interlocked in fights with Hanson's mer-folk, all veiled in a protection spell that won't let them succumb to the arid environment. King Cassius's vampires are surging across the battlefield, switching gracefully into mist and changing back to their humanoid form a step later as their daggers and swords slash through their enemies, leaving mages and merfolk bleeding across the snowy landscape.

The Nether bog is a backdrop to the battle, and the stone palace and village are in woeful condition. Stones from the buildings are scattered across the streets, and furniture from the shops and houses are in burned piles throughout the village. By the appearance of my kingdom, I'd have to guess that King Hanson and his allies got here before my own, disrupting the rather content lives of *my* people, and destroying their possessions.

My blood boils with that revelation, and I tear the sword at my waist from its sheath and start toward the battle, longing for an enemy to take notice of me off to the side, tucked between a pair of trees, and so boldly begin to attack me. I want to push my blade through their abdomen as they beg for my mercy, as they try to retreat, as their last words form and die on their lifeless tongue. But someone grabs me by the shoulder and pulls me back. I whip around to bite their head off when I realize who it is.

"I'm glad you came back, but it may be best if you leave. Find somewhere safe," Adriene begins, pulling me into a tight embrace. There's a long, shallow cut across his cheek. His blood paints half his face red, and the blade of his scythe is already slathered crimson. "When King Hanson broke the barrier between the realms, he split open the sky, changing the weather to align with the Earthen Realm, and now the Banished Realm. He's already killed half of the Shrouds, Emilia. He's more powerful than we gave him credit for."

I push out of his arms and glare at him, shocked and repulsed at his attempt to convince me to run away, to leave my people to fight for themselves. I am queen. I am their defender. I am their first line. And a queen never gives up.

"How did you know we were here, Adriene?" I ask, gesturing to Sky, Sandy, and Ricky.

Adriene lifts his hand and a blue butterfly that's slightly glowing lands on his finger. It flutters its wings twice before settling. "Bartholomew helped me with them. Now they're our assassins as well as our Dark spies. Bartholomew is at the top of the palace right now. He alchemized an arrow to contaminate the snow with an elixir that will send the butterflies into a frenzy as soon as we release them all from the conservatory. The alchemy I used to make the butterflies obedient mixed with Bartholomew's elixir will change their genetics and turn their touch to poison." The butterfly takes off from his finger and flits into the sky, avoiding the snowflakes with an unnatural ease. "Which is why all of you should get out of here—as well as Quicken and Kisha. I don't want you guys to get caught in the crosshairs." He pulls something from his pocket and tosses it to Sky, who catches it with his brow lowered over his eyes. The winter sunlight reflecting off the layer of snow makes his scar brighter. Sky's eyes widen, and his mouth pops open as soon as he realizes what he's holding. "Take that and go back to the place you've come from. I won't have any of you get hurt."

Sky runs his thumb over the rune etched into his stone, pressing his lips into a speculative line before slipping it into his pocket. "No. We're not running away from this. Let us help. I'm fine with a sword. We can hold our own in this war."

Adriene glowers at him, angry at the mere fact that Sky won't listen to him and leave. "You might die."

"Then I'll be dying beside my people," Sky counters.

"We can stay and fight too," Sandy declares, volunteering Ricky and her.

Adriene doesn't question who they are, but he does turn to me for the final answer.

"I'm not leaving, Adriene. These are our people. This is our kingdom. I'm not going to let them destroy it."

He bites his cheek, panning over our faces again, before giving us one stoic nod. "Bartholomew should be firing the arrow and releasing the elixir soon. The weapon room was raided before we got here, so you'll have to find weapons off the dead." He nods toward the palace, where I can vaguely see a man grappling onto the spire and aiming a short bow at the clouds. "Emilia, you should come with me. I can use a hand when releasing the butterflies."

I nod, giving Sky and my family a last look before heading up the slight incline toward the palace. The war rages beside us as we try to sneak around it. An Olympus mage pushes his way out of the battle, raising his sword to strike me down when Adriene's scythe slices through the air. The mage's head lands at his feet. His body slowly crumples, staining the blanket of snow with gore.

We ascend the final incline to the palace, and Adriene wrenches open the servants' entrance, holding the door open for us to disappear inside. The hallway is dimly lit. Brackets containing lit torches are mounted about eight feet from each other down the long passage. Occasionally, another door will appear beside us with small rivers of blood trickling into the hallway, across the patchwork stones. Hanson's army must have caught the servants in their quarters and butchered them. Rage claws at my throat, the desire to grab the merfolk king by his throat and tighten my hands until his eyes drain of life overcomes me, tainting the air around me with my need for vengeance.

Adriene shivers, glancing back at me with black eyes that are slightly glazed, as if he too feels the need to butcher Hanson's people as he butchered ours. "We will get our revenge, Emilia. But first, we need to take out his army. We can't get to him now without someone guarding his back. Many of the Shrouds have died trying." He doesn't sound particularly melancholy about the fact that his kind are dying, their corpses littering the battlefield. They didn't treat him like one of their own though, so I suppose, if I were him, I wouldn't care much either.

Adriene stops at something blocking us from continuing down the long passage. I peer around him to see the bloodied body of a servant splayed across the floor, her brown eyes staring at nothing. With a deep sigh, Adriene steps over her body and continues onward.

I don't... I bend down. Pressing my fingertips to her eyelids, I slide them closed so she can be at peace. I can tell by her appearance, by the wrinkles around the corners of her lips and the crow's feet at her eyes, that she wasn't a malevolent woman. She was kind and harmless and died in a way unbefitting of someone like her.

I glance back up when a silhouette blocks out the torchlight shining down on the woman's slayed corpse. Adriene watches me, expressionless. He reaches down and offers me his hand. When I take his hand in mine, he runs the pad of his thumb across my knuckles. He doesn't have to say anything. I feel the urgency of our task in the energy coming off of him. With a reluctant sigh, I nod, and he's pulling me down the passage and toward the heavy wooden door at the very end.

I cast a last glance at the woman as she's swallowed by the shadows, wondering if that's what I'd look like when I'm eventually killed. If someone would stop at my body and close my eyes, letting me rest eternally. Or would they see the blackness of my eyes and the crown of bones atop my head and think that I was cruel and deserved to be slayed?

Adriene pushes open the door and peeks into the hallway, checking for danger. As soon as he deems it safe, he pulls me through, tightening his grip on my hand until we're across the sunlit hallway and ducking into another servants' passage. I don't know where this one leads, but it must bring us closer to the conservatory.

Loud masculine voices bounce off the walls of the palace as we sneak on by. I can't quite make out what they're saying, but I catch the words *archer* and *palace*. Are they talking about Bartholomew? I hope

we can get to the conservatory and release the butterflies quickly, just in case they *are* talking about
Bartholomew. We can't have him getting shot
down, not when we need him to enact Adriene's
plan.

We near the end of the passage, and Adriene
presses his ear to the door. He finds the doorknob in
the darkness and swings it open.

I recognize this hallway. It's the one that forks
off to the private staircase that leads up to my bedroom. I didn't even realize we were walking up an
incline, venturing further and further up the palace.
But what are we doing here, when the conservatory
is on the main level?

"Adriene," I hiss, squeezing his hand as he tugs
me into the hallway. We dart across it like scared
mice. He straightens up, and glances to the left and
right, before allowing his eyes to travel across the
bronze frame of an oil painting of the night sky. He
runs his fingertips over the gilded corner and tilts
the frame. With a *creeeak*, the section of the wall
with the painting falls open, revealing a secret
passage. He turns quickly, pulling me into it. The
walls are made from round, polished stones and the
floor is slick with moisture. Is the crummy ceiling
leaking over here too? I crinkle my nose as I step
across the moist floor.

The secret passage leads into a small alcove. Spiderwebs loiter in the corners and a single ancient bookshelf has a few dusty, damaged tomes resting on the shelves.

Sunlight filters across the floor, fading into the shadows at our feet. I gawk at the iron-framed window that looks down at the roof of the conservatory that's covered with glittering snow.

"What are we doing up here, Adriene?" I question, tugging on his hand so he looks at me. He frowns and heads to the left of the alcove. I hurry after him, fuming. Why won't he answer me? What are we doing up here, overlooking the conservatory and not down on the level that the conservatory is on? I thought we were trying to free the butterflies so that Bartholomew's elixir affects them.

Adriene presses a series of polished stones into the wall. With another *creeeak* of disuse, the wall reveals a storage room. Chests, dressers, and old, dusty mirrors are covered in white cloths. His footsteps leave tracks in the dust layered on the floor as he crosses to a chest pushed up against a small, grimy window. He lifts the sheet and drops it to the floor, wrapping both his hands around the metal handle on one side of the chest. "Grab the other side —we need to get this chest to the window. Quickly."

I do as he says, locking my hands around the handle and heaving the antique metal chest off the floor. It leaves a patch of clean floor beneath it. Adriene and I groan with the weight of the chest as we hurry out of the storage room and hastily return to the alcove. Before I can even ask what we're doing with the chest, Adriene starts to swing it back and forth. "Now!" Adriene calls. I release the handle and watch as the momentum of the heavy metal chest causes it to crash through the window and the roof of the conservatory.

It breaks apart on impact, leaving a shattered glass roof and a splintered, broken window in its wake.

My hand shoots up to cover my gaping mouth, and my ability to speak leaves me as hundreds of butterflies flutter from the gaping hole in the conservatory roof.

Their wings sparkle with differing colors of magic, glowing across the vibrant membranes and glistening in the falling snow.

"I figured that would release them a lot faster," Adriene says, watching the butterflies as they stream from the conservatory and into the winter sky, heading straight for the battle that's waging on the palace's doorstep. I move to the window, being careful to avoid stepping on the broken shards littering the floor directly in front of it and watch the conglomeration of butterflies as their magical senses latch onto Bartholomew's elixir that's falling and coating the ground in the new snowflakes, making them shimmer a light blue.

"I'm going to go join the fight. Hopefully, the butterflies' poison will deal enough damage to Hanson's army so our people can finish them off," Adriene says, but he sounds skeptical as if he knows that poisonous butterflies won't do much in the grand scheme of war. But we're going to use everything we have... For our people and our home.

Chapter Thirty-One

The palace is swarming with soldiers from Aquartia and Olympus. It seems that Hanson didn't involve other kingdoms in his plans to attack us early. Many of the Shrouds are dead, lying scattered across the palace grounds and throughout the village, getting blanketed by the continuously falling snow. Quite a few of Glaven's soldiers lie beside them, and scattered about the macabre battlefield are merfolk and mages. Very few of the vampires have been slain, which gives me hope that we will win this war.

Adriene tightens his fingers around his scythe as we duck behind doorways and odd bits of furniture to stay out of the sight of the enemies invading the palace.

Adriene presses his back to the wall, holding his scythe horizontally so it doesn't poke above the dresser we're hiding behind. I squat next to him, Aridam poised to gut anyone who comes close enough.

There are footsteps heading up the stairs toward us—multiple sets, I realize as I crane to listen. Adriene stiffens beside me. His grip on his scythe turns white, and his jaw ticks. We exchange a glance just as the source of the footsteps draws near. Adriene's eyes flash as he swerves his scythe toward the person. A startled yelp follows...but there's no blood, not like Adriene was aiming for.

We both pop up from behind the dresser, weapons aimed at the perpetrators.

I drop Aridam back to my side as soon as I realize who it is: Andromeda.

She gives us a wispy, slightly detached smile like her mind is elsewhere. "I'm glad to see you two are still alive." Her voice is croaky, and her lips are chapped and cut. She sheathes her blood-painted broadsword, and I catch the flash of a gemstone rose on her finger. I recognize it from Cassius's study—he was wearing it, and I found it odd that the vampire king would be wearing the symbol of the one thing that harms his species.

Andromeda follows my stare and sighs, her shoulders slumping. Her hair is matted and caked in blood, and her armor has lost its luster. She lifts her hand so the king's ring glints in the light. "King Cassius... He didn't make it out of Cyprion." She blinks down at the ring on her finger, her eyes clouded with sorrow. When she glances back up at us, she lifts her chin and tries to force away her emotions.

My heart sinks to the bottom of my stomach. "What?" I stammer. "What happened? How—"

Andromeda cuts me off. "He sacrificed himself to stop King Hanson from killing any more of his people. His death was in vain." She bites her bottom lip, focusing again on the king's ring that adorns her finger. After a moment of hesitation, she sighs, slipping the ring off her finger and passing it to me. "I think he'd want you to have it. You're going to reunite the realms, aren't you? That's what he would want." Her lips twist up in a half-smile.

I swallow, my throat suddenly thick. "That's my plan," I say, quietly, rubbing my thumb over the curves of the ruby rose. It's smooth against my skin, and my thumb comes back painted red. *Blood.* Is it Cassius's or one of Andromeda's victims? "May I ask, why a rose?"

She smirks, though it's only half-hearted. "His wife wasn't a vampire. She was a mage from Olympus. He wore the rose to remind himself of the other species and the other realms. To make sure that when he thought of himself and his kingdom, he always considered his wife as well—and her home in the Solstice Realm."

I stare down at the rose ring; a whole new light is shed on it. The vampire queen wasn't even a vampire? So…what happened to her? Did she pass away in the battle, or did she die long before?

As if Andromeda can sense my thoughts, she adds, "She died giving birth to their son, Garamond."

Just hearing his name boils my blood. I wonder where he was when Hanson and his army invaded Cyprion. Was he off gallivanting with another woman he'll undoubtedly betray, or was he inside cowering? Or (I doubt) did he join the fray of battle and fight alongside his people?

"We were just doing a sweep of the palace. King Hanson is pushing closer to the steps. If he successfully gets inside the palace, this war is over. We'll lose," Andromeda guarantees. She taps her fingers along the hilt of her broadsword, and the two shorter soldiers that have been standing a good few paces behind her step forward, drawing their swords and pointing the tips to the floor. "Would you like to join us as we finish up?"

Adriene answers before I can. "No. We're going to go outside and stall Hanson if we can."

Andromeda pauses like she wants to say more, but then she shakes her head and starts down the hall, her vampire soldiers trailing after her. After giving her soldiers directions, she calls over her shoulder, "Good luck. Nether and Cyprion rely on you."

"What if Hanson wins, Adriene?" I ask, hating that I have to voice such an atrocity. We *can't* let Hanson win. If he wins, he'll eradicate Nether, Glaven, and Cyprion. Anyone and any kingdom that helps us on this battlefield.

Adriene scowls. "Then the Solstice Realm will never be the same."

"It's already different," I state, turning around to gesture to the snow falling outside the window at the end of the hallway.

With a gruff sigh, he responds. "You're right."

My shoulder stings as the blade from a mage slices my freshly healed wound. I grit my teeth and jam Aridam through her chest, cutting into her heart. She sags against the jagged edge of my blade. I have to kick her corpse while pulling on the sword to dislodge Aridam from between her ribs. She falls to the ground with a soggy sound, squirting blood across the white canvas. The sound is rather satisfying and sends a tingle up my spine. I want to find another person to cut down, another one of Hanson's soldiers to destroy.

Before I have time to gather a breath, a trident is hurling toward me. I duck as the golden flash of metal zips over my head and lodges in a tree behind me. Just as quickly, I'm thrusting Aridam in front of me to block the mermaid's attack. The woman glares down at me with her creepy, two-pupil eyes. She tightens her grip on a small dagger crafted from a coral-like substance. She thrusts it toward me. I step to the side, using the slight momentum her action gave her to swing my blade out and jab her in the side. She falls to the ground, disrupting the neat snow, and proceeds to melt into an indescribable liquid.

Aridam must dispose of its victims in different ways befitting of their species. The shapeshifters turn to ash, merfolk turn to liquid, and a mage—like Aaron—is drained of their blood. I'm not sure if Aaron's death was a special case since he was the Nether king and his title and curse were transferred to me.

The butterflies are flitting about the battlefield, zipping over people's heads, landing on them, spreading their poison, and weakening our enemies just enough that our allies can cut them down. They're oddly effective for being such small, gorgeous creatures. A butterfly flutters toward me, and I jump to the side to try to avoid its dangerous touch. The butterflies must not know the difference between our side and the enemy because it follows my movement, gently landing on my arm. I jerk away, lifting Aridam. The butterfly flutters away, but not before Bartholomew's poison leeches onto my skin. It won't kill—the butterflies can't carry enough of a dose to be lethal—but it does make me slower, an easier target for Hanson's soldiers to kill.

Something whizzes by my head, barely an inch away from the tip of my nose, and I jolt backward, slashing out with Aridam on instinct. I feel the poison spread through my body, slowing my thoughts and my actions, tightening my muscles until every twitch of my body causes me pain.

My blade clashes against another mage's sword, and he uses the extra length his weapon provides him to press forward and slide his sword against mine until the tip of his cuts into my cheek, right below where my previous scar is.

I grunt and leap to the side, ducking as I anticipate him to swing his sword. As soon as his sword has swung a good foot away from my head in the opposite direction and he's caught off balance, I kick his leg out from underneath him and cut his neck with Aridam. The mage sinks into the snow, his glassy eyes staring up at the stormy sky. His body doesn't seem to morph into anything, so I'll have to conclude that mages die like normal people, just quicker because of Aridam's cursed nature, and that Aaron's morbid death was because of the Veiling that needed to transfer to me. My breathing is labored, and every bone in my body is screaming at me to stay still and rest. How am I supposed to continue to fight? I lift my hand to my cheek and grimace when it comes back slick with my own blood. I glare at my hand, my head pounding, and then wipe my blood off on my pants. I suppose now I know how powerful and effective Bartholomew's elixir is, and how much of an advantage our butterflies may actually be giving us. That is—if they can manage to land on our *enemies* and not *us*.

Someone taps on my shoulder, and I hop forward, swinging Aridam around to where the point is flush with their jugular. I blink, taking a quick breath of the air, chilling my lungs. "Bartholomew," I say in relief, bringing my arm back to my side. The man stares at me in contemplation. Does he sense his poison lurking in my blood? "What is it?"

He removes something from his trouser pocket and presses it into my free hand. It's two tiny vials with a familiar liquid inside. "What do you want me to use these for? Is it an antidote?"

He smiles mischievously, pointing through the chaos of war to the trees dividing the bog from the village. "The butterflies can only do so much. They can't kill, but I know something that can." He studies me again, squinting his eyes at the sweat slicking my forehead and my flushed cheeks.

A light bulb clicks in my head, and I stare past

the fighting soldiers, toward the line of trees that hold their own secrets. "Adriene as well?"

Bartholomew nods, patting my hand once more before pulling a dagger from his belt and rounding on the mage sneaking up behind him. He slices the dagger through her neck, and she falls to the ground, pressing her palm to the gurgling wound. Blood patterns the snow around her, and her eyes flick up to meet mine. I can almost hear her beg for my help, but her plea dies on her cracked lips. I smile maliciously, watching her as she falls to the ground and a rivulet of blood trickles from her fatal wound and into the snow. Bartholomew has already disappeared back into the palace. I slip the vials of elixir into my gown pocket and search the roaring battle for Adriene.

I spot Adriene almost immediately as his scythe glints in the fading winter sun, arcing to slice a mermaid's head clean from her body. Her body falls into the snow, her head flying off into the chaos, followed by a horrified shriek when it hits someone.

I surge toward him, ducking and side-stepping and blocking the attacks of the mages throbbing in the war around me. A woman cuts my unwounded shoulder, and I throw my head back as pain courses through my veins and my vision dances with white spots. I growl, rounding my outstretched blade on her in a heartbeat. Aridam slides into her shoulder, and her eyes narrow in anger. Just as she raises her sword to slice at me again, she falls to the ground, dead. I grip my fresh wound, wincing as my blood oozes between my fingers.

I'm half-tempted to spit on her body, but I have more important things to do, such as finding my executioner and fighting our way to the bog.

A dagger slices across my midriff, thankfully only cutting my shirt. But it still makes me see red. I turn on the woman, throwing my body weight into her sword arm and sending her sword into the snow, getting lost under the feet of the pulsating battle. She bares her teeth at me, attempting to bite my wrists that restrain her, pushing against her shoulders and pinning her down in the snow. I bring my foot up to crunch on her wrist, holding it in place so I can raise Aridam above my head and—

I'm thrown off her by another mage; this time, it's a man with muscles corded as thickly as my thighs, and a war-bloodied sword hangs at his side. He helps the girl up, who secures her sword and casts a murderous look at me, a smug smirk pulling at her thin lips, before rejoining the war.

I crawl backward into the snow, watching as the mage takes in my eyes and my crown of bones. A gleeful smile stretches across his stubbled face. His chestnut brown hair appears blonde as the sun hits it. "Queen, is it?" He clicks his tongue as he slowly brings his sword up to point at me. "Well, well, well... Won't I be the lucky one. What would Queen Hera and King Hanson think if I were to bring them your head, mounted on a pike?" His blue eyes flash with murder.

"What if you...didn't?" I suggest, raising Aridam—as if the broken sword will get to him before his long sword gets to me; something we're both aware of, by the cocky glint in his cruel eyes.

"I'd be foolish to pass up an opportunity like this," he says, sugar-coating his voice as the tip of his sword inches even closer to my jugular. "I bet your blood is as cold as you are cruel, *Your Majesty*." Sarcasm drips from his giddy voice.

His sword reaches my throat, digging into the thin skin right above my pulse. It's cold, and the still-wet blood from his last victim slips down the blade, dripping onto my neck and then onto the snow. I wonder, when he kills me, will he become king of Nether and reap the curse from me, or does the Nether monarch need to be killed with Aridam for the curse and the crown to pass on? Will there even be Nether after this war is over? Or will King Hanson obliterate it, completely erase it from the realm? I could see him doing something like that, along with massacring the Nether people.

He blows me a kiss, retracting the sword from my neck and swinging it up and through the air, arcing it toward me. Oh, so I'm going to be be-headed. Just like my father.

The cold breeze that is brought to life by the swinging blade caresses my skin and the sweat and blood that's trickling down my neck.

I turn my eyes to the sky, wanting to see some-thing beautiful before I die; the watercolor clouds, the winter sun, and the snowflakes falling from the sky, enchanted by Bartholomew's elixir, which tints them blue.

Something warm and wet sprays across my face and slips into my eyes. I pinch them shut against the stinging pain and ground the palms of my hands into my eyes, desperate to rid them of whatever is causing this burning sensation.

A hand wraps around my bicep and pulls me from the ground, tucking me into his chest. I stop assaulting my eyes to feel the leather of his uniform and acknowledge his soft hands that are holding me. I blink ferociously, riding my eyes of that horrible substance. I rest my cheek against his leather as he slips Aridam into the sheath at my waist.

There's a head slumped in the snow beside where I was just at. He's not facing me, but I know by the chestnut hair and the fact that I'm still alive that it's the mage who was going to kill me.

I quickly remove the vials of elixir Bartholomew gave me from my pocket and hand one to Adriene.

He raises his eyebrow in a silent question before it dawns on him, and his attention snaps to the bog.

"Let's go win this war," I say, grinning in pair with him.

Chapter Thirty-Two

 driene swings his scythe through the air as I duck, digging Aridam into the mage's midriff as Adriene slices her head off. Her headless body falls backward, staining the snow as we continue forward, pressing our way through the undulating battlefield. The butterflies' poison is waning, but my limbs still feel sluggish, and cold sweat still slicks my face, dripping down into my eyes and making them sting.

He swings and slices while I duck and jab, and eventually, we make it through the battle unscathed. We don't glance behind us as we run for the protection of the tree line, sheathing our weapons and retrieving our vials from our pockets.

My boots squelch in the bog. Adriene helps me pull my leg out as the ground tries to swallow it, creating a nail-biting *squeeeeee* sound. I bite my tongue to stop myself from gagging.

"Do you want me to carry you?" Adriene offers, extending his arm toward me.

I glare at him. "Does it look like I've forgotten how to walk? *No.* Now, hurry up." I use a tree as support to push myself onward.

Adriene bites back a smile. I have a suspicion he likes it when I chastise him. *Weirdo.* "Bartholomew's poison is making you rather...*cranky,*" he snorts.

I raise an eyebrow. "Is it that obvious?" How does he know that Bartholomew's poison got to me? Can he see it in the complexion of my skin or the stiffness of my movements? In response, Adriene flashes me an amused look: his lips stretch up in one corner, and his eyes twinkle with mirth.

The sound of battle rings behind us, making the hair along my spine stand on end. I'm not sure what the others are up to right now...but I hope they are all okay.

A growl resounds around the bog in front of us, bouncing off the ominous trees that jut from the weepy land and drip with lichen. The chimeras must have sensed our return, spurred into alert by the war raging on their doorstep.

Adriene uncaps the vial in his hand, his eyes sliding toward me.

A scream slices through the air, coming from behind us. I don't know whose scream that was, but they're gone now. I shake my head, ridding the scream from burrowing into my mind. I have to focus right now. Adriene and I have to end this war before any more of our people end up dead. Before any more of their blood is spilled on that battlefield.

I catch a wisp of gray fur traipsing behind two trees off to the right. I reach over and pinch Adriene to get his attention, pointing toward the section of the bog the chimera was just at.

It's hunting us, I realize, as a twig snaps off to the left. Something swishes above us, disturbing the branches of the tree directly overhead. Snow falls from the branch and knocks my crown off. I scowl, squinting my eyes to try to spot the monster. A flick of a rattle on a long, scaled tail steals my focus. I point up to the spot in the branches of a tree about ten yards away. Adriene nods, lifting his vial in preparation to take a drink.

I bend down to retrieve my crown, dusting the snow off it and scowling as it sticks to the joints of the finger bones. Adriene says something, knocking me to the ground, as the beat of membranous wings pushes my hair over my shoulder and around my face, blinding me from seeing what's happening. I set my crown back onto my head and try to part the curtain of my hair that's blocking my vision and tickling my skin when a pair of claws encompass me, squeezing my body and lifting me off the ground. My crown falls again, disappearing beneath me as the chimera flies upward, breaking through the canopy of treetops and spreading its wings wide, a shrill howl clawing from its monstrous throat.

The bog is small beneath me. I dig my hands into the chimera's paws, desperately holding on. If it decided to release me right now, I'd fall to my death, splattering on a million branches before landing in a soupy mess on the ground, where I'd inexplicably join the bog. I dig my nails into the chimera's paws, biting my tongue to stop myself from screaming. I'm not scared of heights; I'm scared of falling from them. I'm scared of that small moment in time when I know my death is inevitable, and I have to face it as it hurtles toward me. Or, more accurately, as *I* hurtle toward *it*.

The harsh wind at this elevation and the bursts created by the monster's wings tug at my clothes and my hair, whipping them in the direction of the Nether palace. I grind my teeth, clinging to the monster. The war seems minuscule from this distance; the soldiers are pinpricks on the red-spotted snow. The blue-tinted snowflakes that drift from the clouds above me swirl in the torrential wind as they fall, sparkling and shifting as the elixir's magic courses across them. It's strange to think that something as delicate as a snowflake carries with it a poisonous elixir.

The butterflies are nearly invisible at this distance—but it's obvious they're working, to some degree. Occasionally, they'll land on the shoulder of a mage or a merfolk, causing them to jump around and slash at nothing, their bodies slowing as Bartholomew's poison floods into their systems. If someone's paying attention and can take advantage of their distraction, they'll thrust their sword through them and move on to the next. Unfortunately, the same happens with our people, but since ours are so few now, since Hanson's army butchered the majority of the Shrouds, the enchanted butterflies give us a greater advantage. And we can use every advantage we can get if we're going to win this war.

The chimera that's holding me howls again, summoning two more from the depths of the bog beneath me. I shriek as a moonlight-white chimera with coal-black membranous wings soars at my level. I think it's staring at me…but it's a little hard to tell when its eyes are completely black as well.

The gray chimera holding me, the white one at my left, and the smaller gray one to my right all howl, dropping their wings to their sides and plummeting back toward the bog.

My scream gets whisked away by the roaring wind as the treetops near. This is how I die? I get smashed up on *trees*?

The white chimera extends its wings, catching itself from plummeting further, then swerves to the side, crashing into the one that's ensnared me. The chimera releases me in reflex, and I fall, reaching toward the beasts fighting above me. The wind roars by my ears, taking my sense of hearing. Tears slip from the corners of my eyes and disappear into the rough current of wind, culled by the chill of winter and my impending death.

The gray chimera thrashes in the air, sinking a claw into the white chimera, and staining its snow-colored fur with a spot of red.

Time seems to slow as I tumble through the air, crashing toward the treetops and my inevitable death. There's no way I can survive this. I'm not *immortal*. But at least I don't have to see the treetops speeding toward me. I watch the sky, the mutated monsters battling against the backdrop of clouds and snowflakes. When I die, at least I won't see it coming.

The white chimera uses its large wings to push the gray one back, giving it enough time to plummet toward me. Desperation shines in its black eyes.

Black eyes…that look incredibly familiar.

I study its white fur, its eyes, and the snarl of its lips. *Adriene?*

My eyebrows shoot into my hairline as I realize what I must do. I dig into my pocket, flick the cork of the vial off to be caught in the torrential wind, and then I down the contents. I don't know if I'm too late. If I'm too close to the canopy of treetops below me for the elixir to work, to save me from my impending doom.

My body heats up as the elixir courses through my system. Adriene's still pumping his wings, desperately trying to get to me, fear evident in his wide eyes. The treetops must be a lot closer than I originally anticipated.

I don't close my eyes as my death nears. Instead, I stare up at him, watching him try to save me.

My body aches as the elixir begins to work. My bones feel as if they are snapping. My muscles and ligaments feel as if they are tearing. My blood burns with the magic that's disrupting it.

Dark brown fur sprouts from my body as my skin tears, stitching itself back together as thick as the skin of a wolf. I scream as my fingers grow long black claws and fur coats my skin, growing in clumps from my pores. Wings protrude from my back, golden membranous material stretching low and catching in the wind. I spin toward the treetops, my claws skimming the top of the trees as my wings shoot to the side. I'm a lot closer than I thought. If I didn't turn now, then I wouldn't be alive. I'd be crashing through the trees, mutilated by every branch that hits my body.

A *whooooosh* tells me that Adriene is soaring behind me as well. The gray chimera howls, piercing my eardrums and making my teeth grit. At the same time, countless chimeras all surge from the trees, bursting into the sky with their multicolored wings spread wide and their wolf-snoots pointed toward the storm clouds. The sound of dozens of rattles fills the air as millions of blue-tinted, enchanted snowflakes drift from the sky to paint the dead on the battlefield.

I tilt to the side, my wings drifting to follow the movement of my body. The wet snow makes my coat of fur damp, but I don't feel the chill since my fur is so thick.

The muscles of my back tense as I shift to the side again, finding my momentum in the sky, balancing my movements with the weight of my wings.

When I glance to my left, I note three more chimeras parting the air with their monstrous wings, heading straight for me and Adriene: the imposters among their kind.

A claw catches me off guard, digging into my hide and drawing blood. I growl, thrashing to the side and knocking off the small gray chimera. It bares its teeth at me, flapping its wings and creating torrents of wind that attempt to push me off balance. When it charges toward me, digging its claws into my thighs while a ragged shriek drags free from its throat, I use my wings to beat it off, rolling to the side as they wrap around me, before straightening back out and pressing toward the battle a few yards away from my attacker. If we can just lure them to the battle, they will get drawn in to the excitement of war and join the fray, hopefully taking care of our outnumbering opponents. That's the only way we can win this war. Our numbers have shrunk too small, too fast. With the butterflies giving our people a higher chance and this war being on our home front, we *do* have advantages...but they don't compare to the numbers King Hanson and Olympus have brought. Even with Eirae's soldiers fighting alongside the Nether Shrouds, Cyprion's vampires, and Glaven's mages and human soldiers, our armies don't compare to those in the Gods' Mountain Range who've been taught by seasoned generals, as the Olympus soldiers have been.

Hanson's merfolk army is fueled with hatred and determination, a dreadful combination that speckles the snow-blanketed ground with red.

Adriene fights his way beside me, an auburn chimera is latched on his side and a large silver chimera is stalking him from above, staring daggers down at Adriene, and readying his claws for an attack. I dodge another attack from the incessant gray chimera, barreling through the sky and into the auburn one latched onto Adriene's side. It shrieks, losing its grip and falling until its wings spread wide and it catches the wind. It pins me with an aggrieved stare, and I can imagine all the horrible things it'll do to me if it catches me; the image of claws tearing through the thin membranous material of my wings flashes through my mind, making me wince with how painful it would be. I don't want to experience that. What damage will that leave on my human body once I shift back? How does that work? Would my leg be torn to shreds, or would my human body not sustain any damage?

Adriene veers, dropping further below me, closer to the trees, as the silver chimera rears back and digs its claws across Adriene's back, leaving gnarly red marks in its wake. Adriene screams, throwing his head back as the pain courses through him. His black wings splay to either side of him, and the silver chimera relinquishes its grip. He falls. The chimera watches Adriene cascade toward the treetops with satisfaction. I force myself to dive, ignoring the burning in my thighs and the small gray chimera still trailing after me, determined to maim me some more. I need to get to Adriene, just as desperately as he needed to get to me.

Adriene seems to regain some of his strength, flapping his wings to slow his descent. I let myself drop until I'm below him, just mere feet above the treetops that zip underneath us as we continue toward the battle and the pin-prick-sized soldiers fighting on a canvas battleground. If Adriene loses control again, too overcome with pain to stop himself from falling, I'll be here to catch him—or, at least, assist him while he gets his bearings back and shakes himself from his agonizing stupor.

The silver chimera that tore across Adriene's back howls, drilling through the air toward me. It pushes me out of the air, forcing me to free fall through the trees. It thrashes after me, claws tearing into my sides as my wings helplessly try to save me, but are no use.

The canopy of the trees blurs my vision, branches crisscrossing and overlapping above me. My back faces the approaching ground. If I can't pull out of this descent, my body will turn into a pulp and join the list of the dead in the aftermath of the Solstice War. Will my battered corpse switch back into my human form? Or will my remains be trapped as a chimera forevermore? The wind pulls at my fur, which causes my skin to sting. Tears slip from the corners of my eyes, whisking away in the wind. My hearing starts to ebb from the constant pressure and zipping of the wind, though it's much stronger than human hearing.

The silver chimera tears its claws free from my sides before relishing in another vicious attack; its wolfish lips curl back in a snarl, snow-matted fur and black wings defiant against the green backdrop.

I bring my hind legs up to kick at its stomach to

dislodge its claws from my flesh. The chimera only roars, pushing its paws into me, forcing me down quickly. My back cracks across a branch, and I grit my teeth, white and black spots dancing across my vision. The branch snaps off the thick trunk of the tree, slowing my descent. My spine aches from the contact, sending zillions of sharp, stabbing pains through my body.

The silver chimera's wings spread as wide as they can, disappearing behind the trees as it stares down at me with piercing yellow eyes, triumphant as I fall, assuming that I'll die as soon as I crash onto the forest floor. It finds no need to continue to chase me, to hurt me, when my death is so inevitable.

Wind whistles by my ears, which have shifted with my body to pick up quieter sounds and amplify louder ones. Squirrels rustle in the trees, while birds flutter among the branches and more creatures…cha klas like those imprisoned in the dungeon of the Nether palace lurk deep within the bog, slender paws evading the succumbing nature of the bog and successfully traipsing on solid ground.

I know the ground is coming up on me—and quickly. I don't want to see my death, and since there's nothing to look at above me, save for the intricate web of the forest, I close my eyes and listen.

The world is so loud, bustling with the distant sounds of war, the peaceful songs of birds, and the content wandering of the cha klas.

But it's also so silent… Quiet with my impending demise.

I wonder, if I die, will the faces of my loved ones flash through my mind to comfort me—or will they be distorted, or nonexistent, thanks the Veiling messing with my already weakened mind?

Chapter Thirty-Three

E verything is wet, suctioning to my skin, pulling at my fur, threatening to tear at the thin membrane of my wings. The impact hurt more than I was expecting, bruising every part of my body. I don't know why my bones aren't broken. Or maybe they are, and I'm in such extraordinary pain that I can't feel them at all. That most definitely could be the case—it would make the most sense. But I don't feel like my sensory system is on fire, nor has it shut down. I feel as if I'm paralyzed in a free fall, sinking into the sludge of the bog that's pulling and sloshing against my skin.

I'm not dead. I can't be. But how am I alive? Is the form of a chimera that powerful, that resilient, that it can withstand a free fall from the *clouds*? However, as creatures built to lurk within this forest and with veined wings to take them above the treetops, it would make sense that Adriene and Bartholomew would design them to survive. Still... I shouldn't be alive. I shouldn't have *survived* that long of a fall—but the impossibility won't damper my relief. I don't want to die. I have my friends and my family to save. I have my people to look after, and my kingdom to care for. I have so much to live for.

I don't move. Not that I don't want to, but because I *can't*. It's like my body is rebooting, analyzing, and noting the wear and tear. Everything aches as if my muscles are starting to heal. Whatever is happening, it's painful, as if everything is stretching in my body, but nothing is moving at all.

The thick, gripping sludge that composes the majority of the bog sucks at my skin, urging me farther and farther down. When I blink past the clumps on my eyelashes, the sky speckled between the trees far above me is light blue. Snowflakes sprinkle down, filtered by the numerous trees crossing above the bog, before melting on the warmth of my face. I feel the slight effect of the poison, but it's weaker, hardly noticeable, compared to when it's distributed by the butterflies.

Slowly, the sound starts to come back to me. First, the gentle chirping of creatures nestled in the tree a few feet away from me. Then the gentle pitter-patter of something to my right. When I move my head, struggling against the suction of the bog, I notice the long, slender, navy body of a cha kla. Its wide, furry ears shift toward me as I move, and its feline eyes narrow. Cha klas, at least in Nether, are said to be rather docile creatures. Mainly, they're just content with living their own life and being left alone by others.

After the cha kla tilts its feline nose in the air and its long, white whiskers move on the breeze, it sighs. It doesn't come after me, nor does it spare me another glance, having determined that I'm not a threat. Its thin hips sway in rhythm with its long tail. The cha kla doesn't make much noise, besides the sound of its paws finding solid ground to maneuver the forest.

The sound of war comes next: screams, guttural cries, and the clash of blade against blade.

I can't stay here. I have to get back to Adriene and the others. I need to make sure they are alright. But I also can't move. Not yet. Not when my body feels so broken, leached of all my energy. I lie in the wet, suctioning bog. My skin itches as the thick, sludge-like liquid pulls at every strand of fur. My chest expands slowly, sending shooting spikes of pain throughout my body. I must've broken a rib, if the throbbing ache in my side is any indication. The sunlight slips through the canopy of the trees and across the forest floor, speckling my face with sunlight. Large, dark wings break up the sunlight as the chimeras soar through the sky, skimming the treetops and circling for more prey. Is Adriene still

332

up there? Is he holding his own and concentrating on the other chimeras, or is he trying to find me? To save me, as I know he would? If we switched places, I would do anything to find Adriene—even if it were just his corpse. Gradually, my energy starts to restore itself as my elixir-fueled blood circulates faster.

The thick bog pulls at my aching muscles, trying to coax me to stay in its suffocating grasp. I grunt my refusal, tugging my legs forward until I can pull myself from the bog and onto a section of considerably sturdier ground at the base of a tree. I curl up, catching my breath and pinching my eyes shut against the onslaught of pain from my bruised body. My dark brown fur is slicked with the putrid liquid, and my eyes are heavy, growing heavier and more difficult to keep open by the second. But I need to get out there, I need to...

I force myself to stand, pushing my feet beneath me and raising on my shaky, overexerted legs. I nose the air, catching the scent of blood and sweat coming from the direction I'm facing—the direction out of the bog and toward the palace, I hope.

With my nose still turned to the air and my paws carefully treading on the uneven ground, I make my way toward the tree line and the battle beyond.

All around me, Olympus mages and Aquartia merfolk are falling, brought down by the sharp teeth
and glinting claws of chimeras. Fluttering above the
battle and perching on the shoulders of anyone left
standing are the enchanted butterflies, drawn to the
elixir spreading on the snow. Chaos in tiny, blue
butterfly form.

Adriene snaps his jaws, tearing the throat out of
a mermaid about ten paces away from me. He
throws his head back, discarding the fleshy throat
and splattering the snow with blood. When he
catches sight of my bruised, limping form, he strides
over, shaking the ground with his heavy footsteps.
Though he can't speak to ask how I am, or what
happened, I can tell by the dip of his head that he
wants to—that he's wondering.

I nod once, lifting my wounded paw to show
that it isn't so bad. He doesn't seem to buy it, and I
don't blame him.

He narrows his eyes, huffing and blowing the
fur around his nostrils, but there's not much else he
can do, not in his chimera form. Knowing this, we
both turn toward the surging battle, looking for our
friends to make sure they're unharmed. It's been a

while since we've seen Kisha and Quicken, so hopefully they made it out of the Banished Realm without getting caught up in King Hanson's scheme.

I glance over at Adriene as his legs bend, his muscles coiling tight in preparation. He leaps into the battle, securing his maw around the head of a hovering merman and tearing it clean off. The merman's arm still carries through with the thrust of his trident before he falls limp and tumbles to the ground, lying still as his blood pools across the snow beneath him. The winter sun glistens across the merman's green scales, making the merman shimmer with undeniable beauty even in death.

Would Adriene tell me if something happened to Kisha and Quicken since he lied to me about Emmet O'Hare still being alive? Why did he do that? Was he trying to stop me from bringing Sophia back or investigating Oblivion further? I know Oblivion is dangerous. Most things are turning out to be quite dangerous, especially in this extraordinary world. But if there's even the slightest possibility of Soph coming back, and returning to my old self before the Veiling, shouldn't I try? Why would he stop me from trying? Unless…he doesn't mean what he's said to me numerous times—and he doesn't want to help save me from this curse.

I let these thoughts mull around in my mind as I

search the battlefield for my friends. I need to find them and make sure they are truly okay.

I leap into the fray, biting and slashing at anyone who gets in my way as I search desperately for my friends. Sky, Sandy, and Ricky all said they'd join the fight. I don't know where Kisha and Quicken are, but they don't seem like the type to lift a sword and slick their hands with blood. I also don't know where Victoria and Samantha are. So, I look for the three I know are here.

Something prods me in the thigh, right on the deep claw marks the small, gray chimera left behind. I roar and throw my head to the side, snapping my jaws and breaking their trident. I spit the metal out and stalk toward the petrified mermaid. Her pink scales glitter in the falling snowflakes, and her white skin seems to pale even more with every footstep I take. She gulps, flicking her tail back and forth as if she can't tell which way she should flee. My body aches with every step, with every second of tension from my coiled muscles. But the pain is worth it. The pain is fueling me, encouraging me to give in to my dark desires and blood lust.

My maw snarls to reveal my jaw full of pearly blades, all primed and ready to tear her to pieces. When she blinks and her two-pupil blue eyes close, I strike. I snap my jaw around her arm, crunching down on the bone and sinking my teeth into her soft muscles. They fold like clay around my teeth. The mermaid screams, tears springing from her eyes and falling down her face. But I don't stop. Her scream brings me joy, urges me on, and fuels me with the desire to hurt her more. With her arm still ravaged in my mouth, I toss my head to the side and force her to fall into the snow. Pressing a paw to her chest and pinning her to the ground, I stand over her, heaving with the exertion of violence. I can tell as she opens her mouth that she's going to scream again. No matter how much screams of agony please the Veiling inside of me, I want her to be quiet now. She's distracting me from my goal. Though I'm reveling in my revenge toward the kingdom that's brought me so much worry, I need to find my friends, and killing her is taking my precious time.

Her lips quiver, and her throat twitches with the impulse to move. I take my chance, sinking my canines into the soft, squishy tendons and flesh of her neck. Her blood gurgles around the wounds, filling my mouth with the taste of iron. I crinkle my nose in disgust and thrash my head behind me, tossing her throat into the battle. The severed throat sounds wet as it makes contact, and someone screams, so I assume it must have hit them. I chortle to myself with glee.

The blade of a sword slides into my leg, up to the hilt. I let out a gnarled scream as my leg buckles, driving my hip into the ground. I wrench my leg toward me, glaring at the perpetrator.

It's a mage wearing the crisp armor of Olympus. Her expression is smug; her lips are tilted up in a cocky smirk, and her bright blue eyes sparkle with confidence. She doesn't reach for her broadsword that's buried in my leg. Instead, she unsheathes a dagger from her waist and lifts it into the air. The point glints in the harsh winter sun. She slams her arm down at the same time as I lunge to bury my teeth in her flesh. The dagger slides into my skin and notches my hip bone. I snarl, clamping my teeth even harder on her arm. She's screaming. With every shake of her body, the blade in my hip moves, sending another jolt of agony through me. I need to end her quickly, no matter how much I want to torment her, to make her feel the excruciating pain she's making me feel. The need for her to *shut up* is too great. If *her* agony ends, will mine?

I clamp my jaw down even harder, shattering her arm in my mouth. Blood fills my mouth and drips from the corners, staining my fur. Her eyes roll to the back of her head as I drop her mutilated arm onto the grass. Before she can fall unconscious or die of blood loss, I knock her back and pin her down with a paw to her chest. I watch the mage—who was so sure of her success mere seconds ago—as she comes to the realization that she's not going to make it. That she's going to die right here, right now.

The corners of my mouth tilt up into a cruel, satisfied smile. Blood clumping and dripping from the fur surrounding my muzzle. With one fell bite, her throat is hanging from my mouth and her body stops twitching. I spit her throat out and lick the snow to rid my tongue of that terrible taste, crumbling to my side as the dagger shifts into my hip bone even more.

I glance over at my leg. The dagger is embedded in my hip, so deep that red is spreading quickly around it. And her broadsword completely went through my lower leg. It missed anything super important, but just seeing the tip of the blade on the opposite side as the hilt is enough to make bile climb up my throat.

I collapse to the ground, enjoying the cool snow and how it makes my wounds throb a little less. Maybe I can stay here, staring up at the clouds, the chaotic butterflies, and the enchanted snowflakes fluttering down—a million a second.

Is there any way I can remove the blades myself? If I had opposable thumbs and functional fingers, this would be a different story. But I'm stuck in my chimera form. I don't know when the elixir will wear off or what I'm supposed to do to deactivate it. Maybe Bartholomew turned me into a chimera forever, though that's doubtful. What would be his purpose for doing that? It wouldn't benefit him any.

Just as snowflakes start to clump on my eyelashes and blur my vision, and I've given up any hope of surviving this war, a familiar voice calls out to me and a warm hand brushes my heaving side.

I glance over at him with my solid black eyes, which are now as big as his hand. Sky smiles down at me, blood staining half his face and trickling into the ravine of his scar. He wipes the back of his hand across his face and smears the blood further. A long, jagged cut down his arm confirms that some of the blood is his. But the cut isn't deep enough to stop him from fighting, nor is it deep enough to supply all the blood that paints his skin.

"Hey there," he coos, rubbing a hand across my side. He leaves lines of blood in my already stained fur. "Let me see if I can help you." He smiles kindly before his eyes scan the rest of my body and land on the blades jutting from my leg. He winces, clicking his tongue. "This is going to hurt. But they need to be removed." He studies them some more, his brow furrowing when he notices how deep the dagger went.

Why is he helping me? He can't possibly know that it's *me*. But maybe he's just helping me because he noticed I'm fighting on his side? That has to be it. Or maybe he suspects that it *is* me. Though how could that be?

He gently grips the hilt of the dagger that's buried in my hip. He bites his lip as he readies himself to pull it out, shooting an apologetic glance at me as the blade grates against my hipbone and dislodges itself from my flank. He tosses the dagger aside, running a comforting hand down my side again as I shake in agony. Though relief also washes through me. Now, every time I move, I won't have a blade digging deeper and deeper into my bone. I relax in the snow, enjoying the chill against my overheating skin.

He sighs, wipes his hands off on his blood-stained trousers, and grips the hilt of the sword, studying the way it sliced cleanly through the lean muscle of my lower leg. Without further warning, he slides it out and my leg sinks to the ground. The cold lessens the pain, but even if it didn't, I'm too tired to try to move it. I don't think I can stand. At least I know that Sky is okay, even if I can't check on the rest of my friends and family.

Sky runs his hand down my head, shushing me even though I'm not making a sound—I think it's supposed to be calming, even though it's coming off a little…*weird*.

I nestle my head into the packed snow, my ear twitching as the sound of war around me tries to drown out my every thought.

What I wouldn't do for some *peace and quiet*.

"King Skylar," a too-familiar voice says, leering above my injured body and a blood-speckled King Sky. I knew he was here, but it doesn't make seeing him any less enraging. "Look at you, tending to the poor injured animals." King Hanson hovers above the ground, the tips of his gold trident are stained with layers and layers of blood. I know one of which is mine. His green scales shine in the sunlight and the bright snowy surroundings. His two-pupil eyes dilate as he stares at the young king. His thirst for power, for murder, spills from his eyes and they briefly turn black, flooding to the pigment of coal just like mine. His sneer falls for a moment when he feels the change take place, but he shakes his head and his pearl-adorned hair brushes his shoulders. The bubble of magic surrounding him that is running over his body like a second skin is what's keeping him alive. I wonder, if someone burst it, would he die? Or is the magic impenetrable? Is that even possible?

Sky stands shakily, holding the sword he just pulled from my body. It drips with my blood. This crimson king with fierce blue eyes is terrifying. He could take on an entire kingdom and use the vanquished heads as steps to his throne. Sky, the baker, the brother, and the Runespeaker, has transformed into a face of fury and vengeance.

Sky doesn't move. He lifts his chin, holding his

eyes level with Hanson's, while his black hair swirls behind his head from the wind, and his crown of icicles stands in synchronicity with the surroundings. "King Hanson."

"It's a shame to see you on the other side, Sky," Hanson says lowly, dropping his royal title. "I would've enjoyed seeing Glaven thrive now that a new family has taken charge. Too bad you decided to follow in the Strazenfields' footsteps and turn against your own realm." His eyes darken again as he glares down at Sky. He twists the handle of the gold trident in his two-handed grip. "The Solstice Realm could have turned over a new leaf, started a new golden era. We could have been prosperous, finally rid of those *other* Unnaturals. But then Emilia had to turn Dark too, and corrupt the minds of both you and King Jayden." He *tsks*, shaking his head methodically. "Glaven and Eirae will be next on my list to vanquish. Once and for all, our realm will thrive—free of all those who've threatened order."

"Careful," Sky says, measuring the king's every breath and every twitch of his hands, preparing to defend himself if Hanson strikes. "Your Veiling is showing, Hanson. You say that Emilia is tainting the realm, twisting the minds of the people who call her a friend, and it'll be safe when everyone who contradicts you is dealt with... But look at you, Hanson. Look at your eyes. If anything, the era *you* would lead the Solstice Realm into would be one of Darkness and despair."

Chapter Thirty-Four

*K*ing Hanson's lip curls to reveal his razor-sharp teeth. He clearly doesn't like what Sky said. "Fool," Hanson declares, lifting his trident. "You'll die on this battlefield alongside your friends."

My heart skips a beat. Friends? Does he mean he'll find them and kill them? Or does he mean that he already did? Can they truly be...*dead*? Alongside Sophia and Jaxon?

Sky lifts the bloody broadsword just in time to block Hanson's trident. The handle of the trident clashes with the sharp blade of the sword. Hanson sneers and Sky matches it with a milk-curdling glare. They raise their weapons again, dancing around each other and my still body.

Sky dodges when Hanson reels back to drive the points of the trident through his skull. When Hanson drifts forward, Sky takes the opportunity to thrust his sword upward and try to disarm the merfolk king, to no avail. The attempt seems to make Hanson angrier.

Hanson swings the trident, bumping into Sky's shoulder and knocking him to the ground. His fingers splay in the snow, turning the snow red under his palm, and he squints up at the merfolk king who is silhouetted by the blinding winter sun. "Why are you doing this, Hanson? Do you truly hate the Banished Unnaturals that much?" His oceanic eyes are vibrant in the sunlight, determination and resilience shining alongside the flecks of dark and light blue. Though he's covered in blood and injured, he doesn't seem afraid. He's...brave. Braver than I thought. And he's a survivor, no matter the circumstances. He'll get through this... He'll survive King Hanson. Won't he? But even as the thought crosses my mind, my Soul Sight buds. It doesn't tell me a yes or no, not really. It just throbs in my chest, telling me that there *is a possibility*.

I had an option the night I faced King Aaron. Either I could kill him with the last fragment of Aridam and take his place and his curse, or I could rule alongside him and lose my freedom.

Right now, I have another choice. And I know what I must do.

King Hanson scoffs, throwing his head back so the sun can shine across his triumphant face. "I am restoring order, Skylar Baker. Order is necessary. Order is the way we've ruled this realm since the Great War. You'll understand one day..." His dark lips tilt up in a smirk as he blinks down at Sky, who's sprawled across the ground, defenseless. His broadsword landed a few yards away when it was tossed from Sky's grip. "Actually… That's not true. You won't have the chance." With those words hanging in the tense air between Sky and Hanson, the merfolk king raises his trident and brings the three points down toward Sky's head, prepared to divide his skull and kill the new king of Glaven.

A choice. You have a choice, Emilia. Look for the opportunity.

And so I shall.

I summon all my strength, barring my teeth through the pain of moving. I stand. My legs are shaky and blood drips down my side, but I know what I must do. Without hesitation, I throw my body in front of Hanson's trident. I can feel it as the points dig into my flesh and burrow into the pulsating organ of my heart. A lupine scream shudders through me and my golden wings flow wide, blocking Sky from Hanson's view, making all his enraged focus turn to me.

Instead of stumbling back in shock or withdrawing his trident, he shoves it in deeper, vengeance shining in his black eyes.

I throw my head back, a frenzied scream of utter agony tearing from my throat and freezing all the action on the battlefield. I swear even the butterflies stop their flittering, staying impossibly still in the sky as if frozen in time. I start to sag toward the ground as my lungs empty, but before I can reach the welcoming chill of the snow, white light shoots from the wound in my chest and the punctures in my heart, blanketing the battlefield. More blinding than the sun reflecting off the snow.

King Hanson stumbles back a step, but he doesn't run away, nor does he scream. He watches with intrigue as my bones start to twist and turn and shrink into those of a human. As the fur retreats back into the pores of my skin and my limbs return to normal, though aching and bruised and cut. As the dark brown fur of the chimera melds into my long hair, my once black eyes open to reveal a light blue. I stare straight ahead, hovering a few feet in the air, encompassed by the magical white light. Hanson and Sky are beneath me, as are the rest of the soldiers. The snow directly below me is drenched with crimson blood. Hanson's trident falls at his feet, the damage to my heart healing over with a protective shield created by the mysterious white light. My mind is on fire, heating up as thousands and thousands of memories burst through the gates, fighting to the forefront of my mind.

I gasp, tossing my head back as my body quivers and the curse unravels. I see Sky, Jax, and Aaron when they're little. Right around the time I first met them. You can tell that Sky and Jax share the same parents since they look almost identical. Sky's face is free from the scar he received the day he saved me from Aaron. Now, as I stare at the three Baker Boys in front of me, their child-like faces so round with wonder and joy, I wonder how they ended up torn apart. How Sky became the king of Glaven and a crimson soldier on the battlefield. How Jax ended up dead by his brother's hand. And how Aaron was taken over by the Veiling and donned a crown of bones and gathered an army of soulless Shrouds.

Where did it all go wrong? Or did Aaron's envy grow and thrive and feed off his brothers' happiness? Was the Veiling always inside him, or did it finally click into place the day he killed the Nether king, stole Aridam, and took the Nether throne?

The brothers seem to grow before my eyes, shifting into what they looked like months ago... before everything happened.

Jax is holding the Solstice Map across his arms, beaming down at it with pride and disbelief. His hair swoops toward his chin in the front, but gets progressively shorter in the back. His eyes are identical to Sky's, both oceanic blues, expressive, and hypnotizing. Aaron's soft brown eyes are hypnotizing in their own way. They make him look...kind, sweet, and caring. I suppose it's a good thing that the Veiling turned his eyes completely black. If his

349

eyes were that soft brown, then it would've been harder to kill him, even knowing what he did and planned on doing.

The Baker brothers shift into a mist and drift away as another memory comes into focus: it's my mom. My parents' names flicker through my mind, healing a part of my heart I didn't know was broken: *Alexandra and Igor Strazenfield*.

Their faces, youthful and happy, appear before me, their bodies materializing as a scene unfolds. We're in a grand sitting room overlooking the Glaven village as it bustles with joy and peace. Alexandra, my mom, is embroidering a white cloth in her hands, resting regally on a plush, white sofa. She's wearing an elaborate blue gown with a pair of doves embroidered across her breast; the doves look like they're chasing each other in a circle, but there's something that's strikingly happy about them. Maybe they're chasing each other for a kiss. Mom's light blonde hair is piled on top of her head, and a small tiara made from what appears to be icicles is perched atop the mass. She looks up, her dark blue eyes twinkling when the doors to the sitting room open and a man steps in.

He's familiar, and I instantly know who he is even though he doesn't have a full beard and his icy eyes aren't clouded. His hair is pompous and a lively brown, absent of any gray. His skin is fair, and his cheeks are lightly freckled. He's wearing a light blue tunic that isn't as adorned as Alexandra's gown. The crown of icicles that dons the monarch of the royal bloodline is perched on his head among the gelled waves.

When he grins at Alexandra, his teeth glint in the bright sunlight drifting through the window. I've never seen him happier than when he's staring at her.

A little girl runs into the room, bumping into his legs and causing him to toss his head back, supporting his crown with one hand out of instinct. He laughs. The girl has shoulder-length blonde hair. Her simple purple dress and hands are covered with blue and yellow paint.

"Sophia," Alexandra chides, scooping her daughter up when Soph jumps onto the sofa. She's barely older than a toddler. Possibly four. Alexandra's scolding doesn't reach her eyes. She tucks Soph against her chest, tossing her embroidering aside, and rests her cheek against Soph's head of blonde waves, nearly identical to Mom's.

Another girl runs into the room, laughing and holding a green rose plucked from the greenhouse near the kitchen. She holds it up to her mother, grinning with pride and triumph as if it was so hard to pick the right flower. "I got you something."

Alexandra glances up from Soph, and her eyes

crinkle. She takes the green rose from the girl's grasp and smiles lovingly at it. "Thank you, Emilia. It's so beautiful."

My gaze locks on the girl again. Emilia? That's me? Well, who else could it be? I find myself smiling as little Emilia crawls up onto the sofa and snuggles on the other side of Alexandra—o*f my mom*—and rests her head on Mom's chest. Igor—my dad—moves across the room and sits down at Alexandra's feet, beaming at his family. He reaches out and gently takes his wife's foot, which is clad in a thin, white sock trimmed with lace, and massages the pad of his thumb across the sole of her foot.

The room and the merry family vanish, traveling away on the wind like nothing more than mist. Something hot slips down my cheek and I reach up to brush it away, realizing that it's tears. I'm crying. I grin, my eyes blurring.

Then it all comes into focus again: the battlefield. The dazed merfolk king. Blood-covered Sky. And the hundreds of stunned soldiers all staring at me…and the white light that's slowly evaporating from my body. I fall to the ground, landing in the snow, then tilt my head up to meet the black eyes of King Hanson. His mouth has popped open in shock, and his pearl-adorned hair is billowing gently behind him as the wind's speed wanes. The entire realm seems to fall silent, stretching this impossible moment into an endless expanse of time.

I should be dead. I threw my maimed and battered body in front of King Hanson's trident. *I should be dead.* His trident stabbed my chest, penetrating my heart. *I should be dead.* So, why and how am I alive?

I look over my right shoulder at Sky, whose face is full of grief, relief, and anguish. Is he sorrowful because he thought I died? Because he knows I should be dead? Or is he sorrowful because he knows what I must do? My blue eyes meet his and his expression falters; his mouth dips into a frown and his eyes shine with tears. One slips down his face and crests over his cheek. I know what he wants to ask, too afraid to disturb the quiet that seems to be the only thing keeping the peace: *how?*

How am I alive? How am I suddenly cured of the Veiling?

What just happened?

I need to know, and one day, I will. But today… Today I need to do something else.

When I turn back to King Hanson, who hasn't moved a muscle as he tries to process the impossibility of what just happened, I take in the gawking crowd behind him.

In the front, with his hand prodding a cut on his cheek and his wide and wondrous golden eyes trained on me, is Adriene. He shakes his head, and I can almost read his mind, for I know him so well that I know what he's thinking: *how are we both cured?*

Another question for which the answer is to be discovered on yet another day. For today isn't a day for answering questions, it's a day for change.

As I kneel on the soft blanket of this bloody battlefield, surrounded by friends and foes, enchanted butterflies, and mutated chimeras, my voice is small —yet so incredibly loud—as I say: "I remember… everything." Then, as if out of instinct, I unsheathe Aridam from my waist and thrust it forward, penetrating the merfolk king's magic and sliding the Sword of Death into his sweat-slicked skin. He doesn't say anything as his wide eyes take in the hilt of Aridam and the gurgling stream of blood cascading from his torso, dripping down his tail and etching itself into the curves and hollows of his textured scales. He knows what this means. There is no coming back from Aridam.

He reaches a hand toward me, his mouth twisting to form a vicious sneer, a slew of angry, harsh words ready to spring from his mouth in vengeance. But blood trickles from the corner of his mouth, and the magic bubble that is enchanted to keep him alive when he's out of the water slowly ebbs away, trickling across the ground like nothing more than melted snowflakes. He falls, shaking the ground as thoroughly as an earthquake, and disrupting the stillness that cloaked Nether.

I stare down at the lifeless body of King Hanson of Aquartia. Does this mean the war is over, now that the one leading everything is gone? Can we all finally live in peace? Can the Solstice Realm finally open to all Unnaturals, just as Soph would have liked?

King Hanson's body slowly dissolves into the snow and disappears as if he were never there. Aridam rests on top of the blanket of snow, its blade clean like it didn't just end the life of a king.

I bend to pick it up, lifting the cursed Sword of Death, the feared weapon and vanquisher of life, toward the sky. The sunlight bounces off the clean, glistening blade, reflecting my appearance in the jagged, broken sword.

My dark brown hair is matted with blood and mud, and my skin is covered in grime. Wide in shock are two icy blue eyes.

I'm back.

And I remember *everything*.

After

Adriene paces the length of the sitting room, a drink in one hand and a book in the other. He isn't reading the book or sipping from his glass. He's staring straight ahead, his eyebrows lowered over his golden eyes, and his mouth twisted to one side.

The windows overlooking the forest surrounding Nether let in sunlight that drifts across the floor and the bookshelves lining the walls of the sitting room. A fire roars in the fireplace, giving the room a smoky scent and amplifying the cozy atmosphere. The ground outside is still covered in a thick layer of snow, and floating along the steady breeze is birdsong.

Surrounding a round table on the other side of the room, completely drenched in the winter sunlight, are the rest of my friends. Sky, Quicken, Kisha, Sandy, Ricky, Samantha, and Victoria all talk animatedly with their hands, throwing out ideas and suggestions. The center of the table is covered in open books, with sections underlined or highlighted for convenience.

"Do you really think this is possible?" Kisha asks, hope evident in her voice. For the most part, she stayed out of the war that took place two weeks ago, hiding in the palace with Quicken. They killed a few Olympus mages who wandered too close, or tried to kill them, earning a few bruises and cuts. Nothing in comparison to what Adriene and Sky endured, or even Ricky, who had to have thirty-one stitches in his leg after a broadsword was dragged across it. Sandy was quick to get into the kitchen, preparing everyone a bowl of soup and a tray of buttered garlic bread, speeding our physical recovery along. However, we will never forget the horrors of battle.

My own bruises, though there were many, are now faded to a dull purple and ache less when I accidentally bump them.

My hip and calf still hurt from when the mage attacked me in my chimera form, but it's getting better. It's a little difficult to walk since the mage's dagger chipped away a piece of my hipbone and tweaked my muscles, but with each passing day, the ache and limp lessen.

Adriene stops his pacing to come over to the couch where I am resting, looking out at the serene forest that twinkles with the freed butterflies and the still-falling snow. There must be a foot or two of snow outside now, and a blizzard is predicted to hit Nether in the coming days. We're going to be palace-bound for a while, but after the snow melts, we can safely travel back to the Banished Realm to discuss a treaty and possible alliance with King Garamond.

Adriene tosses the book onto the coffee table in front of us and slouches down on the sofa, resting his hands on his stomach and staring concerningly at the snow.

"You know why I did it, don't you?" he asks, not looking at me. I know why he is refusing to look at me. He's refusing to show me how guilty he is—which I know he is.

"You were trying to protect me," I respond, nodding slowly. "But it should have been my choice, Adriene. I had the right to know, especially since it involved my sister. I'd do anything to get her back." Even saying the words, an ache blossoms deep in my chest, and I bite my bottom lip to stop it from quivering. Tears pearl on my waterlines and I try to blink them away, but they just roll down my cheek. I wipe them off, ignoring Adriene's sharp, concerned gaze. I never want him to see me cry.

"You know what you would have to go through to bring her back, Emilia. Is it really worth it?" I know he's asking because he's worried, but it still rubs me the wrong way. He doesn't have a sibling, so he can't understand what it's like when you lose one, and how desperate you would be to bring them back.

"I...don't know," I answer truthfully, training my attention on our friends at the far end of the sitting room. Right now—and ever since I told them about Oblivion—they have been poring over books, trying to find a way to open the portal to the spirit land; the realm of endless stars. We've only discovered one book on the legend of the Key Masters, but it hasn't given us any new information. Just what Vivienne had told me. When we return to Cyprion to finalize our alliance with the vampire kingdom, we're going to visit Vivienne and Emmett. I know they have more information on Zainey and Oblivion, so I'm going to do whatever it takes to reap it.

"Think on it, Emilia," Adriene whispers, rubbing my hand with his.

It's been a bit strange since my memories returned, since both our curses were lifted. We aren't the same anymore. I have all my memories. I remember everything about all my friends, every moment I shared with each of them.

Before the war... Before I jumped in front of Sky to protect him and King Hanson stabbed me with his trident on the Nether battlefield, Adriene was my familiar, my closest friend, and conniving executioner. We both thrived in the midst of violence and chaos, the shadow of each other. Once, I might have believed we were soulmates—destined for one another. But maybe we are just destined to have converging paths. Maybe he isn't my end, but just a section in the middle of my story.

I'm not sure what we are now. Or what we can be. But I know I'll figure it out. I have to.

"Who did you say the lady was with the scrying crystal?" Sky calls across the room, his hair tied back with a crimson hair tie. His eyes are striking. He forwent wearing the crown of icicles… I think he only made that decision because he noticed how much pain it brought me. That crown, forever in my mind, is my sister's. It looks wrong adorning the head of someone besides her.

"Vivienne O'Hare," I answer, pushing myself up from the sofa and staggering toward the table. My limp is pretty obvious right now, but I know it will get better. Sandy won't give it an opportunity to worsen—she's always shoving food down my throat.

When I get to the table and lean against it, taking the weight off my bad leg, Sandy takes my hand and smiles at me, her eyes glistening with pride.

Even though Sandy isn't my birth mom, and I know she was sent as a caretaker by my father in case something happened to me, I will always love her as my mom. She will always *be* my mom. I miss Alexandra, my birth mother, extraordinarily, but I know she's been gone too long to attempt to bring back. She'd want me to try to save my sister instead. Besides, she's there—in Oblivion—with my father. I want to think that she's finally happy and no longer alone.

"You said that to bring back a loved one from Oblivion, you'd need to confront the seven Key Masters of the sacred realms and complete each of their trials to gain access to your chosen realm, correct?" Sky asks, pressing his tongue into the back of his teeth so his mouth puckers slightly. I notice he starts doing that when he is really focused.

"Right," I say, my body reacting when Adriene nears. I don't even have to see him. My blood warms slightly and the hair along my spine stands on end. "We should go back to Vivienne and Emmett... Maybe he can tell us what the trials were like and what he had to go through. I mean, both of them lost a hand...so it must be dangerous. That is, if you're really considering going through with this."

Sky purses his lips, flipping through a book splayed on the table with the pad of his thumb, though I know he's not absorbing anything within the text. He's just trying to buy himself some time before answering. "He's my brother. Of course I'm considering it."

"You know he won't come out the same…" I've told him about Vivienne before, but I want to make sure he absorbs the gravity of the situation before making his decision. It's hard putting a price on our siblings' lives… But it needs to be done, especially with how gravely it's going to affect our own lives.

He side-eyes me, shutting the book with a loud *thwomp*. "I know. I haven't made my final decision. Not yet… I just…" He shakes his head and lets out a little huff, combing his hands through his hair and leaving sections of his black hair to flop over his forehead and fall into his eyes. Without another word, he leaves the room, muttering something under his breath.

I can see the weight of the decision pressing on him, bending his back and making his once-so-square shoulders droop. Kisha and Quicken share a look before heading after him. Samantha and Victoria, who've chosen each other as their preferred company these past couple weeks, leave the room too. Soon, Sandy and Ricky are scurrying off as well; Sandy to the kitchens to help prepare dinner, and Ricky is off to the conservatory to help with the reconstruction. We're not going to contain the butterflies anymore—now they're free to roam the realm as they wish. Once, our Dark spies. Then our poisonous minions. And now, our friends amongst nature. Most of them, I noticed over the past couple of weeks, have decided to stick close to the palace. I enjoy seeing them flitter around outside my bedroom window and twirl through the leaves of the trees.

Adriene clears his throat as soon as we're alone. I stiffen, hoping he's not going to bring…*it*…up. I'm not ready to discuss it. Not yet. Maybe soon. But not before I've had a chance to rediscover myself, get lost in the flashes of my newly restored memories, and soak in the adventures of my past.

"Do you remember that book I gave you a while ago?" he asks, out of the blue, completely taking me off guard.

I give him a puzzled look, and he gestures for me to follow him. I do as he says, curious.

I almost forgot about the book he had me start reading: the one with the creased spine and time-worn appearance. I don't know why he lent it to me, or what he was hoping to get out of me reading it, if anything.

We pass the kitchen and I peek in to wave to my mom. She grins back, working alongside the chef as they chop vegetables and fruit, preparing the ingredients for dinner tonight. We'll no longer be serving bugs and cha kla eyes in this palace.

There aren't that many people who live at the palace anymore; most of the Shrouds were killed during the battle, resulting in empty rooms and quiet hallways. I find it peaceful… I didn't particularly like the Shrouds, finding them rude, grotesque, and shrewd. I wince. That isn't a very nice thing to think—no matter how true.

We bound down the steps and into the dungeon, which no longer reeks of urine and blood from the tortured cha klas. Now, the room where the cruel actions took place has been transformed into a nursery of sorts, to heal and help the poor creatures thrive.

Surprisingly, barely any of the cha klas that the Shrouds kidnapped from the bog died when they mutilated them, taking their feline eyes to eat—a delicacy I had never heard of, nor have I ever indulged in. Adriene and I are personally assisting Bartholomew and another woman—Clara, I believe —on healing and taking care of the cha klas.

The light from the lanterns that line the dungeon flickers across the dark, patchwork floors, and across our bodies as we head toward Adriene's room at the very end.

I stop before his door to peek into the cha klas nursery. Bartholomew is in the middle of coaxing an elixir down a slinky navy cha kla's throat with an eyedropper. He looks up when the door creaks and smiles. His brown eyes shine. I'm not used to seeing him with colored eyes. After I sacrificed myself for

Sky, I didn't only free Adriene and me from the Veiling… I freed the entire Solstice Realm.

A woman is standing on the opposite side of the table from Bartholomew. She has dark blonde hair and copper-colored eyes. When she turns and smiles too, a single dimple dots her right cheek, and her face is covered in freckles. Underneath a white medical coat, she's wearing a beige wool dress that falls to her ankles and a pair of brown combat boots. I assume this is Clara—though I've never met her before. Bartholomew only told me he asked a skilled veterinarian from Eirae to assist him.

"How are they doing?" I ask, scanning the cages set up around the perimeter of the room; each one is customized for the needs of the cha kla inside it.

Bartholomew shrugs one shoulder as the cha kla hisses, ears standing erect. "They're making progress, healing up. But some of them are rather stubborn." He directs that statement at the one struggling to free itself from his arms right now. He attempts to gently wrangle it into submission, but the creature refuses to give in.

"That makes sense. They're probably terrified of being touched—of people in general. I can't imagine what they went through at the hands of people under my roof… Under my rule," I say, forcing past the emotion that threatens to choke me. Guilt coats my tongue and warms my chest. I could have done something. I could have stopped it as soon as I found out. But I didn't. I reveled in their agony. I bite my lip, disgusted at myself, even though I know I couldn't have helped it. The Veiling that coursed through my body made blood and violence please me.

Bartholomew nods, his expression darkening a fraction with sorrow.

I turn to Clara, thrusting my hand toward her to shake. "It's nice to meet you at last, Clara. I'm so thankful you're helping these creatures. Hopefully, they can be returned to the wild or at least gain some sense of freedom soon." I offer her a small smile.

She grins back, broadcasting a mouth full of pristine white teeth. Coming from Eirae, I'm not surprised that her teeth are flawless and pearlescent. "It's lovely to meet you too, Your Majesty. I've heard great things about you from King Jayden."

"You know the king?" I ask, tilting my head slightly. It makes sense that the residents of Eirae know the king, but why is Jayden so acquainted with a vet? So much so that they have conversations about *me*.

She chuckles. "I've only started interacting with him a couple months ago. He's searching for a dog to adopt and wanted my help to find him one that needs a home and needs to be spoiled."

I grin at that, finding the mere idea of King Jayden and his precious hound endearing.

With a wave, I leave them and the cha klas alone, finding it's too depressing to be in that room right now.

Adriene is waiting for me in the hallway. He probably heard the entire thing. We're going to have to have *that* conversation soon to diffuse the tension that's taut between us. Are we meant to be together, or are our paths supposed to overlap for just the middle of our stories and not until the very end?

He doesn't say anything as he opens the door to his room and grabs the book resting on his desk. It's just as worn and creased as I remember. The person on the cover, with long, brown hair and a broken sword clutched in her grasp reminds me of someone. Someone unexpected.

"You asked me how many times I've read this book," Adriene says, breaking the silence as he thumbs through the pages. He leans against his desk and tosses the book to me. I catch it, scanning the cover again in the dim lantern light. "And, at the time, I didn't answer. But now, I think it's time you at least receive one piece of the prophecy."

I arch an eyebrow, sitting down on his bed and opening the book. Why is it so creased and worn then, if he has never even read it? "Then why—"

"It's been in the Nether palace for a long, long time. Ever since my creation," he starts to explain. "It's prophesied that the book follows the life of a destined monarch; one who is said to rule Nether into another era… One who is said to break the curse of the Veiling that has flooded the Nether monarch's blood for generations." The corner of his mouth tilts into a smile that's an odd mix of sad and mischievous. "No one can read it, save for the destined monarch. It's my job to test the new monarchs to see if they are the change our kingdom needs. No one has passed—until you." He nods toward me, brushing his wavy white hair out of his eyes. His lips twist into a teasing smirk, though I have no doubt how serious he's being. He's held onto this book for generations to fulfill a prophecy and find Nether's true heir?

"I passed? How do you know that?" I ask, sitting up straight and giving him my most perplexed look, demanding to know how I passed—what exactly I *did* or *didn't* do.

He sits down on the bed beside me, a decent distance away, and points to the page in the open book I'm holding.

"Can you see the text?"

I nod. "Yeah…"

"Well, no one else can. Only the prophesied." He smiles genuinely, his golden eyes sparkling in the lantern light. "Only you can read the text. It's you, Emilia. You were destined to save this kingdom, and in turn, save this realm."

I swallow, sweat slicking my brow that has nothing to do with the temperature of the room and everything to do with the great weight that's been thrust on my shoulders. I set the book aside. I was destined to save not only Nether, but the entire Solstice Realm? Maybe Adriene and I have been connected, long before either of us even knew it. Maybe there's hope for us yet, or maybe we're not meant to be soulmates in the romantic sense, but friends who have each other's back no matter what. I know that this next chapter of my life will give me answers, and soon I'll figure out exactly what I'm destined to do, with or without my sister by my side.

I study the cover of the ancient tome, noting the long, dark brown hair and jagged sword clutched in her hand. That's me. I'm on the cover of this story. I flip it open to scan the contents, to see if I can finally understand the lost girl in this book. That lost girl is me, and this is a recounting of my life. I read the first page with a new sense of understanding, tears filling my eyes when my mother's and my father's names are inked on the page. When I flip to the nineteenth chapter, I find that all the pages are blank. The events of my nineteenth year are yet to be determined. Will it be filled with the happiness of my reunited family or the hardships of grief and despair?

I smile up at Adriene, my blue eyes twinkling with excitement. This next chapter is mine. It isn't foretold, nor is it manipulated under the threat of war.

"What are you going to do now, Emilia? You already saved two kingdoms," Adriene asks, taking the book from my hands and setting it back on his desk. He steps toward me, a coy smirk taunt on his lips.

I grin. "Now, it's time to save my family."

To be continued…

Depiction of a cha kla, illustrated by Daphne Paige

~Acknowledgments~

This book was a whirlwind to write, and a whirlwind to edit. Emilia and her friends go through so much in this book, and I can't wait to give you the finale and finally show their ending.

Thank you so much for reading *Return of Eve* and *Banished by Darkness*, and tagging along on Emilia's wild adventures. If it weren't for you, these books would still be locked away in my imagination, instead of in your hands. To keep up to date on book three, follow my Instagram @daphne.paige.books. And, while you're waiting for the next installment, consider checking out my other stories!

A massive thank you to my editors and proof-readers, and everyone who had a hand in bringing this book to life. I literally couldn't do it without you.

To Nonni and Mom, my biggest supporters and dedicated readers. You both mean so much to me that I can't even put it into words. Which is saying something...because I'm a writer… That's literally my job.

And to Papa, Doug, Sydney, and Jacob, thank you all for the tiny things. The awkward *"congratulations on another book."* The fangirling over the characters and cover with me. Reading my stories a week or two before release to help me catch any last edits. And for being there, no matter the circumstances.

Daphne Paige has always loved writing; watching and learning from her mother, who's also a writer. With the majority of her time spent writing, the breaks between stories makes her remember she has an actual life away from her characters. During those breaks, she loves to play video games, hangout with her various pets, and watch classic black and white films with her family. Daphne lives in Oregon helping her family with their popcorn business.

~More By the Author~

Kingdoms and Curses:
The Heiress of Gaia (January 2022)
The Empire's Witch (December 2022)
The Prince of Klymora (July 2024)

Jess (April 2023)

Emilia of the Solstice Realm:
Return of Eve (February 2024)
Banished by Darkness (September 2024)

www.ingramcontent.com/pod-product-compliance
Lightning Source LLC
Chambersburg PA
CBHW021129260626
47169CB00005B/1529